THE GOD SWORD

By Paula Baker and Aidan Davies:

The Hawks Trilogy:

Prequel: *Raptor's Call*
Book One: *Rebels of Halklyen*
Book Two: *The God Sword*
Book Three: *The White Wolf*

Dirt Town

Scan to get your free copy.

Grab your FREE copy of *Raptor's Call*, a prequel to *The Hawks Trilogy* today and join the fight for justice.

https://dl.bookfunnel.com/yftog4t8if

THE GOD SWORD

THE HAWKS

BOOK TWO

PAULA BAKER

&

AIDAN DAVIES

MacFay Books

The God Sword

For information contact:

MacFay Books
103 Heron Dr.
Penticton, BC
V2A 8K6
bakerdavies.ca

Map Art by Anna-Jo Grandbois
Cover illustration by Daria 'Frealyr' Kovalenko
Cover design by Kusanagistudios

Typeset in Garamond

ISBN: 978-0-9917900-2-9

For Ray.
1935 - 2013

CHAPTER ONE

Dancing

THE MUSIC WAS UNLIKE ANYTHING Flint had ever heard. They never danced like this in Abbarkon. He grinned at how he and his partner must appear. The dwarf girl who had pulled him up from his spot on the benches barely came up to his elbows. Her feet were a blur of motion and he kept his eyes fixed on them as he tried to follow every step.

It was only his hours of footwork training in the rebel village of Halklyen that gave him any chance of keeping up. However, what she was doing took far more coordination than fighting with two swords. Perhaps the Hawks should start including dance in their training regimens. It would certainly help with speed and coordination. Flint did not doubt that the little dwarf girl would be formidable with a sword in her hand. All the dwarves looked as if they were born warriors.

The pattern of steps began to make sense to Flint, and he realized she was repeating the sequence. Once he had it figured out, it was easier to match her rhythm. He let out a whoop and lifted his gaze. It was one of the first moments since Cadmon's death that he had felt genuinely happy.

As his eyes wandered over the circle of dwarves, guilt welled up in him. But, to his surprise, it did not make him back away from the dance. As the sweat flowed down his back, Flint realized that Cadmon would have been pleased to see him having fun. The man who had been his teacher and guardian would not have wanted Flint to give up on the joys of life.

He would have encouraged him to embrace the happiness. Cadmon had spent the last dozen years of his life fighting to protect the little freedoms of every citizen of Abbarkon—whether they knew it or not. As the leader of the rebels in Halklyen, he had believed fiercely in the war against Martokallu. He had also known the risks.

Since Cadmon's funeral and King Sebastien's coronation, events had tumbled on top of each another. The problem was that no one knew for certain whether or not Martokallu was dead. When he vanished from the top of the hill with one of Flint's swords dangling from his stomach, everyone wanted to believe he had been defeated. However, his Followers still held positions of power throughout the kingdom.

That was why they needed the God Sword. And that was why a dozen Hawks had made the long trek down to the dwarven country of Tsaralvia.

Flint still found it difficult to believe that Egbert, the little man who made all the Hawks' weapons and had created the marvellous Hawk vehicle, was far more than a simple blacksmith. Egbert's father, Adler, had been the Hammer of Dworgunul. That meant that Egbert might have grown up to hold the most important hereditary post in Tsaralvia.

Unfortunately, Alder had not enjoyed his role in the Temple of Dworgunul and he ran away, leaving the duty to his twin brother, Harbert. Nonetheless, despite his dislike of the job,

Adler had passed along his learning to his son.

Suddenly, Flint sensed a shift in the rhythm. His eyes shot back to his partner's feet. She giggled and began to add more complex steps to the dance. Clearly, she had been taking it easy on him. It took every bit of his warrior's training to follow her flashing feet. The music increased in tempo, and he strained to match her every move.

The blood pounded in his ears, hammering in time to the beat of the drums, while the fiddles wove a melody that propelled his feet in a pattern of endless repetition. Finally, a flourish of running notes brought the music to the end and Flint sagged in relief. Looking around, he saw that he and the girl were the only remaining dancers.

The dwarves burst out cheering. With a sheepish smile, Flint produced a self-conscious bow for the applauding crowd. The girl had no such reservations. She grinned at their audience and dropped into a deep curtsy.

Flint searched the watching faces for his friends. Kjell, the newest Hawk, sat on a nearby bench with his usual blissful expression in place as he gazed back at Flint. The man was odd—but he had proven himself useful on more than one occasion.

Once one of the most powerful Followers of Martokallu, Kjell had awakened from injuries that should have killed him. Instead, his body had healed itself, while also freeing him from the enthralment that had ruled his existence for over two hundred years. Since then, he had revelled in every aspect of human life. His desire to have fun made him an excellent travel companion.

Next, Flint spotted Hackett and Igon, who both towered above everyone around them. Although they appeared to be enjoying themselves, Flint noted that their casual conversation masked a careful watchfulness.

A flick of Igon's eyebrow led Flint to glance over to the

shadows where he picked out the shape of Dell slouching against a tree, away from the firelight. It did not matter that it was too dark to see him clearly. The jester's smile would be in place. It was painted on a mask that hid terrible burn scars as well as any expression that might have told Flint what he was thinking.

However, knowing Dell's thoughts was less important than finding out whether they had implemented the plan. Flint watched for Dell's signal. When the man deliberately rubbed a hand across his ear before sliding off into the shadows, Flint's stomach fluttered. They were doing it.

Bringing his attention back to his dance partner, Flint reached for her hand. She gave it to him with an adoring smile and laughed as he bowed over it in his best impression of the courtly manners that he had seen at King Sebastien's coronation celebration.

"You must excuse me, my lady," he said. "It has been a long day, and I fear tomorrow will prove even more exciting." Knowing she would not understand a word, he continued his playacting, smiling widely and looking steadily into her eyes. "I thank you for the dance." He brought her hand to his lips before letting it fall. As she giggled, he backed away from the fire, raising a hand in farewell.

Squeezing through the gathered dwarves, Flint scooped up his baldric from where he had set it when the girl pulled him up to dance. He eased his arms through the webbing and shrugged to settle the double swords on his back. His face remained impassive, but as always, the act of wearing the swords reminded him of Cadmon's dying wish.

Flint still had trouble believing that the man had bequeathed Rising Star to him. Egbert had made the sword for Cadmon from metal that fell from the sky. Nonetheless, Flint was grateful for the keepsake. He had loved Cadmon like a father.

Dancing

Every evening, on the long trip south to Vaarndal, Flint had drawn his swords and run through the drills that he and Cadmon had developed. It had not taken long to accustom himself to the new, longer blade and he found it worked best in his right hand. The added reach was devastatingly effective when he sparred with Igon or Gode.

As Flint slipped out of the circle of light, the drums started up again and the fiddles joined the chorus. He stood still for a moment, letting his eyes adjust to the darkness before heading toward the inn where he and the other Hawks were staying. Urravon, the Cheveralian messenger who had drawn them into this quest, was probably already back in his room. He had made it more than clear that he did not enjoy their company.

The Hawks had been in town for three nights already and each evening as the music and dancing began, Urravon disappeared. No one saw him again until the next morning. How was he spending his time? The fellow did not know what he was missing.

Flint on the other hand, had thoroughly enjoyed the evenings of song and dance. From the moment of their arrival, when Egbert introduced himself as the son of a Hammer of Dworgunul and entranced his listeners with a story, the townspeople of Vaarndal had welcomed the Hawks.

During the day, the visitors took over the town square where they practiced with their weapons while most of the town's children and many of the adults watched. There had also been meetings that Egbert arranged with the town leaders where the discussions had centered on the political climate of the area.

Then at sunset, fires were lit in the square and the musicians brought out their drums, viols, and shawms. It seemed the whole town joined in the celebrations that ran late into the night.

As the music faded into the distance, silence pressed in

around him. Everyone was at the party. Still, Flint scanned his surroundings, searching the shadows for watchers. When he was certain there were no witnesses, he changed direction and headed for the shrine, where he expected to find an excavation underway.

CHAPTER TWO

Grave Robbers

FLINT SLID FROM SHADOW TO shadow as he crept closer to the stone structure built up against a sheer cliff. The town of Vaarndal huddled next to the base of the mountain and the Disciples of Dworgunul held the big slab of rock sacred. It was the chief reason Egbert had chosen it for their first stop in Tsaralvia.

There had been a brief visit to the library of Oruk in Abbarkon. The library had been a fantastic discovery. Over a hundred years earlier, Martokallu had ordered the destruction of every book in the kingdom except for one copy of each, which he had hidden in the remote mountain cavern. Working from no more than a rumour, Halvor and the other Hawks had found it and killed the Followers guarding it.

They had spent two full days at the library, where Egbert devoted the entire time to studying books that Galo, the old librarian, found for him in the stacks. Galo was still the slightly forgetful old man Flint remembered from their first discovery of the library, but the interest in his books had rejuvenated him.

A faint gleam flashed from the rear of the stone building and Flint corrected his course. The others were waiting for him. When he got to the wooden door, he found it tightly sealed in its stone frame. With one last check over his shoulder, he reached for the handle and then hesitated. What if things had gone wrong inside the crypt? Stepping back, he drew Rising Star in a ripple of steel.

At that moment, a breath of cold, damp air blew past his face as the door swung open.

"Are you coming in or not?" Fleta hissed. "We've been waiting long enough." She glanced up at his sword, where he held it poised, ready to swing. "Exactly who are you planning to skewer with that? Put it away."

She tugged him inside and he slid the sword back into its scabbard. The drop in temperature made him shiver in his sweat dampened shirt. Although, it may have been more than the cold. There was something decidedly unnerving about the church's under-croft, which held the tombs of the Hammers of Dworgunul.

As he stared into a darkness that made the starlight outside appear bright, Flint heard the door close behind him and a bar drop into place. A brisk scratching noise brought a flash of fire and revealed Egbert bent over a torch.

When he got it burning properly, the blacksmith held it aloft and said, "Trouble getting away from the gathering, my boy?" He winked at Flint and grinned. "We wondered if you would make it in time."

The others chuckled as Flint blushed. "Well, I'm here now," he said. "What next, Egbert?"

They had decided not to ask for permission to visit the crypt. Egbert knew the townspeople would be protective of their sacred site which was accessible only to sworn officers of Dworgunul. If the Hawks were going to search it, they had to do it secretly.

"I believe we will find what we are looking for in the oldest cave," Egbert answered, waving the torch toward a low doorway. "This building was added much later. The books tell of a casket covered with a carving of Narzar, the fifteenth Hammer of Dworgunul. It is said that he did the work himself, while he was still a young man. It shows him dressed in full armour with a three-headed dog lying at his feet." As he spoke, Egbert led them toward the back wall.

Flint trailed along behind Fleta, Gode, Hackett and Cwenhild through a narrow corridor crowded with carved limestone coffins. The heavy stone sarcophagi filled most of the room, each sealed with a lid decorated with a carved image of a dead Hammer. The hair on the back of his neck rose and he wanted to draw his swords. Was it just the idea of being near so many entombed bodies? Or was there really something sinister in the room?

Only the tramp of their boots on the stone disturbed the thick silence until Fleta muttered, "This is the creepiest place I've ever been."

The others laughed nervously and as if her words had released them from the spell, everyone began to speak at once.

The voices were too loud in the small space and just as quickly, they all fell quiet again.

Egbert broke the tense silence. "If you think you sense something malevolent, it is most likely true." Ignoring their anxious glances, he added, "Keep your eyes open. The Hammers of Dworgunul are charged with protecting the stories and secrets of Tsaralvia. Do not believe for one instant that the responsibility ends with death."

Flint's eyes strained out of his head as he tried to see beyond the circle of light provided by the torch. He sensed something just beyond his field of vision and his nerves felt stretched to the breaking point. Deciding he did not care whether the others thought him a fool, he drew both blades.

Instantly, there was an answering hiss of metal as the others drew their own weapons.

"Easy there," murmured Egbert. "We are just looking." He turned to find the armed Hawks bristling with tension. They stared wildly back at him, but Egbert's calm gaze did much to settle their panic. He cocked his head to the side and lifted an eyebrow. With a shrug he went back to examining the coffins.

Two steps later, he stopped and held his torch close to a sarcophagus beside the aisle. "This is it," he breathed.

Flint could not see past the others who crowded in beside Egbert.

Fleta blew out her breath in a huff of disappointment. "How can you tell?" she asked. "It looks the same as all the other graves."

With a touch of irritation Gode muttered, "They all have a carving of a person in full armour with an animal at their feet. I've already seen two other three-headed dogs."

Egbert raised an admonishing finger. "Yes, but none of the others actually say, 'Here lies Narzar, the Fifteenth Hammer.'" He reached out a callused finger to rub the carved letters entwined into the carving of the armoured warrior.

Cwenhild leaned in. "You can read that? What language is it?"

"Tsaralvian, of course," Egbert answered. "It was the first language I learned to read."

"How many languages do you know, Egbert?" Hackett asked.

Egbert considered the question. "Hmm, I speak thirteen, but a few of those may be a bit rusty. I can read four more that I have never spoken aloud." He lifted a shoulder. "It says here, 'death carries secrets that will change the world'."

Cwenhild shuddered. "Can you feel it?" she asked. "This is the creepiest spot in the whole crypt. It makes my skin crawl."

Egbert handed her the torch. "I agree," he said. "Something is trying to talk to us. Something or someone. Let us have a peek, shall we? Gode? Fleta? Will you give me a hand?" From his belt, he produced a steel prybar and thrust it under the lip of the lid. "When I lift, you two push it aside."

Gode and Fleta slipped into place at his side and gripped the sarcophagus lid.

A fleeting look of worry crossed Egbert's face before he took a deep breath and leaned his weight on the prybar. A terrible creaking noise signalled the beginning of movement and he gasped, "It is coming free."

Flint's stomach clenched as Gode cried, "Push!"

He and Fleta strained to shove the loosened lid aside. At first, it did not budge, until in a sudden rush, the stone began to slide. Once it started, there was nothing they could do. It crashed to the floor in a rumble of shattering rock.

Everyone froze while the echoes faded.

Cwenhild broke the spell. "That was more dramatic than necessary," she said, tilting the torch so that the light fell into the coffin.

Flint craned in for a better look. A skeleton lay on the bottom of the stone box. How would the bones help in the search? What if they had disrupted Narzar's final resting place for nothing?

Fleta bent closer and asked, "What's he holding?"

CHAPTER THREE

Raising Ghosts

FLETA REACHED INTO THE COFFIN and grasped the flat metal disc entwined in the bony fingers of the skeleton. Her first tug yielded nothing, and Egbert caught her arm before she tried again.

"Careful there, lass," he said. "This may be a secret the Hammer is loath to give up." He leaned in and squinted at the disc. "Something is written here, but I cannot make it out." Straightening, he tugged on his beard braids. "Before we pull it free, there are words that must be spoken."

"Is it something from one of the books we brought?" Fleta asked.

"It has never been written down," answered Egbert. "But I am the son of a Hammer. I know the words."

Everyone stared at him with identical expressions of bemusement. Egbert, their blacksmith, held the knowledge of a priest.

Egbert drew his hammer and raised it high. Placing one finger on the disc, he drew in a long breath, and began to speak. "Ot heug mah, Martell ya gruofoug. Nuef wosen yaarik. Aarognal nue a okel zed daiw."

He stopped but maintained his pose with his hammer held aloft. Flint hardly dared breath as the hair on the back of his neck stood straight up again.

Then, a light began to glow just outside the circle of illumination provided by the flickering torch. With an effort of will, Flint suppressed a desire to bolt from the under-croft.

Egbert did not relax his stance as the light grew in both size and brightness. It began to move, whirling faster and faster, gathering form, and becoming almost solid.

Abruptly, the motion ceased and the figure of a muscular elf appeared. He hovered above the stone floor and a ghostly bow was slung across his back while he held a glowing sword ready in his hand.

While the apparition hung in the air, glaring with wild eyes, everyone froze, holding their breaths.

Then, without warning, the elf attacked.

Gode dodged the whistling assault, danced aside and swung his axe. His blow went right through the attacker's body and he stumbled against the corner of the sarcophagus. As he lost his balance, his axe fell, spinning away into a corner.

The air filled with a booming laugh as the ghostly figure drew back for another strike.

Flint dove forward and Rising Star clanged against the downward strike of the ghost's sword. After watching how Gode's axe sailed through the body of the ghostly elf, Flint was shocked to find his hilt locked against the attacker's sword. He whipped his second sword at the ghost's shoulder, and it slipped through without resistance.

While Flint struggled to maintain his balance, the ghost let out another unnerving laugh.

A chill rippled down Flint's spine and his mind darted around, trying to understand. Was it because Rising Star was not made from earth metal? Or was it that Rising Star had struck the weapon and not the person? He shook the questions away and concentrated on holding against the ghost's power.

Minutes ticked by and the ghost did not move. Sweat poured down Flint's face, but he did dare back off. Inches away, the ghostly eyes studied him with no sign of laughter.

Just when Flint decided he could not hold a second longer, the ghost's scowl vanished, and he released the pressure.

Gasping with relief, Flint sagged and he let his sword dip to the floor.

"Thou art righteous of heart," the ghost said in a hollow voice. "I warn thee, though. The path thou seekest will not end well." Rising, he floated over the coffin with its skeletal remains. "Takest the map, young Flint. I shalt not stop thee." He emitted another echoing laugh before bowing formally and sheathing his sword with a flourish.

After narrowing his eyes at Flint one last time, he grasped the medallion around his neck. At once, he began to spin, swirling into a pinpoint of light and vanishing.

Gode's breath hissed out into the deafening silence and he whispered, "Did you see that?"

"Did I see it?" Flint asked, collapsing against the sarcophagus. "He knew my name! He was staring right in my face, not even breathing. I've never felt such strength. Not even from Martokallu!" He swiped at the sweat running down his face. "He wasn't trying to defeat me. He never pushed back. Not once. He held my blade and no matter how much I tried, he just matched my strength and kept me in place."

Egbert tugged on a beard braid and pursed his lips. "He was testing you," he murmured.

"Testing me?" Flint demanded. "Why would an ancient priest need to test me?"

Egbert peered into the coffin and his face was unreadable as he studied the remains of the fifteenth Hammer. "To see if you are worthy of bearing the secrets," he said. "Mind, he is not a priest. He is one of those who protect the God Sword."

Fleta leaned against Egbert. "Do you think the disc is the map he was talking about?" Her efforts at nonchalance were betrayed by her shaking voice. Visibly overcoming a reluctance to touch it, she reached down to grasp the metal circle and this time, Egbert made no move to stop her.

It took a firm tug and the finger bones that had held so tightly to their burden, relaxed at last and rattled to the bottom of the coffin. Fleta stepped back with her prize and the tension in the crypt eased. Nothing more was going to happen.

Straightening, Egbert took the metal disc from Fleta. She had been trying to make out the markings and handed it over reluctantly.

Egbert took his time puzzling over the inscription until Fleta could bear it no longer. "Does it tell us where to find the God Sword?" she demanded, looking over Egbert's shoulder.

Egbert grimaced. "I do not think it will be as straightforward as that," he replied. He gazed at their hopeful faces and sighed. "Perhaps, while we have a moment away from prying ears, I should tell you a little more about the God Sword."

Flint glanced around the crypt. "Do we have to stay in here?" he asked. Sweat was cooling on his skin and he wanted nothing more than to escape outside into the warm evening. He needed to shake off the terror that had gripped him as he stared into those ghostly eyes.

One side of Egbert's mouth lifted in a wry smile. "You have nothing to worry about now, young Flint. Have you forgotten you just received a blessing from a Protector of the God Sword?" He settled a firm hand on Flint's shoulder and looked him in the eye. "No, we need not rush away. This is the perfect place. We have not had a chance to speak privately since we left Kallcunarth." His brow furrowed as he looked back to the other Hawks. "We cannot trust the Cheveralian messenger."

Gode chuckled humourlessly. "Urravon?" he asked. "I hardly think you need tell us that. He sticks his long nose into every conversation. I haven't said anything more interesting than a comment on the weather since we left Kallcunarth."

Calmed by Egbert's hand on his shoulder, Flint said, "Every time I try to talk to someone, he shows up. He usually pretends to be busy with something else, but it's obvious he's listening, so I change the subject."

Cwenhild set her hands on her hips and stretched her back. "I don't think anyone has said much in front of him. The man is not at all likable. We don't trust him, and he doesn't trust us."

Egbert glanced at the guttering flame of Cwenhild's torch "Perhaps you are right, Flint. We will find another location and another time. We best return to the inn before our absence is noted." He slid the disc inside his shirt and gazed sternly around at his listeners. "Need I remind you to keep this find between us? I believe it is best if we say nothing aloud so that scrawny big ears will have nothing to report."

Sitting at the window of his darkened room, Urravon watched six more Hawks slip into the inn's courtyard. A short time earlier, he had seen the others return along with the few other guests in town. He had assumed then that the celebration in the main square had ended. What had delayed this group?

With a grunt of disapproval, he stepped away from the window, moving slowly to avoid drawing attention. The Hawks were already wary of him and he did not wish to give them any more reason to suspect he was not on their side.

Almost a year had passed since the High Priest chose him above all the other junior acolytes. It had been a glorious day.

However, during his time with the Abbarkonians, his pride and pleasure at the recognition had soured. In his dark room, Urravon cringed to recall how he had showered the High Priest with coins and begged to be the one to travel through the mountains to Abbarkon. How naïve he had been.

He shoved his hair off his forehead. Had the offering even been necessary? Perhaps no one else had volunteered. He could believe that. Lately, he spent much of his time wishing he were safely home in Neveral. Never had he imagined how difficult life would be among people who did not put Dreff first in everything. The evening's celebration was just another example of their frivolity.

Perhaps it would be easier to bear if they were making progress in the search for the God Sword. It had taken him nearly a year to track down Egbert. When he finally found the man, he had convinced himself he would be home withing a few weeks. However, as far as Urravon could see, the Hawks had discovered nothing useful about the holy blade. The past few days had been nothing but dancing, talking, and showing off.

Pushing his frustration away, Urravon returned to the sacrifice he was performing. In preparation, he had fasted since the previous evening. The light-headedness was surely a sign that Dreff was near.

Since sundown, he had knelt on the hard floor before the rabbit he captured earlier in the day. Catching a live rabbit was not easy. But learning to move in silence and to strike with speed was a requirement for a Follower of Dreff.

Focusing his energies on the life force of the rabbit, he drew his ceremonial dagger. The rabbit squirmed away from his grasping hand, but he tightened his grip behind its skull and lifted it from the wicker cage.

CHAPTER FOUR

Bandits

EGBERT POINTED TO A TREE and said, "Grat."

Obediently, the others echoed, "Grat."

Riding out under a brilliant blue sky, Egbert had resumed their language lessons. During the stay in Vaarndal, everyone had tried out their new words but for the most part, it had been an exercise in frustration. As a result, Egbert's students were much more attentive than they had been on the earlier leg of the journey.

Egbert pointed to his axe and said, "Copor."

"Copor," answered the group.

Riding off to his side, Fleta copied more than Egbert's pronunciation. She imitated his posture and facial expressions as well—to the amusement of the others.

An air of festivity accompanied the group. At breakfast, Egbert had announced that they would leave immediately for Tsarval. Flint had not missed the look of irritation that flickered across Urravon's face when Egbert offered no further explanation.

Everyone knew about the map they had found in the crypt—everyone except Urravon—and there was no way he could ever guess. But the air of supressed excitement had him peering suspiciously at everyone.

As usual, Urravon did not participate in the language lesson. He rode near the back and pretended it was he who ignored the Hawks rather than the other way around. But his eyes had taken on a sullen cast and he watched everyone with an intensity that bordered on mania.

Tired of being stared at, Flint caught Fleta's gaze and choked back a laugh. She was a deadly accurate mimic and had captured Egbert perfectly.

He nudged his horse to a trot. "Fleta, let's scout ahead," he called. It would feel good to let his horse run. The slow speed that Egbert preferred was beginning to chafe. "I heard about bandits along this road. There are a few spots where they set up ambushes." As he spoke, Flint kept his eyes on Fleta, but he felt the questioning looks from the older Hawks.

Fleta smoothed her expression when Egbert turned to her. "That sounds like a good idea," she said with a bright smile.

The corners of Gode's mouth twitched. "Absolutely," he said. "A fine idea." Then he lowered his eyebrows. "We'll see you back here in a few minutes."

"You got it," called Flint. Giving a wave, he sent his mount galloping down the road with Fleta close behind. When she came even with him, he leaned close to his horse's neck and urged him to greater speed. The forest flashed by as they surged around a series of curves.

After only a few minutes, Fleta hauled on her reins and called, "Hold up! We're supposed to be checking for ambushes."

Flint sat up and slowed his horse to a trot. "I needed that!"

he said with a grin. "But, you're right. We better take a look."
He peered off into the woods. The widely spaced trees
provided little opportunity for cover. There was no sign of
anyone. "Have you had a chance to talk to Egbert since last
night?"

Absently, Fleta ran a finger across the handles of her
daggers as she studied her side of the road. "No, not since we
left the crypt," she answered. "I wonder what he wanted to
talk about before he decided we should hurry back to the inn."

"Yes, that's what I want to know." He grinned sideways at
her. "Maybe I should have invited him to come along for a bit
of a run," he said. "Then I could have asked him my
questions."

Fleta giggled. "I'm sure he would have loved to join us. You
know how he enjoys sitting on the bouncing back of a demon
horse determined to send his spine through the top of his
head." The last bit was delivered in a perfect imitation of
Egbert's pretended outrage every time someone suggested
riding more quickly.

They laughed and Flint studied the dust for signs of recent
travel. Nothing was visible that he had not been able to see
when he rode with the group, but he felt better for being away
from Urravon.

"You had a chance to look at the disc," he said. "I only got
a glimpse. Tell me what you saw."

Fleta let her eyes drift over the forest as she considered. "It
had carvings on both sides as well as on the rim," she said. "I
was surprised at how heavy it was for the size of it. On one
side, it looked like a map, but the other side was covered in
writing." She grimaced. "It was nothing I could read."

"Do you reckon Egbert can read it?" he asked.

"He is the son of a Hammer," she answered with another
imitation of Egbert's ringing tones.

Flint laughed and then pulled his horse up short, leaning

down to study the dirt.

"What is it?" Fleta asked. "What do you see?"

"It's probably nothing, but it looks as if someone headed into the forest here. How many horses would you say went this way?" Flint dropped down from his saddle and released the reins. His horse immediately began to crop the dry grass at the side of the road.

Fleta joined him and squatted by the tracks that showed clearly in the dusty ditch. "It looks like four or maybe five riders," she said. "Maybe more." She stood and squinted into the forest. It was denser than it had been earlier. "I thought you made up that story about bandits. Is it true then?"

"Well, I wasn't sure how serious it was," he answered. "I spoke with a man who had heard from someone else, who had the story from another person about an attack along the road to Tsarval." He tried to keep his tone light, but a shiver ran down his back.

"I can see why you didn't give it too much weight," Fleta said, striding toward her horse. "But I don't like this. We should get back."

"I agree," said Flint.

They galloped along the forest road back the way they had come. Flint was surprised to see how far they had gotten ahead of the main group. He expected them to be closer. Every time he rounded a bend, he was disappointed to find the road empty. Pricked by real worry, he nudged his mount to greater speed.

"Where are they?" Fleta shouted over the thunder of hooves. She pressed her horse to pass Flint and they hurtled around another curve.

They were back where they had left the Hawks. Sword crashes filled the air along with grunts and muffled screams. Flint's eyes flew over the crowded road, searching for his friends. Every Hawk was upright but they were engaged against a much larger force. Flint counted fifteen attackers, plus four unmoving forms in the dust. Removed at a safe distance from any fighting, an expensively dressed dwarf sat astride his horse with a sword held loosely across his knees.

Flint drew the long sword Cadmon had left to him and aimed at a dwarf on the edge of the crowd. The attacker had cornered Egbert who desperately parried a succession of sword blows with his hammer. Using the momentum of his horse, Flint dismounted in a flying leap.

Eyes wide, the dwarf turned in time to catch the sword through his throat. Flint hit him with such force that the blade cut cleanly through and came free in a spray of warm blood.

Egbert staggered back and wiped sweat from his forehead with the back of a blood-spattered hand. Panting hard, he wheezed, "Thanks for that, Flint but I almost had him."

Flint opened his mouth to answer and then spun away as a dwarf aimed a two-handed sword at his head. Off-balance, he blocked the blow with Rising Star. Without stopping, he reached back and drew his second sword. It sent him into a spin. Knocking the dwarf's blade to the ground, he stabbed forward with his second sword. His blade struck his opponent's eye socket and the tip slid through until it ran up against resistance at the back of his skull.

Shaking the limp body free from his sword, Flint watched Fleta climb to her feet from her landing spot on top of a burly dwarf dressed in a once-elegant red coat. Two separate dagger wounds in the dwarf's back told him that Fleta had thrown the weapons before she landed.

Kjell used the moment of Flint and Fleta's arrival to back away from the fight. His hands a blur of motion, he nocked and released two arrows. The instant they struck, squarely hitting two of the attackers, the men burst into flames. Shrieking with pain, they reeled amidst the combatants, causing others to dance out of their way to avoid the fire.

Dell jumped up from skewering a dwarf with his bladed gauntlet and plucked a small, round grenade from a pocket. When one of the burning men stumbled past, he touched the fuse to the flames and it sputtered to life. Stepping away from the chaos, he let the fuse burn down until he judged it short enough. Then he lobbed it at the mounted dwarf on the side of the road.

A perfect toss, the grenade landed in the gaping pocket of the dwarf's waistcoat. Before he could react, it exploded.

CHAPTER FIVE

Protectors of the God Sword

THE EXPLOSION PROPELLED BODY PARTS and bits of flesh into the air. After a ghastly instant when the sky turned red, the gore rained down. The bandits recovered first. With the obliteration of their leader, they lost all desire to continue the fight. Almost as one, they turned and bounded into the woods where they mounted horses and crashed off through the undergrowth.

None of the Hawks made any move to pursue them. Flint swept his gaze over the gruesome scene and let out a long breath. Everyone was upright. That had to count for something. With all the blood, it was difficult to tell if anyone was injured.

His attention went to the bodies on the ground. The man Dell had blown up would have nothing to tell. He was obviously dead. However, one of the motionless bodies might provide some useful information.

Flint leaned close to Fleta and muttered, "Get Gode, Kjell and Dagur. Set a perimeter guard."

"Good thinking," she said, moving off to pass on the message.

"Check for survivors," Flint shouted. "Maybe someone will tell us why they attacked."

"We only need one," growled Egbert.

As everyone bent to the grisly task, Flint knelt by the side of one of Dell's victims. His throat had been torn open and he was well past help. Reaching out to close the wide startled eyes, Flint wondered who would miss the man. Did he have a family?

"This one's alive!" Cwenhild shouted. "Egbert, come and talk to him. He doesn't understand me."

Egbert wiped his bloody hammer on a dead dwarf's shirt before rising. Thrusting the weapon in his belt, he trudged over to Cwenhild.

Flint followed. He wanted to hear what the dwarf had to say.

Egbert squatted beside the burly man who was no more than thirty years old. Pale and sweating, he had a gaping wound in his chest. Cwenhild had pressed her hands against the injury, trying to slow the bleeding while the man struggled weakly against her efforts.

"Tell him to hold still," she said. "Without help, he's going to die."

The dwarf leveled a dark gaze at her while Egbert settled on one knee and said, "Heug gar. Nuef yasen yaarif. Plosen sha bi eld vousen geyler ren bakak."

Relief flashed in the dwarf's brown eyes. Almost at once they clouded over with pain as Cwenhild attempted to fit the ragged edges of the wound together. By the look of it, the man had been on the receiving end of Igon's flail. He laboured to breathe with his chest a mess of torn flesh. No doubt he had broken ribs as well.

Without lifting her head, Cwenhild said, "Bring my medicine bag. This is going to need sutures."

"I'll get it," Hackett said from over Flint's shoulder and he hurried off to where Fleta had rounded up the horses.

It did not look as if the dwarf would survive long enough to benefit from any medical treatment. His lips were turning blue, and blood trickled from one corner of his mouth.

"Find out what they were after," Flint said. "We need to know if they only wanted money or was it something else that made them attack."

Glancing up, Egbert's eyebrows knit together. Then he looked back at the man and asked a question. The conversation that followed was lengthy on Egbert's side while the injured dwarf replied in brief gasping answers. At first, he appeared to refuse to answer Egbert's questions, but as his breathing became more and more tortured, he lost his reluctance. Egbert remained gentle and calm. Eventually, the dwarf's story came in brief, fragmented sentences.

Hackett reappeared with the medical bag and set it beside Cwenhild.

Trying not to disrupt Egbert's interrogation, she muttered, "There's salt in the yellow bag. Pour a bit in a canteen and wash out the wound. Flint, wash your hands and give me a needle and cat gut. They are in an orange case."

As Hackett doused the dwarf's chest, sluicing blood and dirt from the cut, Cwenhild lifted the hand that had been applying pressure. A spurt of blood jetted out and the dwarf gave a gurgling sigh. Cwenhild pressed her hand back on the wound but his chest did not rise again.

Egbert sat back on his heels and said, "He is gone." Squeezing his eyes shut, he wiped a dirty hand across his face. He looked exhausted.

Did he tell you anything useful?" Flint asked. His hands

were as clean as he could make them with the water from his canteen, but he had not had time to get out the equipment for suturing the wound.

"Well, yes. I suppose he did," replied Egbert, rising stiffly. "This was a planned attack." He thrust his chin toward the mass of destroyed flesh on the side of the road. "That dwarf was the leader." He paused and drew in a deep breath. "Do you remember what I told you would happen if anyone found out that we are looking for the God Sword?"

Flint set his hands on his hips. "You said there was a secret group within Tsaralvia who would do anything to prevent its discovery." He narrowed his eyes and gazed around at the carnage. "Is that who they were?"

Egbert looked up as the other Hawks gathered around. Only Fleta, Gode, Kjell and Dagur remained on guard, facing the woods on either side of the road. He nodded. "Protectors of the God Sword," he said. "The others were bandits recruited to fight us. The leader of the Protectors convinced them it would be worth their while if they joined up together." Surveying the corpses, he sighed. "I wonder how many of these bodies were bandits and how many were Protectors."

Abruptly, he stopped speaking and stared into the distance. Then, with a grunt, he grasped the dead dwarf's hand and turned it over. A blue rune was tattooed on his palm.

"What does it mean?" asked Flint.

"Protector of the God Sword," answered Egbert with a sigh, as he arranged the dwarf's hands at his sides. "We need to check them all."

It did not take long to examine the remaining corpses. Of the eleven dead, five bore the rune tattoo. For the dwarf who Dell blew up, there was not enough skin remaining to check, but the dying dwarf had called him the leader, so they added him to the count.

"I saw twenty attackers when we arrived," said Flint. "The

Protectors of the God Sword must have figured they needed more people on his side to guarantee a win." With no attempt at modesty, he added, "They've heard about us."

Egbert pulled on his beard braid and asked, "Yes, but who told them?"

"Maybe they took note of our weapons and decided we posed a threat," Cwenhild suggested. She looked pointedly at Flint's double blades.

"Maybe they saw us training in Vaarndal," said Igon. He had kept well back while Egbert spoke to the man he had hit, and he still looked shaken. They trained to fight but no one took any pleasure in the deaths.

Suddenly, Fleta drew two daggers and shouted, "Drop your weapons and move to where I can see you." With a rasp of steel, everyone whirled toward the woods.

For a moment, there was only silence, and then with a rattle of branches, Urravon crept out of the woods. The Cheveralian messenger looked pale and dazed. Everyone lowered their weapons as the slight man tottered onto the road.

Everyone except for Fleta. She kept her daggers trained on him as her face twisted in indignation. Finally, she lowered them and demanded, "What were you doing in the woods anyway?"

Urravon shrugged as he stared mutely at one of the mutilated dwarves.

Gode answered for him. "Never mind. Not everyone is a warrior."

Flint studied the Cheveralian and his unused sword. Grinding his teeth, he bit back a scathing observation and sheathed his swords with a grunt. As if it was a signal, the other Hawks put away their weapons as well.

Taking a deep breath, Flint surveyed the scene. "We should do something about these bodies," he said.

Cwenhild sighed. "You're right. We can't leave this mess

for the next travellers to find."

Flint narrowed his eyes at Dell. "Do you have any ideas?" he asked.

Dell's eyes crinkled, a sign he was smiling. "I might," he said. "Give me a minute." He started toward the woods and then stopped and called, "Kjell, would you give me a hand?"

CHAPTER SIX

Fire Starter

BACK ON THE ROAD, FLINT found himself studying his own horse's tracks. The dust told the tale of his eager gallop away from his friends and the frantic ride back.

It had been a grisly cleanup, but the hole Dell blasted in the forest floor had made the burial easier. Remembering it, a corner of Flint's mouth lifted. Dell had asked Kjell to fire an arrow into a pile of kindling and tossed a grenade into the resulting fire.

The blast produced a crater and the Hawks had hauled all the bodies over to the hole. Covering them had not been easy without proper shovels. In the end, Egbert had convinced Gode to use his war axe to split a log to use as scrapers.

After the battle and the work of burying the dead, they had briefly considered spending the night there. But no one had wanted to stay so close to the grave.

With dusk descending, they were still searching for an

acceptable campsite. Two potential spots had already been passed over as undefendable. Weariness was beginning to wear on everyone as they pressed on, hearing only the horses' hooves on the hard-packed surface.

The road curved gently and then as it straightened out, the forest opened into a meadow with a creek running through it. As one, they halted and scrutinized the landscape.

Flint broke the silence. "Good water, space to hobble the horses, room to distance ourselves from the trees," he said. "This will work."

With a rumble of agreement, they dismounted.

"Hackett and I will take first watch," said Igon, handing his reins to Flint and unhooking his flail from his belt.

Hulda watched him stalk off along the perimeter and said, "It's getting dark. Fleta and Kjell, help me get a fire going."

Gode took her reins. "Good idea," he said.

While the others tended to the horses, Fleta helped assemble the makings for a fire. Dropping an armful of wood beside the ring of rocks that Kjell was arranging, she asked. "Is it your bow that makes the fire? Or the arrows? Or is it something you do yourself?"

Kjell sat back on his heels. "I never thought about it," he answered. "The bow is the same one I used as a young soldier." He rubbed his chin. "I can choose an arrow from anyone's quiver and get the same result." Grinning, he leaned forward. "That is a really good question." In the middle of the circle of rocks, he created a small mound with a handful of tinder. "Ever since Martokallu made me a Follower, my arrows flamed. But I don't have the link with Martokallu anymore, so my arrows shouldn't flame." He paused, gazing into the distance.

He grinned up at Fleta. "I wonder—" he said, before hesitating again. Working quickly, he stacked small sticks against the tinder and added larger pieces of wood around the outside. "I always just expected the arrows to flame. I wonder—" he repeated as he stared at the tinder.

A moment later, it burst into flames. Fleta and Hulda jumped back in disbelief while Kjell sat back with a satisfied smile. Quickly, the fire spread and took hold, bringing with it a welcome warmth.

"How did you do that?" demanded Hulda.

"I don't know," answered Kjell, lifting his hands with a chuckle. "I imagined the flames in the tinder, and poof, there it was."

"Poof, indeed," murmured Fleta as she threw another log onto the fire. "This is a skill with possibilities. How much control do you have? Can you start a fire anywhere or does it have to be right in front of you?"

"I don't know. Until I tried it just now, I didn't even know I could do it without the arrows." Kjell shrugged. "I thought it was a spell Martokallu put on my bow."

Hulda and Fleta exchanged a look. Kjell's casual reference to the monster who had enslaved thousands of men and women was something they still mistrusted.

Kjell spent over two hundred years as a Follower of Martokallu and sometimes it was difficult to believe he had truly separated himself from that link. However, his actions during the battle against Martokallu, Hain and the other Followers, coupled with his open and friendly nature had led to his general acceptance by the Hawks. He seemed genuinely delighted to join the fight against his former master.

Hulda rose. "How about I set up a couple of targets where a fire could be contained?" She lifted an eyebrow as she started across the meadow. "We don't want to start a forest fire." Several yards away, she scraped a circle in the dirt with her boot and kicked the uprooted dry grass into the middle. "Try to light this," she called.

Seconds later, the grass kindled, and she hurriedly stamped out the flames.

Fleta let out a whoop. "That's amazing!" she shouted. "Try going to the other side of the meadow."

Hulda crossed the creek on a series of stones that stood above the water and jogged over to where Hackett was peering into the woods.

"What's going on?" he asked.

"Watch this," she said. Using her heel, she scraped the grass into a circle, once again leaving the ground bare around it. As she stepped back, the grass burst into flames again. "What do you think of that?" she asked, shaking her head.

Hackett gaped. "How did you do that?" he demanded.

"It's not me," she answered, looking up at him. "It's Kjell." She raised her eyebrows. "It's magic." She let it burn for a moment, before stamping on it with both feet, and trotting back to the cooking fire.

"How do you do it?" asked Fleta as she added dried meat to a pot of water.

Kjell shook his head. "I have no idea."

"Maybe it was never Martokallu's power," suggested Hulda. "Maybe you're a mage like Orma. Do you have any other powers?"

The fires had not gone unnoticed. Gode jogged up with Egbert and Cwenhild on his heels.

"What's going on?" asked Gode.

"We have another mage in our midst," said Fleta. She gestured to Kjell. "He's a fire starter."

Gode cocked an eyebrow at Kjell. "What does that mean?"

With a shrug, Kjell said, "Don't look at me. I have no idea how it works."

"How can that be?" demanded Gode.

Kjell took no offense at his tone. "I don't know, but if I look at something and imagine the flames, it lights on fire."

Gode pushed his hair off his forehead. "That could be useful," he murmured as he settled beside the fire. "Do you suppose you have other powers too?"

Cwenhild settled down beside him. "When I was young, my mother tested me for magic," she said. Her mouth twisted and she shrugged. "There were no signs. How about you, Kjell? Did anything unusual happen when you were a child?"

Fleta leaned forward. "Orma said when she lost her temper, strange things happened—usually something got broken, and she got in trouble."

Kjell eyebrows shot up. "Yes!" He nodded emphatically. "That happened to me all the time. To avoid the punishments, I decided I would never get angry." He scowled and murmured, "That worked fine until I became a Follower. Anger is standard when you're a Follower."

Silence descended over the circle as they listened to the crackling fire until Flint asked, "Cwenhild, did your mother ever talk about how she learned magic?"

Cwenhild looked up from where she had been staring into the flames. "She said her mother made her practice juggling—without her hands."

"There is your answer," said Egbert. "Find yourself three pebbles, Kjell. It is time for you to become our mage."

CHAPTER SEVEN

The Hammer

WELL BEFORE THE SUN REACHED the highest point in the sky, they rounded a bend in the road and spotted the city of Tsarval. Across the distance, the white stone buildings glowed in the sunlight. Only Kjell was uninterested in the sight. He walked at the rear of the procession juggling three small pebbles.

Gode had taught him the basics the night before and as soon as he had the rhythm, Kjell made tremendous progress. Initially, he struggled to move a single pebble with his mind. The first tiny shift had been greeted with a roar of applause from his audience.

Flint glanced back. The pebbles were flowing in a circle, like water from a fountain. He was about to call out his congratulations when Kjell stumbled. The flight paths tangled and the stones collided in midair, dropping to the ground.

Still, he had improved tremendously since they left camp

that morning. Flint smiled as Kjell bent to retrieve his pebbles. A mage might be useful.

Then, he spotted Urravon and his smile vanished. The man was staring at Kjell with his face set in angry lines. Kjell might be oblivious to his hostility, but Flint was not.

Dropping back, Flint fell in beside Kjell. He watched the cycling pebbles for a moment. "It might be best—" he began and stopped when the pebbles cascaded to the ground.

Kjell grinned as he knelt to pick up his pebbles. "It's getting easier," he said.

Flint returned the smile. Despite his initial suspicions, he could not help liking the former Follower of Martokallu.

Leaning close, Flint murmured, "It might be best if you hold off with the mind practice for a while. We're almost at Tsarval."

Riding into the huge city, Flint could not imagine how they would find Egbert's uncle. Inside the great stone gates, a maze of streets greeted them. Flint had never seen so many people in one place. They all moved at a determined speed, while staring curiously at the Hawks, who were the only humans to be seen.

Flint tipped his head close to Fleta and asked, "How are we going to find anyone in this place?"

Wide-eyed, Fleta lifted her shoulders and shook her head.

Egbert took one look around the crowded square and headed toward a knot of old men playing a board game. Without hesitation, he dismounted and approached them on stiff legs. Flashing a smile, he began an animated conversation.

Flint had not learned enough Tsaralvian to understand what they said, but he recognized a few words. From the gesturing, he knew Egbert was getting directions.

Turning back to the Hawks, Egbert clenched his fist in triumph. "It's not far from here. We can probably walk."

"It's faster to ride," said Gode.

Egbert grimaced. "You're probably right. It just feels better to be on the ground." With a sigh, he thrust his foot into his stirrup and hoisted himself aboard.

The real surprise for Flint was the size of the house Egbert led them toward. It was a palace. But it made sense when he thought about it. After all, Egbert was related to one of the most powerful men in Tsaralvia. Nonetheless, it was a bit of a shock.

As they approached the tall, stone building, Flint tried to envision how different Egbert's life would have been if his father had stayed and kept his position as Hammer of Dworgunul.

Fleta echoed his thoughts. At his elbow, she whispered, "Can you imagine walking away from all this? Egbert's father must have really hated the job."

Egbert's mind may have been running along similar lines. For the first time he seemed uncertain. The front stairway, with its twelve wide steps, led to a pair of enormous, ornately carved front doors that were set into a stone archway. Flint could not imagine climbing those graceful stairs to knock.

The problem was solved for them when the doors swung wide and four Tsaralvian guards stepped through. Dressed in red tunics and white trousers, they formed up in a row, two on either side. Armed with short swords at their waists, they came to attention and pounded their tall pikes on the stone steps. As the noise hung in the air, a fifth man appeared.

He was dressed in a long red robe. Golden embroidery glinted in the sunlight and wide sleeves concealed his hands. A white stole hung around his neck and as he took his place behind his honour guard, he straightened his shoulders and gazed out over the square.

Even if they had not been watching a house where Egbert's

uncle lived, there would have been no doubt that this was the man they sought. Older and shorter than Egbert—with more grey in his beard—he looked very much like his nephew. Even the beard braids were the same.

Harbert stepped into the open space between the guards. With practiced ceremony, they descended the steps, their eyes darting around the square. Except for the Hawks, there was surprisingly little activity after the bustle of the earlier streets. It left them exposed and obvious.

The Hammer of Dworgunul studied the group as he marched down the steps. Briefly, Flint felt the deep-hooded eyes probe his face before they flicked on to Fleta. When his examination reached Egbert, the man froze in his tracks. His brow furrowed for a moment before he broke into a joyful smile.

The guards took two more steps before they noticed he had stopped. A command snapped out and they halted, coming to attention with another thump of the pikes.

His eyes wide and a smile stretching his mustache, Harbert started down the stairs. Ignoring his guards and the ceremonial procession, he made a beeline toward Egbert, who dismounted and stepped forward to meet him.

The guards kept pace, but they too were staring at Egbert.

With complete certainty, Harbert spoke. The Tsaralvian words moved far too quickly for any of the Hawks to understand. But Egbert answered him, leaning forward, and waving his arms.

Whatever was said was enough to cause the guards to allow their hands to drift away from their sword hilts—although they kept careful watch on the Hawks.

The conversation continued until Harbert's face suddenly fell. He reached out to grasp his nephew's arm and they shared a long moment of silence. Flint guessed he had just learned his brother was dead.

Switching languages, Egbert beamed at the Hawks and explained, "He recognized me immediately." Dropping his gaze shyly, he added, "I have been told I look like my father."

Gode laughed. "And your father and the Hammer were identical twins."

Egbert shook his head in wonder. "Harbert looks just as my father did."

"And you too, look just like Adler," said Harbert. "Perhaps a little more..." He stopped and rubbed his round belly, his eyes bright with teasing. "...than when he left here when we were eighteen."

Flint's eyebrows rose. The Hammer of Dworgunul was fluent in Abbarkonian. After a moment's thought, he realized he should not be surprised after what he had learned about Egbert's facility with languages.

"Well, it has been a long time since I was eighteen," Egbert replied, a wide smile plastered on his face as he rubbed his own belly.

The two of them stood staring at each other until Gode cleared his throat.

Straightening, Egbert waved vaguely to the Hawks. "I should like to introduce my friends and talk with you about why we have come," he said. His eyes slid sideways to the guards. "Do you have some time and a place where we can speak?"

"Of course, of course," replied Harbert. "Right now, however, I must perform a ritual at the temple." He gestured to one of his guards. "Perhaps, Niviit could show you to our guest rooms. You can rest there for the afternoon. Please, join me for supper this evening. We can talk then."

The Hammer held Niviit's eyes in a brief unspoken communication before the guard bowed and turned to face the Hawks.

Egbert brought his hands together at his waist and bowed

to his uncle. "Thank you," he said. "I look forward to our visit. We will happily accept your invitation for supper."

In reply, the Hammer bowed briefly before resuming his formal posture. Then, with his three remaining guards, he carried on toward the temple.

The Hawks watched until he vanished behind the doors. Then they turned expectantly to Niviit.

He brought his right heel down and snapped to attention with his pike held upright at his side. "Follow me," he said in Abbarkonian. Spinning neatly on his heel, he marched to the corner of the house.

Flint grinned at Fleta and muttered, "Even the guards in Tsaralvia receive an extensive education."

She nodded distractedly as she dismounted and followed Niviit to a metal gate that guarded the space between the Hammer's home and its neighbour.

The dwarf fished under the collar of his uniform and produced a chain from which hung a heavy key. Unlocking the gate, he swung it open on silent hinges and stepped aside.

"After you," he said with a wave of his hand.

Egbert led the way and one by one, the Hawks guided their horses into the narrow opening. Flint went last. Behind him, he heard the gate clang shut and a key grate in the lock. His heart sped up and he wanted to reach for his swords. However, when he turned to look back, he could see nothing beyond his horse's broad back.

Nor could he see anything ahead besides the back end of Fleta's horse. There was no choice but to continue toward the thin strip of sunlight ahead. When he reached the end of the passage, he blinked against the sudden brightness and his fear vanished.

He had entered an enormous cobbled courtyard that easily accommodated the Hawks and their horses with plenty of room to spare. A stable took up the back part of the property with a high stone fence shielding the area from the street.

Niviit shouted a command in Tsaralvian and several young boys and two elderly men appeared from the stable. The dwarves stopped and stared at the party of armed humans with their dusty horses. Niviit gave another order and the boys stepped forward to take the reins of two horses each.

"If you show us where, we can take care of our mounts ourselves," Gode said.

"You are guests of the Hammer," responded Niviit. "Do not be concerned. Your horses will receive the best of care."

As an old man reached for Egbert's reins, he froze, his eyes wide. Waving his free hand, he began to speak.

Egbert stared, his face going stiff before he answered in Tsaralvian.

Briefly, the old man looked pained, and he bowed his head. After another few words, he clapped Egbert on the shoulder and led the horse into the stable.

When Egbert turned, he found the other Hawks waiting expectantly. Scrubbing a hand across his chin, he said, "He recognized me. He taught my father his blacksmith skills."

Gode clasped Egbert around the shoulders. "You'll get another chance to speak with him."

"If you please," Niviit said, bowing in Egbert's direction. "Follow me. I will take you to your rooms where you may rest."

CHAPTER EIGHT

Prisoners

"MAYBE YOU'RE RIGHT," FLINT ADMITTED. "It makes sense that Harbert would want to know for certain Egbert isn't here to reclaim his inheritance. What if Harbert has a son who expects the position to be his one day." He lifted his eyebrow at Egbert. "Maybe you're next in line for the position of the Hammer."

From the moment the door closed behind them, and they heard the snick of a key in the lock, the Hawks had been discussing methods to escape from the room. The fact that it was not merely a room but a whole suite of rooms did nothing to temper their indignation at being locked in. They were perfectly comfortable in the central sitting room, with its four adjoining bedrooms and a bathing area with hot water piped into a pool large enough to accommodate at least three people.

However, their comfort was not the issue. For the most part, the discussion was not about how to escape; they all agreed there would be no difficulty with that. The debate centered on whether it was advisable to leave. On that point, they were divided into two even camps. There were those who believed that the act of locking them in meant they had to break out, and those who argued Harbert had no reason to trust them but neither did it mean they were in any danger.

Initially, Flint had been a vocal member of the first group. However, after listening to Cwenhild, he had changed his mind.

Dell hovered near a window protected by an ornate grill. The decoration on the iron rungs did not make it any less a prison. Turning back to the discussions, he announced, "I can set a grenade here. We'll take cover in the bedrooms. We'd be out in minutes."

Egbert raised his hands in exasperation. "Of course, we could be out of here in minutes," he exclaimed. "The point is we don't want to escape. We want to speak with Harbert. If he wishes us to stay in these lovely rooms for a few hours before supper, we can do that." He scowled. "Harbert is taking a natural precaution. If we break out, why would he make time to speak with us?"

Gode laughed. "You make a very good point, Egbert. I agree. Let's take it easy this afternoon and look forward to supper."

Dell flopped onto a couch and crossed his arms. "Fine," he said. "We'll wait."

Egbert shook his head and settled onto a couch. "There is time for a bath," he said.

Rising from a couch, Fleta said, "I propose the women get the bathing room first."

"I agree," said Hulda. She had been prowling the suite, examining the furniture and wall hangings. Now she wandered back into the main room from one of the bedrooms. "If we were to break out, it would be messy. Let's wait until suppertime and see what's planned for us. If we still want to break out later, we can."

Gode had been exploring as well. "I think we can agree to wait and see what happens," he said. "But I also believe we should not let down our guard. Igon, Dell, Hackett and I will take first watch."

When Flint's turn to use the bathing room came, he studied the setup with interest. Hooks for clothing lined the walls and a shelf in the corner was heaped with large blue towels. However, it was the bath itself that fascinated Flint.

Sunk into the center of the room and made of the same polished rock that covered the floor, it was about twelve feet long and five feet wide. Two metal pipes brought water in through a wall. The first one poured steaming hot water in at the far end of the pool. He stuck a finger in and pulled it out with a yelp. Who would get into water that hot?

A second pipe half-way down delivered cold water. That was where he chose to enter. Unlike the hot-water pipe, which was either on or off, a lever at the cold-water outlet allowed the flow to be regulated. Flint adjusted it so that the water around him was pleasantly warm and scrubbed himself clean, watching the dirty water flow away from him toward a drain at the low end of the tub.

When the water around him ran clean and clear, Flint inched past the cold-water pipe toward the hottest water. He got as close to the inflow pipe as he could stand and then with a sigh, settled back on the submerged bench that ran around the edge of the pool

He was on the verge of sleep, relaxed and blissful when he jerked upright at a rap on the door. Water sloshed over the edge onto the floor as Gode strode into the bathing room, bringing with him a blast of cooler air. Flint regarded him blearily.

Gode laughed. "I hate to disturb your beauty sleep," he said. "But I believe it is my turn. Everyone else out there is sweet-smelling and relaxed and they can't stop talking about this wonderful bath. I hope it hasn't turned their brains to mush, because I left Hulda, Fleta and Cwenhild on guard duty."

Every muscle in Flint's body, including his tongue, had turned to jelly. He struggled to answer. "Argh," was all he managed, as he levered himself up. Making his way to the cold-water tap, he opened it to full flow and stuck his head into the stream of icy water.

Shocked into wakefulness, he shook his head, his hair sending droplets around the stone-lined room. In possession of the ability to speak once more, he said, "I guarantee that whatever you've heard about this bath doesn't give it full justice." Reaching for a towel, he climbed out at the cooler end. "Has Egbert been talking about how he might build one? I can imagine finding time for it at home."

Gode tossed his clothes aside with a chuckle. "As a matter of fact, he was. His father built one in their village when he was a child. At that time, he couldn't appreciate it like he does now." He set his axe in reach of the edge of the tub and slipped into the water at the cool end of the tub. Splashing some water into his face, he started scrubbing the dust and crusted blood from his skin. "So far, it isn't much different from a lake in summer."

Flint settled his coat over his clean shirt and slid his arms through the webbing of his scabbards. Reaching for the door handle, he answered over his shoulder, "Just wait, you'll see."

"The Hammer is back," Cwenhild called from the sitting room window that she had claimed for its view.

Kjell stuck out his hand and caught the four stones he had been sending through the air in a regular cascade. For almost an hour, he had kept the rocks floating without allowing a single one to fall. Sliding the pebbles into a small bag he had tied to his belt, he continued to ignore Urravon.

The messenger was the only person who had not taken advantage of the bathing room. Instead, the slight man remained in the upright chair he had chosen when they were ushered into the room. Except for the time Kjell spent in the hot water, Urravon had passed the afternoon watching Kjell juggle. Kjell appeared not to notice, but everyone else saw the look of distaste on the elf's face. Apparently, he did not approve of magic.

Flint roused himself from the couch where he had settled after his bath. He had doffed the double scabbards but his blue shining sword, Rising Star rested near his right hand. Grabbing up the baldric, which still held his second sword, he joined Cwenhild at the window.

Below, Harbert and his three guards marched across the empty square. All four men glanced up at the window and for a moment, Flint stared into a pair of brown eyes that were almost exactly like Egbert's. Involuntarily, he glanced at Egbert where he reclined on one of the couches. What would the blacksmith look like in the red robes of a Hammer of Dworgunul?

"Do you suppose it's suppertime?" asked Flint. He was hungry and bored. It had not been an unpleasant afternoon, but there had been no offers of food and nothing much to do after his bath except sit and wait. "You don't suppose he means to keep us locked up here forever without feeding us?"

Stretched out on a couch with his hands tucked behind his head, Gode answered, "I'm sure the Hammer's plan was to imprison us in this beautiful suite of rooms with only bathwater to sustain us."

Egbert snorted. "Harbert invited us to supper," he said. "And I expect he meant it."

A sharp rap on the door brought everyone to their feet. Igon, who had taken the chair near the door, rose with his flail dangling from his right hand.

Flint drew his second sword from its scabbard and Dell slid a dagger from its sheath. The others stopped short of drawing their weapons, but every hand rested on a hilt.

A moment later, the door swung inward, revealing the same guard who had locked them in several hours earlier. Niviit affected not to notice the bristling weapons and suspicious looks as he bowed from the waist and clicked his heel sharply on the stone floor.

Rising, he swept his gaze around the room and announced, "Supper will be served in a quarter of an hour. The Hammer invites you to join him in the dining room."

Flint suddenly felt awkward, standing with his two swords. He met Niviit's eyes and returned a small bow that was not much more than a nod. "We would be honoured," he said.

"Perhaps your weapons could remain in this room?" suggested Niviit.

Flint looked pointedly at the sword hanging at Niviit's side. "Will you be armed?" he asked.

"Yes. However, I will not be seated at the dining table. I guard the Hammer." Niviit's expression did not waver.

"Perhaps a compromise then," suggested Gode, moving to Flint's side. "Igon and Dell will remain armed and the rest of us will leave our weapons here."

Flint glanced up at Gode in appreciation. It was the perfect compromise.

Niviit narrowed his eyes before giving another crisp bow. "I would be pleased to lead you and your honour guard to the Hammer's dining room."

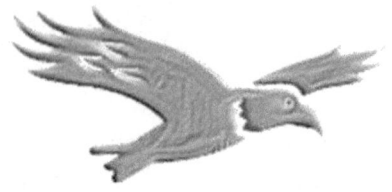

CHAPTER NINE

Supper

FLETA STUDIED EGBERT. IT WAS a wonder to her that the man who had raised her in a three-room cottage, would—if circumstances had been different—have grown up in this palace. It was beautiful. Everywhere she looked, she saw another work of art or one more architectural feature that told a tale of wealth and ease.

When Niviit led them into the grand dining room, two armed guards were the only other occupants. Dell and Igon took positions opposite the dwarven soldiers and settled into a staring contest.

Fleta missed her daggers. Her hands fluttered to her waist as she examined the enormous dining table with its elaborate place settings. There was room enough for all the Hawks and a dozen more people besides. She looked sideways at Flint and muttered, "Should we sit?"

He shrugged and then his shoulders twitched. She almost

smiled at his discomfort. He missed his weapons too.

"Be welcome," Niviit said. "Sit where you please." The man barely came up to Flint's shoulders, but his heavily muscled body and intelligent eyes gave him an air of authority. He was used to being obeyed.

Fleta guessed the elaborate chair at the head of the table was meant for the Hammer. She glanced at Egbert. Would he know what to do? So far, he had navigated every part of the visit expertly.

He was studying the table with the same intensity he brought to a problem at his forge, his head cocked to one side and his eyes narrowed. Making up his mind, he tugged his beard into place, strode forward and seated himself to the right of the Hammer's place. After scooting his chair up to the table, he looked at the others who hovered near the door.

Raising his eyebrows, Egbert smiled and said, "Please, join me." With a sweep of his hand, he indicated the empty seats. "There is room for everyone."

With obvious relief, the Hawks rushed the table and seated themselves just in time to see the carved doors at the far end of the room swing open.

Two more guards entered and snapped to attention, bringing their heels down sharply on the floor.

Struck by the ceremony, the Hawks struggled to push back their heavy chairs so they too could stand.

An instant later, the Hammer swept into the room. He had changed his red robe with its wide floppy sleeves for a green one that fit more closely. "Please, please," he said, opening his arms wide. "Be seated. You are my guests. I apologize for not being here to greet you." His warm smile tightened when he spotted Igon and Dell standing ramrod straight against the wall.

The new guards eyed the armed visitors and settled across from them, standing with their legs braced and their arms folded across their chests.

Dell shifted his weight and allowed his coat to fall open, revealing the row of daggers. If the tension in the room had not been so high, Fleta would have laughed at the obvious showmanship on both sides.

The Hammer settled into his chair and fixed his eyes on Egbert. "Nephew," he said, "I am very pleased to have you here, in the house of your father."

Egbert raised his eyebrows and answered, "Your welcome this afternoon was most unexpected."

The irony in his voice was obvious and Harbert acknowledged it with a matching lift of his own eyebrows. "Your visit took me by surprise and as much as I might have wished to stay and talk earlier, my responsibilities required my presence this afternoon." Harbert let his eyes travel around the table again, and his glance stopped at Urravon, who still wore the dusty clothes of the road.

The others also turned to examine the Cheveralian, who cringed under their scrutiny. The movement caused his lank hair to part and with a start, Fleta saw that the man's ears were pointy. He was an elf. How had she not noticed before?

"It is an interesting group you have brought to my home, nephew," Harbert said.

"Well, uncle," Egbert paused. He cleared his throat and tugged on a beard braid. "May I call you 'uncle'?"

"Of course. You are my brother's boy," answered Harbert. His face softened. "I never thought I would hear of him again."

Egbert sat up straighter. "Uncle, there is a story behind our arrival." His eyes shifted to the guards. "Though, perhaps this is not the best time to share it."

At that moment, the food arrived. The aromas drew everyone's attention. Fleta watched Igon force his eyes from the platters of food and back to the task of watching the dwarven guards. She caught his eye and winked, which earned her a wry smile.

Dell was not distracted by the food, although with his naturally suspicious nature, he switched his focus to the servers. They moved around the outside of the table, setting overflowing plates in front of each person. When they stepped back, only the sounds of eating could be heard as everyone settled down to enjoy the feast.

Harbert did not join in the initial rush to eat. Instead, he leaned back and watched his guests, his hands folded across his belly, a smile lingering on his face. Mid-bit, Fleta noticed, and horrified, she set down her knife and fork with a clatter.

Harbert's head jerked back as he realized her fear. Hurriedly, he picked up his own utensils and quickly ate several bites of food.

Relief swept over her. The Hammer did not intend to poison them. Embarrassed by her suspicions, she lowered her head and shovelled a load of creamed potatoes into her mouth.

Harbert cleared his throat. "I would be interested to hear what has brought you to my door," he said.

Not to be rushed, Egbert chewed and swallowed before taking a sip of mead. "We have questions we hope you will be able to answer," he said. "You might say we are on a quest."

"A quest?" Harbert echoed. "That sounds interesting." He had begun to eat, but he set down his fork and knife, picked up his tankard and held it up in salute. He waved it at the guards. "I imagine your people know the substance of your query. Please feel free to share in front of my men. They are sworn to Dworgunul."

At the god's name, the guards and Harbert drew a swirling pattern over their hearts with their right hands. Fleta tried to decipher the design. Was it a figure-eight?

Egbert looked startled by the gesture. "My father used to do that whenever he told stories of Dworgunul," he said. "I'd forgotten."

"We bind our hearts to Dworgunul," Harbert said. "Please, feel free to share your story."

Egbert studied the soldiers before lifting his napkin to his lips. "This is not related to our quest," he said, "but may I ask, do I have any cousins?"

A fleeting look of sadness crossed Harbert's face. "No," he answered.

Egbert held his uncle's eyes and Fleta knew he was thinking of his own lack of heirs. Clearing his throat, he said, "Our quest is related to the story of Dworgunul." He watched Harbert's face. All the dwarves made the small gesture again, but his uncle's expression did not change. After another moment's hesitation, Egbert blurted, "We are searching for the God Sword."

Fleta was not sure what reaction she had expected, but it was certainly not laughter. She snapped her mouth shut while Harbert produced a belly laugh that sounded a great deal like Egbert's guffaw. Glancing around the table, she saw that every Hawks wore matching expressions of shock.

Finally, wiping tears of laughter from his eyes, Harbert subsided until he emitted only the occasional snort. "So, you are on a quest for the God Sword," he said. He tried to appear serious, but one corner of his mouth twitched with a suppressed smile that threatened to erupt into laughter again.

Taken aback by his uncle's reaction, Egbert drew a calming breath and asked, "Perhaps, you have heard of our troubles with Martokallu?"

When his uncle nodded soberly and settled back in his chair to listen, Egbert relaxed. "We believe the God Sword could be used to destroy Martokallu," he said. "In a battle earlier this year, young Flint—" He thrust his chin in Flint's direction. "He put a sword into Martokallu. We do not know if it was fatal. As soon as he was struck, the fiend disappeared from the field of battle."

Sitting straighter in his chair and looking directly at the Hammer of Dworgunul, Egbert declared, "Abbarkon is not prepared to go back to how it was under Martokallu's rule."

Harbert was listening intently now, all traces of humour gone.

Gesturing down the table toward the elf, Egbert said, "Urravon visited us in Kallcunarth on the day of King Sebastien's coronation. He knew enough about the God Sword to pique my interest. After speaking with him, I did some investigation myself." He stopped for a swallow of mead and asked, "Do you know of the Library of Oruk?"

When his uncle shook his head, Egbert pursed his lips. "I thought not. That is a bit of story in itself." Settling back in his chair, Egbert focused on a statue of an armoured warrior and said, "About a hundred years ago, Martokallu confiscated all the books in Abbarkon. Recently, we discovered that rather than destroying them—as most people believed—he had a hidden library built in the mountains."

Harbert's eyebrows rose again, but still he said nothing.

Fleta recalled the rooms they had passed on the way to the dining room. There were books everywhere. The Hammer's collection probably matched the Library of Oruk.

"On our way here, we stopped at the library to search out any information about the God Sword. So far, I know the sword is said to have been crafted by Dworgunul himself."

Again, hands went automatically to hearts.

Egbert cleared his throat. "I also know that Dworgunul made the sword for Abbarkov at the end of the great war of the gods when he asked for help killing Dreff."

At this announcement, Urravon jerked his tankard and golden droplets splashed across the white tablecloth. When Egbert turned to him, the elf remained rigid except for a single muscle that twitched in his cheek.

Egbert finally looked back at his uncle. "It proved effective in stopping the battle between Abbarkov and Dreff," he said. "Although, of course, Dreff was not killed." He glanced at Urravon who squirmed at this disrespect to his god.

Pressing his lips together, Egbert looked away and sipped from his tankard. "After that, when the gods decided they could no longer live among men, the story becomes more confusing. But of course, you know that." He glanced sideways at his uncle and dropped his eyes. "Some sources say Abbarkov took the sword with him when he retreated from our world. Others indicate the sword was left with guardians who were to keep it safe until it was needed again."

Egbert looked directly at his uncle. "Some sources name the Protectors of the God Sword, an ancient brotherhood, who maintain the sword in secrecy."

At the mention of the Protectors, Harbert suddenly looked uncomfortable.

Egbert saw the look and pressed on. "Is there any chance you know something about the Protectors of the God Sword planning an attack on us?"

Harbert wiped his face clear of all expression as he returned Egbert's challenging stare. "As a matter of fact, I did hear something about that," he said, mildly. "Although at the time, I had no idea it was my own nephew searching for the sword."

Egbert studied his uncle's face and broke into a grin. "I guess my arrival here must have come as something of a surprise. I can almost understand why you locked us up for the afternoon."

His smile broke the tension and Flint said, "It was a good thing you convinced us to not to break out, Egbert. We would have missed this delicious meal."

Fleta could not resist. "And that bath," she said with a sigh. "I hope you've figured out how it works, Egbert, because you have to build one when we get home."

CHAPTER TEN

History Lesson

THE REST OF THE MEAL passed more easily. Cradling a tiny coffee cup in his sturdy fingers, Harbert settled back in his chair. His trained voice took on a sonorous quality, ensnaring his audience while he wove together the strands of the tale of the war between the gods.

"Abbarkov and Dworgunul became allies against Dreff," he said. "The Worshippers of Dreff had chased the dwarves into the mountains of the Chain of Thollcrawnow and seized all the land south of the mountains. The alliance of the dwarves and the humans brought advantages to both sides. The mages among the humans were able to provide long-range communications, while the dwarves brought enormous skill with weaponry. It made them a powerful team. Naturally, it did not hurt that it was now two against one—instead of a war with enemies on every side."

Harbert sipped from his cup and set it aside, clasping his

hands across his belly before picking up the tale. "The gods did not have any qualms about squandering the lives of their people. Tens of thousands died during the years of fierce fighting."

Even when telling a story, Harbert spoke perfect Abbarkonian. Egbert's accent was far more pronounced. His speech held traces of the melodic dwarven language despite his having grown up in Abbarkon. It must have been the way his father spoke.

"It is difficult to separate good from evil during a war," Harbert continued. "A rift grew in the ranks of the elves. There were those who believed Dreff could do no wrong while a growing number of elves believed Dreff had become twisted and evil. In secret, this group began to actively oppose the Worshippers of Dreff."

Harbert waved a finger at his rapt listeners, his eyebrows dancing mischievously. "Obviously, it is difficult to hide a rebellion from a god." He tilted his head and grimaced. "Dreff was arrogant. He did not respect his elves. In the end, he was blind to what was happening."

Urravon sat stiffly throughout this recitation, his eyes focused on his untouched coffee cup. He looked as if he were personally under attack.

Harbert's eyes flickered over the elf, and he said, "An elf named Gan gained the trust of both a human and a dwarf when he was taken prisoner. He was a remarkable man. Together, the human, the dwarf and the elf ended the war.

"Gan carried a diamond said to have special properties. Dworgunul set the diamond into the hilt of a sword he made for Abbarkov. That sword allowed Abbarkov to defeat Dreff and banish him from the world."

"That was the end of the war." Harbert shrugged. "When I tell the story, it sounds so simple and straight forward. But it was a time of disruption and death. Too many of the important yet tiny details that make up an everyday life are left out." He shrugged again. "It is better to live in boring times."

Lifting his cup, he saluted his listeners. "Nonetheless, the three companions have gone down in history as heroes. In appreciation, Dworgunul presented each with a gift. The human, Kunnegarde accepted a mask that allowed the wearer to see people's thoughts. For Gan, there was a medallion that granted the ability to live as a ghost long after the body has gone to dust. Finally, Tul, the dwarf, received a mace that made the bearer invincible in battle. As well, because he was Dworgunul's own creation, Tul was endowed with immortality."

Flint sat up straight and stared around the table. The memory of the medallion hanging from the neck of the ghost in the tomb at Vaarndal was clear in his mind. Meeting Egbert's eyes, he was surprised when the blacksmith merely blinked slowly and gave him a bland nod.

Understanding bloomed and Flint tried to control his face. Egbert already knew the origin of the medallion and he did not intend to share that part of the story with his uncle.

Flint missed the next part of Harbert's tale as he tried to puzzle out Egbert's secrecy. They had come for information so surely it would be useful to ask questions. Glancing around the room, he saw Niviit studying him with a heavy-lidded stare.

Returning the look with a lift of his eyebrow, Flint attempted to appear impassive. He did not think it worked and he felt the heat rise to his face. Certain he was doing nothing to help their cause, Flint forced his attention back to Harbert.

"After the battle between Abbarkov and Dreff," the Hammer said, "the gods chose to leave the world. As you mentioned earlier, nephew, legends say Abbarkov left the God Sword behind, with special guards to preserve it in the event it was needed again. Beyond that, I do not believe there is much more I can tell you."

Harbert lifted his tankard and drank deeply. Wiping his mustache with his napkin, he said, "Nephew, we have much to catch up on. I want to hear about my brother." A look of pain flitted across his face.

"And I would like to tell you of him," Egbert answered.

Harbert regarded his other guests. He had not missed the yawns everyone politely tried to conceal. The hot bath followed by a lazy afternoon and a heavy meal had left everyone feeling sleepy.

"Perhaps you would be more comfortable in your rooms?" suggested Harbert.

Dell bristled at what was so clearly a dismissal, but Egbert quelled him with a glance. "Harbert and I need to talk," he said quietly. "Do not worry about me. Return to the rooms and I shall see you later."

Gode pushed back his heavy chair and said, "Harbert, Hammer of Dworgunul, we thank you for your kind hospitality."

Harbert answered just as formally. "Be welcome in my home. I thank you for bringing my nephew to me." He turned and smiled fondly at Egbert. "I look forward to hearing his tale."

With that, Niviit stepped to the door and waited while everyone stood. Flint was glad Niviit led the way. The hallways had no simple pattern, and he quickly became lost. When the dwarf finally reached their suite, he opened the door and stood aside to let them enter.

Two servants with trays laden with generously portioned meals stepped out of the shadows and followed them into the room.

Igon reached out to relieve one of the dwarves of her load. Smiling broadly, he said, "You must have read my mind. That was the hardest spell of guard duty I've ever pulled." Leaning over the tray, he inhaled deeply and sighed. "This is a special treat."

The second servant handed her tray to Dell who took it without comment.

Niviit bowed low and after waiting for the servants to withdraw, he stepped into the hallway and pulled the door closed.

Leaning forward, every Hawk listened for the snick of the lock. When it did not come, a barely audible sigh rustled through the room.

Igon settled at the table and happily dug into his supper. Ever conscious of his burn scars, Dell moved to where he would not be observed. Settling next to a window, he faced away from everyone and slipped his mask aside to eat.

Flint flopped onto one of the couches. "I'm stuffed," he announced. "I can hardly keep my eyes open."

Fleta tossed a blanket on top of him. "Cwenhild, Hulda and I are taking one of the bedrooms," she said. "Good night."

While the others spread out around the suite claiming beds and couches for the night, Urravon unfolded his bedroll on the floor of a closet. As soon as he had everything in place, he closed the door. Flint snorted and tucked the blanket more firmly around his shoulders. In moments, he was asleep.

Flint opened his eyes to the sounds of people moving around the suite. His first thought was of Egbert. Had he made it safely back to their rooms? His question was answered a moment later when the man wandered into Flint's view.

"Sleeping beauty has awakened," Egbert announced, with a chuckle. "We wondered whether we would have to load you on your horse and haul you away."

Flint wanted to ask what Egbert had learned from Harbert, but his mouth snapped shut when he remembered Urravon. With a stretch, he asked a different question, "Are we leaving this morning?"

"Right after Kjell finishes his magic lesson," answered Egbert.

"Who's teaching him?" Flint yawned and stretched before tossing back his blanket and jumping up from the couch.

Egbert smiled proudly. "Uncle Harbert."

"Harbert's a mage?" asked Flint in surprise.

"No, but he has read a number of books on the subject." Egbert waggled his eyebrows at Flint. He was unusually cheerful. "He is giving Kjell a few ideas about how to train his powers. I am going down to the forge to talk with Nulebar. He knew my father well and taught him smithing."

Despite his chipper manner, Egbert looked tired, and Flint suspected he had been awake most of the night. He was wearing his chainmail and carried his hammer on his belt.

"Are you going to show him your armour?" Flint asked. "Do you want me to show him Rising Star too?"

Egbert tilted his head and grinned self-consciously. "I would appreciate that," answered Egbert. He picked up his saddlebag and headed for the door. "When you are ready, come by the forge."

Flint was left alone in the room. How had he slept so late? As he folded his blanket, Fleta arrived.

"You're awake," she said and waved a large sandwich in under his nose. "I brought you breakfast. We're leaving in about an hour, so eat up and we'll go see to our horses."

"Egbert wants me to drop by the forge to show his father's teacher Rising Star." Flint took an enormous bite and spoke through his mouthful. "You should come too. You can show off your daggers and we could wear our chainmail. Egbert was wearing his when he left." Flint stuffed the rest of his breakfast into his mouth.

Fleta's face twisted. "When I made that sandwich for you," she said, "I was not imagining it would only last two bites." Clicking her tongue, she turned away and moved to the couch where Gode had slept.

Arranged along its length were eleven neatly folded piles of clothing. "I can't believe it!" she said. "Someone washed our clothes. They must have been delivered while we were away at breakfast." Picking up her pile, she pressed her nose into the fabric and inhaled. "It will be nice to have clean clothes to put on when we arrive at our destination."

Flint's head jerked up. "Do you know where we're headed?" he asked, stuffing his own freshly laundered clothes into his bag.

"All Egbert said was that he thinks he has a plan," she answered as she squirmed into her chainmail.

"Well, that's a start," replied Flint, pulling his own chainmail over his head. Fleta moved to help him fasten it when the door burst open. Flint dove for his sword belt and came up with a blade just as Gode entered.

"Greetings of the day, sleepyhead," the big man called, raising his eyebrows at Flint's sword. "You were expecting someone else?"

Flint lowered his weapon and grinned back. "Who's to say I wasn't expecting you?" He slid the sword into its sheath, shrugged into his baldric and buckled the straps over his chainmail.

Gode surveyed Flint and Fleta with a frown. "Are you heading off to battle?" he asked. "What's with the armour?"

"Egbert went down to visit his father's teacher," Fleta answered. "We're going to show off some of his handiwork." She turned her back to Flint so he could fasten the buckle on her armour and finished strapping on her dagger belt with its row of six perfectly-matched gleaming blades. "You should come too. Show him your Hawk axe." She made some final adjustments to the belt and turned to grin at Gode. "Too bad we didn't bring the Hawk. That would have been something to show off."

"That's just what we need!" exclaimed Flint with a shudder that was only partly feigned. "Can you imagine riding inside that tin can, rattling along these roads? It was bad enough on the day we assassinated King Abelard."

Fleta looked offended. "It worked exactly like it was supposed to," she said. "It wasn't designed to be a luxurious riding carriage."

"Tell you what," Gode said, interrupting their bickering. "We'll all dress in full armour. The Hawks shall stand for inspection before we leave, and Egbert can be very proud of his fine work."

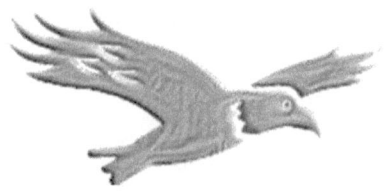

CHAPTER ELEVEN

Protectors

THE SUN SHONE STRAIGHT DOWN into the white cobbled courtyard. When everyone had assembled, Gode used his best parade ground voice to call them to attention. Light gleamed from forged armour and weapons as the Hawks straightened and stood rigidly, staring straight ahead. It was an impressive sight. Only Kjell and Urravon did not take a place in the row.

Kjell declined because after two hundred years at court as commander of the King's Guard, he had spent more than enough time standing at attention. Besides, he had no Egbert-crafted armour or weaponry to show off. Dressed only in leather trousers and a loose-fitting shirt, he leaned against the stable wall, watching Egbert proudly lead Nulebar and Harbert down the row.

Though still powerful and heavily muscled, the old blacksmith showed signs of age in his stiff gait. His warm brown eyes lit with interest as he studied the metal creations.

On Gode's command, every Hawk drew their weapons and held them on display.

While Flint stood stiffly with both blades extended, the elderly blacksmith halted in front of him. After peering up at Flint's face, Nulebar bent to study the sword that had been Cadmon's pride and joy.

Flint fought against a shudder of grief as he examined the top of the little man's head. Cadmon should have been the one showing off his sword. He tightened his lips against the lump in his throat while Nulebar lifted a gnarled finger to trace along the swirls that spelled out "The Rising Star."

Nulebar lifted his head and asked a question in rapid Tsaralvian while Harbert took his turn to study the sword.

Egbert answered in the language of his father and Flint guessed he was explaining how Cadmon had found the meteor and how much work it had been to smelt the metal.

When Nulebar bent to examine the sword again, Flint broke his rigid posture and offered Rising Star to the master craftsman.

With a bow, Nulebar accepted the sword and stepped away from the line of warriors. After hefting it a few times to get a feel for the balance, Nulebar brandished the sword in a series of attacks and defenses that revealed his skill as a swordsman. Raising an appreciative eyebrow, he turned back to Egbert.

This time the conversation was long, and judging from Egbert's gestures, they were discussing how he created the perfect balance in the weapon.

Suddenly, the thunder of many hooves rang from the cobblestone street outside Harbert's home. The Hawks broke from their parade ground formation and looked at each other while Kjell leapt nimbly onto the high wall with one of the stable boys at his heels.

Wearing his chainmail coat, Gode did not attempt the climb but called up to Kjell, "What is it? Can you see?"

The child who had followed Kjell so eagerly, answered in a high-pitched voice, "They wear the emblem of the Protectors of the God Sword."

Everyone swivelled to look to Harbert whose stony face revealed nothing.

Egbert reacted first. "Kjell, get down from there," he shouted. "Hawks, we will take our leave now—through the back gate. It is us they are after. No point riding straight into a fight if we can avoid it."

Kjell and the boy both turned on Egbert's command but before they could jump into the safety of the interior courtyard, something punched Kjell in the stomach. Looking down, he was surprised to find the fletched end of an arrow protruding from the same spot Hulda had shot him. Wrenching it free, he glanced down at the boy.

He had his grubby hands wrapped around the shaft of an arrow embedded deeply in his own belly. Having watched Kjell pull his arrow free so easily, he tried it himself. He was unable to pull it out entirely, but the movement caused blood to spurt from the wound.

The boy's eyes went wide as the blood drained from his face and he crumpled to his knees.

Another arrow sped past his head as Kjell stooped to gather him in his arms. "Let me help you," he whispered, and then, careful to avoid jostling him, he leapt lightly from the wall and laid him on the ground.

Glancing down to assess his own injury, Kjell was not surprised to see the skin had already closed over the arrow hole. He had lost only a dribble of blood. Injuries never bothered him for long.

The boy, however, was not so fortunate. His breathing was shallow and a faint sheen of sweat covered his skin. Uncertain if it would help, Kjell covered the wound with his hand. His theory was confirmed when the flow of blood slowed. Somehow, he was responsible for the healing.

Taking a chance, he grasped the end of the shaft and drew it quickly from the boy's stomach. A gush of blood followed, but as soon as he placed his hand on the wound, the blood stopped, and the skin began to knit together.

Kjell studied the healing process until he was torn from his reverie by Egbert's urgent shout.

"Kjell, we must go now!"

For a moment longer, Kjell held his hand in place before standing up. Dizzy, he staggered and reached out to steady himself on the fence.

"Come on, Kjell," Egbert shouted from atop his horse.

By force of will, Kjell dismissed the faintness and ran to his horse, where it waited alone at the hitching post.

Unwinding the reins, he threw a leg over the saddle, kicked his horse into motion and followed Egbert. Except for the swish of a horse's tail disappearing around the corner, no one was in sight. Gripping tightly with his knees as he pushed away a wave of nausea, he urged his horse to a gallop and pounded out of the alley.

Flint whipped his defending sword around in time to protect his left side. The moment he had entered the square, a brawny dwarf who moved with frightening speed had attacked him. Around him, the crash of battle told him the other Hawks were similarly engaged.

Knocking aside the attacking blade, Flint took advantage of the dwarf's temporary loss of balance. He kicked his foot free of the stirrup, set his boot firmly on the dwarf's chest and pushed.

It was not a move he had practiced before. Yet, it did not seem right to kill a Defender of the God Sword. After all, they were protecting the very talisman for which the Hawks were searching.

The dwarf flailed his arms but Flint's boot pushed him past the point where he could recover his balance. All at once, the weight of his heavy sword and armour toppled him to the cobblestones.

Whirling his horse, Flint searched for another opponent and saw Kjell and Egbert race around the corner. Egbert hauled his horse up short and scanned the crowd, his eyebrows in a sharp vee.

A dwarf sent his mace crashing against Gode's axe. Only the dwarf's braided brown beard was visible beneath a highly polished helmet. The man rose in his stirrups and brought the mace down again. Gode barely defended himself and as he lost his balance, his axe flew from his grip.

Weaponless, Gode urged his horse back, but before he could protect himself, the mace rose again. Without hesitation, Kjell lifted his hands and a blast of fire coursed through the air to ripple against the dwarf's shield. Surprised, the dwarf scowled around to find the source of the flames.

When he spotted Kjell, whose extended arm still pointed at him, he let his mace drop by his side and stared at the former Follower of Martokallu.

Gode started to dismount to pick up his lost axe, but at that moment, Egbert shouted, "Ride, Hawks! This is not a fight we need to win." Driving his heels into his horse, he fled the square.

Taking advantage of their adversaries' astonishment, most of the Hawks raced after him.

Gode grabbed Flint's arm as he turned his horse. "Cover me," he called. Leaping down, he scrambled after his axe where it had lodged in a storm drain grate. Without letting go of his horse's reins, he tried to wrest it free.

However, at that moment, the dwarf who Flint had pushed off his horse, regained his feet and charged Gode with his blade ready.

"Leave it, Gode," Flint shouted. "Let's go."

After an anguished moment, Gode threw himself onto his horse and they fled.

Tul pulled thoughtfully on one of his beard braids while he sat on his horse and watched the last of the Hawks disappear around the corner. His men milled around in confusion for a moment and then turned to him for instructions.

He made them wait while he examined the burn mark on the front of his shield. Hooking his mace through a loop on the front of his saddle, he used his thumb to wipe away part of the black stain. It came off easily, revealing the painted rune behind it.

With the shadow of a smile, he shook his head and said, "Let them go."

CHAPTER TWELVE

Revelations

AT THE GATES OF TSARVAL, the guards' startled expressions were almost enough to make Flint laugh aloud as he and the other Hawks galloped past. It was the first time he had ever run from a fight.

It made sense though. Egbert had the right idea. The Defenders of the God Sword were not the enemy. He snorted. Someone should tell them about the ghost in the crypt that had approved of Flint and granted the Hawks access to the map.

The map. Had Harbert known what it meant? Glancing at Egbert, he was not surprised to see the older man struggling to maintain his seat on the galloping horse.

They would have to rein in soon if they wanted to save both the horse and Egbert's backside. Igon and Dell rode on either side of the smith, prepared to catch him if he bounced out of the saddle.

Twisting around, Flint peered back. "No one's following," he shouted.

In relief, Egbert slowed his horse to a walk and the others did the same. Looking much more comfortable at the walking pace, he leaned out of his saddle to wrap a powerful hand around Gode's arm. "You will need a new blade," he said.

"Egbert, I am sorry to lose that axe," Gode said with a frown. "It was stuck. If I'd stayed, Flint would have had to fight." He pressed his lips together. "You were right to call a retreat. The Defenders of the God Sword are not our enemy."

"No need to worry." Egbert patted his arm. "I know how to make another just like it. The moment I find a forge, I will get to work."

Gode's throat worked. "And, in the meantime?" he asked. "All I've got is this." He drew a dagger from the sheath tied to his saddle. Another example of Egbert's fine work, it was too small to be truly impressive.

He untied the thong holding the sheath in place and attached it to his belt. Then he began to practice drawing the weapon and brandishing it about before sheathing it again.

When he glanced at Flint, his expression darkened. "Something funny?" he demanded.

"Well," answered Flint, drawing out the word. "I couldn't help but notice that your sword is awfully small." Reaching back, he drew Rising Star from its scabbard. "Perhaps you would feel more confident with a larger weapon."

Gode blinked. "You would lend me Rising Star?" he asked.

Flint snorted. "No." With a flourish, he drew his second sword. "But I might be persuaded to lend you this blade if you ask nicely."

Gode's eyebrows drew together. Then, with a laugh, he relaxed. "You make a tempting offer," he answered, stabbing the dagger toward Flint. "But this is a blade I know. I trust it'll be enough to fend off any attackers."

Fleta leaned over and gripped Gode's elbow. "Take the sword, Gode," she said, meeting his eyes. "That dagger isn't enough for you in a real battle."

Cwenhild nodded. "She's right. You're an axe-wielder, Gode. That little eating knife is not going to work when you have a real opponent in front of you. Take the sword."

Gode's hands curled into fists. Then he drew in a deep breath and released it in an explosive sigh. "I thank you for your kind offer, Flint," he said, stretching out a hand to accept the sword.

Handing it over with a grin, Flint said, "My pleasure.

Gode scowled and settled the blade across his knees.

"When we stop for the night, I'll help you rig a scabbard for it," Egbert said.

"Speaking of stopping for the night," said Fleta. "Where are we headed?"

"There is no easy answer to that question," Egbert replied, squinting down the road.

Flint's shoulders slumped. He had really hoped Harbert would set them on the next leg of their journey. Perhaps they should give up and head home.

"Harbert read the disc," Egbert said.

Biting his lip, Flint straightened and stared at Egbert. "What did it say?" he asked.

Egbert cocked his head to the side and chanted,

> "Otel zed sug da zed chuca,
> Otel zed yocol da zed coanch,
> Vocanf plif vout yarca,
> Gidat zed satal da zed harca."

Gode rubbed a hand across his face and tugged on one ear. "And does that mean anything to you?" he asked.

"It is ancient Tsaralvian," Egbert replied. "The language has changed since the days when the disc was made. Let me translate for you." He closed his eyes and recited,

"On the top of the world,
On the bottom of the land,
Find what is hidden,
Behind the grief of the hand."

Dell rolled his eyes. "They're pretty words but they're not terribly useful. Do you have any idea what they mean?"

Egbert's forehead wrinkled and he tugged on a beard braid. "It is supposed to tell us where to find the map that shows where the God Sword is hidden. However—" With a grimace, he broke off and shook his head. "Harbert was not certain."

"Did he have any suggestions?" asked Cwenhild.

"He said we should head to Livanum," replied Egbert. "After that, I have a vague idea about where we should go." He gave a quick sideways glance at Urravon and changed the subject. "As to where we will spend the night—"

Urravon, who had been edging his horse closer to the center of the conversation, chose that moment to interrupt. "I know a place to camp," he said, his voice rusty with disuse. "We can be there in about three hours."

When Urravon led them off the road onto a tree-lined trail, Flint heard them first. A single note cut through the rustle of the wind in the trees. "What is that?" he asked.

Before anyone could answer, they entered a wide meadow. Kneeling in tidy rows, several hundred fully-armoured men and women faced the setting sun with their palms up and their eyes closed. They were humming and the noise combined into a solid layer of sound.

Not everyone in the camp was involved in the prayer. Six sentries stepped onto the path to challenge the Hawks. Their faces were concealed behind the long hoods of their white linen surcoats.

The largest of the sentries stepped forward and the lowering sun glinted off his polished breast plate. "Welcome,

Urravon," he said. "We have been expecting you."

At this greeting, most of the Hawks swivelled to stare at Urravon. He ignored their surprise. "Thank you, Talagon," he murmured breathlessly. "I am glad to be back amongst the Faithful." With a smile, he gazed around the camp.

Gode's grip tightened on the sword in his lap. "Expecting us?" he demanded. "And who are you to expect us?"

The tall elf turned to Gode. Pushing back his hood, he revealed pointed ears and black hair. An eyepatch cut from the same leather as his trousers covered one eye, but the good grey eye studied him coldly.

After a moment, Egbert answered for him. "They are Followers of Dreff. Same as young Urravon here." His brow wrinkled as he considered Urravon's evident pleasure. "No doubt, they have been in communication throughout our travels."

Urravon jerked upright and his glazed expression vanished as he crossed his arms and jutted out his chin.

Egbert's lips thinned. "Perhaps there is someone in particular here who is expecting us?" he asked.

Flint enjoyed the ripple of discomfort that flitted across Urravon's face. His hand twitched toward Rising Star. For a moment, he almost regretted his generosity in lending his second sword to Gode. What would he do with his left hand?

Out of the corner of his eye, Flint saw Fleta shift her position and adjust the scarf around her waist to allow better access to her throwing blades. No one had yet reached for a weapon, but they were ready.

If it came to that, it would be a bloody fight. The Worshippers of Dreff outnumbered the Hawks by at least forty to one.

CHAPTER THIRTEEN

Worshippers of Dreff

TALAGON DID NOT FLINCH WHEN Egbert suggested that Urravon was a spy. The leader of the sentries inclined his head and fixed Egbert with a menacing one-eyed glare. "Come with me," he said and turned on his heel.

Egbert glanced at Flint and murmured, "Let us see what this is about. Perhaps young Urravon has brought us to the people who can help solve the mystery of the disc."

"Perhaps," muttered Flint. He fell in beside Fleta whose fingers fluttered over her concealed daggers. It was obvious Urravon had led them into a trap.

Kjell studied the camp. What were the elves doing on the wrong side of the river? And why had they gone to such trouble to lure the Hawks into Tsaralvia. What did they want?

And then, in a flash, he understood.

The elves needed the disc. And they would never have been able to retrieve it on their own. Only someone like Flint had the brave innocence necessary to earn the disc and its concealed message.

Taking up the rear, Kjell glanced over his shoulder at the five sentries who were ushering them further into unknown territory. He would have dearly loved to draw his bow, but it was not yet time. There was no point in provoking a fight. The Hawks were terribly outnumbered. They would have to rely on Egbert's diplomacy skills to get them safely out of the situation.

Urravon paid no attention to the Hawks' scowls as they made their way through the camp. It was the first time Kjell had seen the boy smile. Everything about the camp seemed to please him.

Unable to ignore the sensation creeping up his spine a moment longer, Kjell placed his hands on the back of his saddle, lifted himself and swung his legs around to ride backwards. It felt odd, nonetheless, he thrust his feet into his stirrups and narrowed his eyes at the sentries.

The Hawks were good people and he sensed that the Worshippers of Dreff were not. From the elves, he got the same impression of evil that Martokallu had given off. With a start, he realized the Hawks had become his friends. It was a strange idea. How long had it been since he felt anything like loyalty? In his days as a Follower, he had always considered himself loyal to Martokallu. But it was not true. The connection they had shared had not been loyalty. It had been a compulsion to serve.

The praying elves finished their devotions and rose as one to watch the Hawks parade past. The strangeness of their silence was striking. Were the elves surprised by the visitors or was such stillness natural for the Worshippers of Dreff?

It made the hair on the back of Kjell's neck stand up. He glanced over his shoulder. Ahead of him, Cwenhild riffled her fingers through the arrows in her quiver as if to reassure herself that she had a good supply. Hackett's knuckles showed white where they gripped the haft of his axe.

Abruptly, Kjell's horse stopped. They had arrived at the entrance to an enormous white tent. Talagon called out a greeting and immediately, an older elf stepped out.

Tall and thin, he wore the same style of robes as the sentries, except his were black, as was his polished chest protector. A smile creased his face when he saw the assembled Hawks.

Spreading his arms wide to encompass them all, he called, "Welcome. Welcome." His smile broadened further when he spotted Urravon in the group. "Urravon, my boy. Welcome. And congratulations on the completion of a successful mission."

Urravon flushed in pleasure and Kjell watched with alarm as the tension went out of all the Hawks. Hackett's hand relaxed, while Flint heaved a sigh and let his shoulders slump forward.

"Welcome to the camp of the Followers of Dreff," the man purred. His voice was rich and hypnotic. "I am Radomil. It is such a pleasure to have you here."

Egbert swung slowly off his horse and tested his balance cautiously when he touched the ground. "Greetings of the day, Radomil," he said with a smile as he stretched out his right hand. "I am Egbert Martell of Abbarkon."

The elf reached forward and grasped Egbert's extended hand with both of his. "Yes, of course, Egbert. How wonderful to meet you at last! I have heard so much about you." Normally, his effusive tone would have caused some raised eyebrows among the Hawks, but no one seemed to be put off in the least. "Urravon tells me you are a brilliant smith as well as a knowledgeable historian."

With a pleased smile, Egbert glanced at Urravon, but the younger elf did not take his eyes off his leader.

"Please, please, be welcome in my tent," Radomil said, sweeping back the flap and gesturing for the Hawks to precede him. "We have much to talk about."

Unhurriedly, the Hawks dismounted. They moved as if in a daze, slight smiles held in place. Several young men appeared and without question, the Hawks handed over their reins.

Egbert was the first to duck under Radomil's extended arm, and one by one, the other Hawks followed.

Kjell hopped down from his horse and cut in line, blocking the way. Only Hackett, Dagur, Hulda and Igon remained outside. Kjell touched each person firmly on the shoulder.

As if awakening from sleep, they blinked and stared around at the rows of Cheveralians who continued to watch in silence. Every hand went to a weapon.

Before they could draw them, Kjell said, "Why don't you stay outside and keep watch for us? Shout if you see anything unusual."

Hulda's eyes darted around the camp, and she cleared her throat before looking directly at Kjell. "Yes," she said. "I see what you mean. We'll be right here if you need us."

As Kjell turned to follow the others into the tent, Hulda reached out and grasped his arm. "Thank you, Kjell," she whispered.

Kjell grinned and ducked into the tent. He found the Hawks seated in a circle. They reclined at ease on pillows and not one hand hovered near a weapon.

At the door, Radomil studied the four Hawks who had remained outside, before turning a curious gaze on Kjell.

Cocking his head to the side, Kjell said, "I believe they will be more comfortable where they are." His customary smile vanished, and he made a tour around the tent, touching each person on the shoulder as he passed. The effect was immediate.

Flint and Gode sprang to their feet and stood back-to-back,

each brandishing a sword. In the meantime, Cwenhild and Fleta rolled to the edge of the tent and drew their daggers. Dell was the first to understand the danger. While everyone else stared around in bewilderment, he threw himself at Radomil.

Kjell brought him up short. "Dell," he called. "Hold on a minute."

Dell skidded to a stop, his gauntlet inches from Radomil's throat. "Why wait?" he demanded. "Are you on his side, traitor?"

Cwenhild said, "Kjell saved us. He's not a traitor. Didn't you feel the enthrallment Radomil put on us? It made me stop worrying." She scowled. "I never stop worrying."

"I felt it," Dell ground out. "Give me one good reason not to finish this scum right now."

Egbert rose stiffly from his pillow. "There are at least three hundred reasons beyond these tent walls. Let us talk before we act."

Radomil tilted his head in acknowledgement. "My apologies for acting rashly. It is difficult to know whom to trust, but having seen the clarity of your purpose, I believe we can work together."

It was hardly an apology for using his powers on people who had, for all intents and purposes, arrived at the camp by invitation. Perhaps if Kjell did not have two centuries of experience with men and their battles, he might have reacted differently, but he chose to let the elf's arrogance pass.

Not taking his eyes off Radomil, Kjell rested a hand on Dell's arm and said, "I believe our host has tested our dedication to the cause. Perhaps he was uncertain upon our arrival, but I expect his examinations have not found us wanting. We should be able to work together to meet our common goal."

Dell shook off Kjell's hand, but he said nothing as he stepped back from Radomil and let his gauntlet drop to his side.

His face set in stern lines, Egbert moved to the other side of Dell and met Radomil's eye. "I understand you might have good reason to be cautious," he said. "Especially when we are involved in such an undertaking." He swept his gaze over the other Hawks.

The tension in the tent abated somewhat and Kjell settled himself on a pillow. "Shall we discuss what brought us all to Tsaralvia?" he asked with a smile. He did not enjoy returning to the role of negotiator. It felt too much like his time with Martokallu.

Egbert tugged on a beard braid before drawing in a deep breath and dropping to a pillow.

Radomil too sat down and beamed up at those who remained standing. "Please, join us. It is true. We have much to talk about."

Gode glanced from Egbert to Radomil, his face impassive. Making up his mind, he sat facing Radomil. But he kept Flint's sword across his lap and showed no sign of relaxing.

Flint gnawed his lip as he exchanged a long look with Fleta. Without a word, they sat together, holding their blades ready. Cwenhild narrowed her eyes at Kjell and lowered herself to a pillow as well.

Only Dell remained standing, rage and suspicion pouring off him. Radomil affected not to notice the snick of metal on metal as his bladed fingers flexed.

Kjell leaned forward and said, "Since we do share a common purpose in the search for the God Sword, perhaps you can help us in our quest?"

Radomil shifted. "I am pleased you have come. I shall do whatever I can to support your progress," he said. "Knowing the importance of this weapon, we have tried on our own to find it, but owing to the difficult relations between the elves and the dwarves, we were unable to proceed very far. Still, we have learned a great deal along the way, and that is why I asked Urravon to bring you here today."

His face bland, Egbert studied Radomil. "We too have learned a few things along our travels," he said, looking around at each of the Hawks. It was obvious he was trying to decide whether to risk confiding in the man. Taking a deep breath, he sat upright in his nest of pillows and recited,

"Otel zed sug da zed chuca,
Otel zed yocol da zed coanch,
Vocanf plif vout yarca,
Gidat zed satal da zed harca."

Radomil hummed and said, "Behind the grief of the hand?" He scratched his chin and tilted his head back to gaze at the canvas ceiling of the tent.

Kjell watched Cwenhild stare at Radomil's exposed neck as she fingered a dagger. Did the elf have any notion of his danger? Or was he testing them?

Finally, Radomil looked back at his visitors. His broad smile returned as his fingers formed a steeple. "Behind the grief of the hand," he repeated. "I believe I know where that is."

CHAPTER FOURTEEN

Ambush

FLINT COULD NOT FORGET THE flood of confusion that had hit him when Kjell touched his shoulder and pulled him out from under Radomil's control. Even thinking about it left him nauseous. Radomil's invasion of their minds was inexcusable.

Still, the elf leader had made no further attempts to slide into anyone's consciousness. Perhaps because he knew Kjell was insusceptible to his charms. Or maybe he really had only been checking their intentions.

In any case, Radomil was the least of their worries as far as Flint was concerned. Talagon, the lead sentry, seemed far more dangerous. When Radomil ushered them out of his tent, Talagon had taken charge again and led them to a tent set aside for their use. It was nothing the elf did that bothered Flint. It was more how he looked at the Hawks—as if they were kittens that he planned to drown.

Shaking off the disturbing memory, Flint forced his

attention back to the trail. His position at the back of the party allowed him to watch their rear, as well as keep an eye on the ridges above the path.

All day, he had been nervous, although there had been no sign of anything unusual. He kept telling himself that there was nothing to worry about. His nerves were nothing more than the residue of their time with the Followers of Dreff. The elves were a strange lot. Something about their silent prayers set him on edge.

Flint studied the back of Urravon's head and wondered for the hundredth time why they had allowed the sneaky little elf to continue to ride with them. Obviously, he was Radomil's spy. Why had Egbert agreed to take him along?

Urravon had caught them unaware and led them into a trap. It might have been worth it though. If Radomil was right, they were on their way to the next step in their quest.

Though why would someone who had grown up in Cheveral, on the other side of the Renncasfo River know more about the landscape in Tsaralvia than the Hammer of Dworgunul? Why had Harbert offered only a general idea about where to find 'The grief behind the Hand'?

Watching how the Cheveralians acted around Radomil reminded Flint of what Kjell had said about Martokallu and his Followers. Did the elf control the Worshippers of Dreff the same way?

A tiny movement on a cliff above the trail caught Flint's attention. As he strained to see something more, an arrow bounced off the front of his saddle. He sucked in a breath and scanned the ridgeline, searching for his assailant, before he remembered to call a warning. "Take cover," he yelled. "It's an ambush!"

At that instant, a figure dressed in robes the colour of straw appeared high on the cliff.

"I am Gadrith," he thundered, thumping his staff on the

ground so that light shimmered from the ring on its end. "I am the foremost Lieutenant of the great and powerful Martokallu." He raised his sword and swept his glowing green eyes across the Hawks. "You have displeased the Master, and for this, you shall die."

Flint forced himself to look away and studied the canyon wall, searching for a route up. Then he heard the twang of Hulda's bow string. In the same instant, Kjell sent a fireball hurtling upward.

Dodging both missiles, Gadrith leapt forty feet down to the road and landed like a cat. As he raised his sword, he smiled in anticipation. "Make your farewells!" he boomed, his voice echoing off the rock.

As if in answer to a command, two dozen Followers emerged from their hiding spots in the bushes beside the path. Without warning, they attacked.

Gode made a flying leap from his saddle and landed on Gadrith's back. The tall, thin Follower stumbled under his weight, twisting as he fell. Scrambling to maintain his advantage, Gode sat on his chest, pinning his arms to his sides. Then, finding himself in no position to swing a sword, he punched Gadrith in the face.

Meanwhile, Dell threw himself into the fray, slashing at every Follower within reach. They fell back under his initial fury but surged forward a moment later.

Flint faced a huge Follower whose glowing blue eyes gazed greedily at him. Two sword clashes later, Flint realized he was in trouble. Big trouble. Without his second sword, his arm was tiring from the power of the blows, and he was continually off-balance.

Hulda and Cwenhild galloped out of immediate danger before pulling up and firing arrows back at the attackers. The Followers ignored the bolts that stuck out of their rotten armour and continued to fight anyone within reach.

It quickly became clear that while the Hawks might take down a few Followers, there were too many to defeat without casualties on their side.

Dell fought himself into a clear spot and shouted, "Kjell! Come to me. Everyone else, ride!"

It took a moment for Flint to react. Then, he battered back a jarring blow and sprinted for his horse. As he threw himself on its back, he saw the other Hawks dashing away.

Safely out of reach, Flint pulled up and called, "Wait until everyone is clear!"

Breathlessly, Fleta shouted, "Gode! We have to help him."

Sitting atop Gadrith, Gode was unable to do much more than continue to pummel the pinned man. After throwing one final brutal punch and spattering dark green blood everywhere, he pushed himself up and launched himself at his horse.

Freed at last, Gadrith whipped his staff in an arc, knocking Gode's feet out from under him. As Gode hit the ground, Gadrith rose, spitting green blood. But he was too slow. In a flash, Gode scrambled up and vaulted onto his horse.

Kjell had avoided any hand-to-hand combat, choosing to remain out of reach and fling fireballs at the attackers. Moving along the edge of the battlefield, he covered the Hawks' retreat. When he reached Dell, he grinned. "You have a plan?" he asked.

Dell bounced a grenade in his palm and shifted his eyes up at an overhanging ledge. "I do," he replied.

Following his gaze, Kjell said, "That should do it." He stretched out a finger and pressed it to the fuse of the grenade. When it started to sizzle, he whirled away and fired an arrow into the chest of a charging Follower. Unlike Hulda and Cwenhild's arrows, his had an effect. The Follower clutched the haft and screamed as he burst into flame.

The sound was enough to cause two other Followers to skid to a halt and stare warily at Kjell.

He smiled and called, "Hello, boys! It's been too long!" Nocking another arrow, he held it casually. "We're leaving now. There's no need to follow us." He glanced at Dell. Only a tiny amount of fuse remained. "How's your arm?"

"Good enough," replied Dell and he heaved the grenade up onto the ledge.

The moment it landed, they bolted.

Gadrith stepped back as the dust cleared. He was beginning to understand Martokallu's insistence that the Hawks had to die. The damage they had already caused to the Master's plan was upsetting enough but their continued defiance was truly galling.

Martokallu rarely gave reasons for his orders. Gadrith shuddered to recall the Master's barely suppressed anger as he explained to Gadrith what needed to be done. Something about the Hawks' current mission disturbed Martokallu greatly.

Gadrith recalled the grating voice instructing him not to underestimate them. Standing amidst the ruins of his carefully planned ambush, he struggled to understand how they had slid out of his trap. It had all been so clear to him when he set it up. The Hawks were warriors. They would fight to their death. He had never anticipated their decision to run away. And the idea of explosives that could set off landslides had certainly not entered into his calculations.

Looking around at the Followers who had died in the battle and the following landslide, Gadrith realized he had better see who could be saved before he continued the pursuit. He could not speak with the Master, but he could heal.

He would start with himself. His attacker had made a mess of his face. Along with several gashes that had opened when the man smashed his fists against his cheekbone, his nose was broken and blood was gushing into his mouth.

Covering his face with his hands, Gadrith released a surge of power. The initial blast was cold but as the skin and bones knit together, it turned warm, and he felt a rush of energy.

When he pulled his hands away from his face, he pictured the faces of the men who had escaped his trap. One of them had looked remarkably like Kjell. But how could that be? Kjell was dead. He had died at the hands of the rebels.

He would never admit it when Martokallu was near, but Gadrith had celebrated Kjell's death. Lorund's and Hain's too if the truth be known. He had believed their deaths meant he would finally be chosen to ascend to the rank of General.

Gadrith cringed to recall how excited he had been. He had been confident that his healing powers and loyalty had finally been recognized. With every step toward the throne room, he had imagined how his life would change with the promotion. The Master would begin the process of raising him up by enhancing both his body and healing powers to make him one of the most powerful Followers.

His enhanced strength would virtually ensure his immortality. And he would not permit himself to grow careless as Hain, Kjell and Lorund had done. The best part was that he would develop the powerful mind-link with the Master. He, Gadrith, would become Martokallu's closest confidant and ally. Gadrith would be seated by the Master's side when he finally achieved his goals.

But that had not been why Martokallu called for him. Gadrith's dream shattered when Martokallu treated him as no more than a messenger. Instead of bestowing him with great power, the Master sent him to follow the Hawks into Tsaralvia and kill them.

As he studied the devastation surrounding him, Gadrith cursed Martokallu's decision to send him on the mission without a General. With Martokallu's vision, it would have been a simple matter to find where the Hawks had gone. He had chased them for days before landing on the perfect spot for an ambush. And look what had come of that.

He would have to improvise. Scanning the uninjured Followers, he chose two at random. Pointing with a long, grey finger that displayed cracks of dark-green light, he commanded, "Pursue the Hawks. Leave a trail we can follow."

Without hesitation, Shallak and Korgun scrabbled over the rocks that blocked the road. Gadrith watched until they gained the other side of the debris and settled into a mile-eating trot. When they disappeared around a corner, he turned back to the injured bodies that littered the ground.

"Hold it out," said Cwenhild.

Gritting his teeth, Igon released his grip on his right forearm and stretched it out to her. The moment he let go, blood began to seep from the deep gash that ran from wrist to elbow.

She clicked her teeth. "We should stop so I can sew it up," she said.

Gode shook his head. "Not yet. It's better if we put some space between us and the Followers," he said. "Can you patch him up while we ride?"

"Tie it up," Igon said. "I'll be fine."

Cwenhild lifted an eyebrow. "I suppose it doesn't hurt at all?"

Igon grimaced. "I didn't say that." Then he grinned. "But it'll feel better if I don't have to look at it."

"Less messy, too," agreed Cwenhild. Twisting around, she rummaged through her saddlebag. With a cry of triumph, she produced a roll of clean white bandage and a small linen packet with a purple flower painted on it. Taking Igon's arm in her lap, she upended the bag over his cut.

He hissed as the white powder settled in the wound, but the bleeding slowed at once.

"That should take care of any nasty infections you might have picked up from the Follower's blade," Cwenhild said, wrapping the bandage snuggly around his arm before tying it off. "I'll look at it again when we stop. It will need stitches."

Fleta edged closer to Egbert and murmured, "I had to leave three blades behind." Her shoulders drooped. "Now I know how Gode felt when he abandoned his axe. It's like I left part of myself behind."

Egbert leaned over and wrapped an arm around her shoulders. "I am glad it was only blades you had to leave behind," he said. "I can always make more of those. The important thing is your safety." Suddenly, he grunted and stood up in his stirrups as he turned to dig into his saddlebag. "I almost forgot," he said, pulling out a leather-wrapped bundle. "I brought a couple of extras, just in case."

Fleta's face lit up. "Egbert, I can't believe it! I thought I'd have to make do with three blades. It didn't seem like nearly enough." Taking the package, she untied the cord holding it closed and unrolled the leather to reveal four daggers that matched the ones already sheathed at her waist.

Out of the corner of his eye, Flint watched her choose three new blades and slide them into her empty sheaths. Continuing his surveillance of the surrounding area, he said, "Haven't I always warned you about the hazards of tossing your weapons around?"

"Hey," called Gode. "I wouldn't get too smug about your choice of weapons. It could happen to anyone." He kept his attention on the back trail despite his teasing. "By the way, young Flint, thank you again for the loan of your little blade. I didn't get a chance to use it yet, but I'm sure it will come in handy sometime."

They needed to take a break soon. Since the ambush, they had pushed the pace as hard as they could despite Igon's injury. The big man sat limply in his saddle, cradling his arm, and looking pale. As well, the horses would need a rest. Plus, everyone was hungry. Flint was dreaming of supper. It would do no good to run themselves into exhaustion.

Just then, the trail opened into a big meadow. Egbert gestured at the wide-open space and the creek that ran parallel to the road. "This will do just fine," he said. "The creek will provide water and the meadow will give us plenty of time to see any visitors before they get too close."

It was exactly the invitation the others had been waiting for. In no time, horses lined the creek, drinking their fill while Kjell helped Hulda start a fire and Fleta worked with Cwenhild to stitch up Igon's arm.

It was not likely to be a restful night, however. After a hurried supper, Hackett, Dagur and Dell offered to take the first watch.

"I'll join you," Flint volunteered even though he was dead tired. If there was a choice, he always preferred first watch because it was so hard for him to wake up.

Enviously, he watched Fleta curl into her blankets as he walked away from the fire and into the darkness.

CHAPTER FIFTEEN

Discovery

SHALLAK RAISED HIS HEAD TO see past the low bushes that surrounded the wide-open meadow. The Hawks were bedded down for the night. It would be a perfect time to attack. But the disastrous ambush earlier was enough to warn him off.

Besides, their orders had been clear. They were to follow the Hawks and leave a trail. No skilled trackers accompanied the Followers, so Shallak and Korgun had left a very obvious trail. Shortly after setting out, they had passed some cliffs of bright red clay. There, they loaded a bag with some of the fine sand that had collected at the bottom of a rock-slide. Every five hundred steps, they left a small pile of the red sand. Gadrith and the others would catch up with them shortly.

Moving almost imperceptibly, Shallak backed up to where he had left Korgun. He did not want to alert the four hunched shadows who stared alertly into the darkness, so his progress was necessarily slow. When he finally reached a point where he would not be seen, he stood and gestured for Korgun to follow him.

"They're staying the night," he said.

Korgun glanced toward the camp. "Should we kill them now?"

Shallak shook his head. "Gadrith told us to follow and leave a trail," he growled. "We will wait for the others to catch up."

For an instant, Korgan looked disappointed, but in the next instant, his face cleared, and he settled on a fallen log. "So, we wait."

Egbert reached down to rub his sore backside. No matter how many days he spent in the saddle, he had not become accustomed to the discomfort of riding. The sun had dropped very low in the sky and still they had seen no sign of the trail that was supposed to lead to a mountain that looked like four fingers of a hand. He hoped they had not missed it. Radomil told them that the trail was seldom used so it was probably entirely grown over.

Grimacing, he nudged his horse to a trot to pull up beside Gode. "Do you think we have missed the trail?" he asked.

Without raising his eyes from the side of the road, Gode answered, "I hope not. But it's hard to know." He looked up and met Egbert's eyes. "The thing that I've been wondering is why didn't Harbert tell us about this fortress?"

"I have wondered the same thing," said Egbert, smoothing his beard braids. "Perhaps my dear uncle was not convinced of our sincerity."

Gode gripped Egbert's arm. "Then, we will have to prove it to him," he said.

Swallowing against a sudden lump in his throat, Egbert opened his mouth to reply.

Flint's shout interrupted him. "I found it!" he cried. Dismounting from his horse, Flint used the toe of his boot to nudge aside the undergrowth. The barest trace of a path led off to the south. Flint handed his reins to Fleta and drew Rising Star.

At the sight of the sword, Gode called, "What are you expecting, Flint? It doesn't look like you have much to fear in that tangle of brush."

Flint grinned over his shoulder at the big man. Then he whirled and took a vicious swing at the overgrown trail. The sharp blade cleaved cleanly through the undergrowth. Shooting a look of triumph at Gode, he began to hack his way into the forest.

"I suggest we wait here," said Egbert. "The boy is a little over enthusiastic with that blade."

A moment later, Flint shouted in triumph. Before anyone could follow him, he was back. Ducking under the last branch, he stepped clear of the trees and asked, "Did Radomil say that he'd been on this path?"

Egbert's brow wrinkled. What had the man said? Finally, he shook his head. "No, I do not believe he said that," he answered. "By the look of it, no one has been here for years."

Fleta swung down and peered into the hole. "Why is that important?" she asked.

"I just thought he might have mentioned that the path is cobblestone," answered Flint.

Egbert's head jerked up. "Cobblestones?" he asked, leaning forward to gaze down the path. "So, at some time in the past, this path led somewhere important." Sweeping a bright blue gaze around at the others, he grinned. "This is it. I know it." He stood in his stirrups and sighed. "I almost hoped it would be so overgrown we would have to lead our horses the whole way.

Flint laughed. "You'll get your wish for this first bit," he said. "And who knows? Maybe if you're lucky, there'll be other overgrown spots too!"

"I don't want to camp anywhere along here," Gode said as he peered into the undergrowth of the heavy forest. Lush vegetation grew right up to the cobblestones. Only the tightly fitted stones prevented the road from being overrun as well.

Ever since turning off the main road, they had been climbing through a series of switchbacks. It was getting dark and there had been no sign of a mountain that looked like four fingers of a hand.

Hulda said, "We'll need to rest the horses soon. We should stop at the next creek we come to."

In the lead, Fleta dismounted and knelt to peer at something on the road.

Leaning forward in his saddle, Egbert asked, "What is it?"

She scrubbed at the stone with the elbow of her coat before sitting back on her heels. "I think it's writing," she said.

Egbert slid his leg over his saddle and dropped heavily to the ground. He rubbed his backside and stretched before squatting beside Fleta. Squinting in the dim light, he exclaimed, "It is words! It is the same ancient Tsaralvian as the disc. By the Hammer of Dworgunul, it is hard to see. I wish I had better light."

At once, Kjell leapt from his horse and produced a ball of fire that hovered above his palm. "Your wish is my command, my good sir," he said grandly.

Egbert laughed and smiled up at him. "You've learned a new trick, Kjell." Sobering, he glanced back at the road. "I wish Uncle Harbert were here. I could use a hand deciphering this message." He looked up at Kjell and cocked an eyebrow. "Can you make that wish come true, too?

Kjell lifted one shoulder and Egbert grunted as he went back to studying the engraved letters.

Flint and Cwenhild dismounted and peered back the way they had come. It was impossible to see anything in the gloom. For all he knew, the Followers could be right behind them. A cold finger ran up his spine as another thought occurred to him. The Protectors of the God Sword could be hidden by the darkness as well. His fingers flexed and then, not caring if he looked nervous, he unsheathed Rising Star.

Cwenhild looked up at him and pulled her bow from its sling. "Better safe than sorry," she murmured as she nocked an arrow.

While they stared into the darkness, the others crowded around Egbert who muttered to himself as he ran his fingers over the words.

"Can you read it?" asked Hulda.

For a moment, Egbert did not answer and then he muttered, "Magic will lead the way."

Kjell's flame faded. "Magic will lead the way?" he asked. "That's what it says on the road?"

"Or are you just thanking Kjell for his light?" Fleta added.

"Magic will lead the way," Egbert repeated, staring over Fleta's shoulder. "If I have translated it correctly, that is what the message says."

Igon and Hackett came to stand shoulder to shoulder with Cwenhild and Flint. Without, leaving her post, Cwenhild called, "Are there any other messages on the road? Because, if not, we should move along. This doesn't seem like the safest place to stop."

"Good point," Fleta said. "Kjell and I will walk ahead to look for other messages. Who knows? It might be important." She set off, leading her horse, bent almost in half as she peered at the cobblestones.

At the rear of the party, Flint was reluctant to turn his back on the darkness. "Lead my horse, will you, Igon?" he said as he settled himself backwards in the saddle.

"You do know how odd you look," Igon replied.

Flint laughed, glad of the release. His back and neck were stiff with tension. "When I saw Kjell do this at the Camp of the Worshippers of Dreff, it looked like a good idea," he said. Now, it just feels rather desperate. It'll be better when we start moving more quickly."

As if in answer to his wish, Fleta let out a hoot and mounted her horse. "I think we found it!" she shouted as she rushed ahead.

Igon called, "Hold on, Flint!"

As they sped up to a bouncing trot, Flint gripped the saddle. He lost a stirrup for a moment and pitched sideways before righting himself. Forcing himself to relax, he found the new rhythm and the ride smoothed out.

Suddenly, the view opened up and it was not nearly as dark. They had climbed above the tree line. He glanced over his shoulder as Igon slowed.

Lit by the last rays of the setting sun, a mountain with four slender peaks poked above the horizon.

CHAPTER SIXTEEN

Magic

EVER SINCE GODE PRODDED HIM awake, Flint had been peering into darkness, listening for anything that might indicate the Followers had caught up. He and Igon had settled some distance apart, Igon looking back and Flint looking forward.

Before stopping, the Hawks had put some distance between themselves and the edge of the forest. The Followers would not catch them unaware again.

To his surprise, Flint was enjoying the last shift of the night. Normally, he tried to avoid early morning watch because he found it so hard to wake up, but Fleta had wanted to sleep in and she had teased him into volunteering.

Once he was up, it was not so bad. In fact, there was something almost pleasant about watching the night turn to dawn. As the sun lit up the mountain, he began to study the scene more carefully. The evening before, they had watered their horses at the stream but he could see there was a small mountain lake as well. When the sun crept over the mountain, the water lit up with a brilliant turquoise colour unlike anything Flint had ever seen. The setting could not be more beautiful.

He switched his attention back to the edge of the treeline and scanned the area for motion, but nothing caught his eye. Turning to study the mountain again, he noticed a shape that looked like the outline of a door.

"Igon," he called quietly, "do you see that thing over there that looks like a door?"

Igon swivelled to look where Flint pointed, and replied, "It doesn't look like the rest of the rock around it." He squinted, trying to see through the distance. "Is it made of metal?"

They both moved toward the base of the mountain for a few paces and then stopped as they remembered their responsibilities.

Flint grinned and said, "I think it's time for everyone to be up anyway."

With a twinkle in his eye, Igon let out a loud whoop and waited for the reaction.

At the noise, the Hawks bolted out of their blankets with weapons drawn. They stared around, wide-eyed, and ready, searching for an enemy.

Igon and Flint burst out laughing.

Realizing there was no immediate danger, the others shook their heads and grumbled as they rolled up their blankets.

Catching sight of Dell as he tucked his dagger away and relaxed his gauntlet, Flint suddenly understood that he might have set himself up for some rude awakenings in the future.

"No. No," he called, pointing toward the mountain. "It's not a joke. We woke you up to show you something. Can you see a door?"

It was time to get moving. For far too long, Gadrith had been patient, but that was over. Either the others would keep up or he would kill them himself. He had done all he could to heal their injuries, and it was time to catch the Hawks.

On his command, they moved into a single-file procession, scrambled over the landslide debris, and started down the road. They looked good. Strong. There was nothing to worry about. Despite the deaths, Gadrith still had plenty of Followers. Even though the ambush had not worked out, he had learned all he needed to know to guarantee a victory the next time. He would find the Hawks and kill them.

As they settled into a trot, they came across a small pile of red sand left neatly where it would not be missed. Cheered, Gadrith kicked at the marker, scattering the sand across the road. Shallak and Gorgon had done their job. He would catch the humans before the end of the day.

It was definitely a door—a metal door that reflected the sun in a blinding beam of light that guided them up the mountain. As they drew nearer, the excitement built. Nonetheless, no one forgot the threat of the Followers. Most people kept a better eye on what was behind than what was in front.

When they finally arrived, Egbert was the first one off his horse. "There is no handle or keyhole," he said, leaning close to study the polished surface.

Gode joined him. "What do the words say?" he asked, brushing his fingers across the letters inscribed along the top.

Egbert shook his head. "They are not in any language I know. They look more decorative than informative."

Dell reached into a pocket and withdrew one of his small grenades. "We could blow it open," he suggested.

Egbert looked offended. "We cannot do that. An explosion might trigger a landslide inside that would bury any hope of finding the God Sword."

Dell stepped aside with a shrug and Fleta, who had been

standing back, shifted closer. She touched the door. "Do you see this?" she asked, tracing a swirl that ran around a circle.

Egbert leaned in, his brow furrowed. "By the Hammer of Dworgunul, girl," he burst out. "That is it!"

He hurried back to his horse where he rummaged in his saddlebag and extracted a cloth-wrapped bundle. Returning, he held up the disc they had taken from the grave of the Fifteenth Hammer. After giving it a polish, he fitted it onto the outlined circle.

At the touch, it snapped into place and stuck.

Egbert stumbled back. "By the Fire of Dworgunul," he whispered.

The disc began to spin.

They had found the key! Everyone held their breath as they waited for the door to open.

But nothing changed.

The disc continued to spin until it appeared as a blur, but the door did not shift. The spot in the middle of the disc began to glow with a brilliant white light, and again the feeling of expectation built.

Nothing.

Egbert's shoulders sagged. He stepped back and swept his gaze around the door's frame. Everyone else backed up too. Several turned to survey the tree line, searching for any sign of Followers.

"There has to be a clue that tells us what to do," said Cwenhild. "Egbert, what did it say on the disc, again?"

Egbert scrunched up his face in an effort of memory and recited,

"On the top of the world,
On the bottom of the land,
Find what is hidden,
Behind the grief of the hand."

Fleta balled up her fists and kicked the door. "But that only tells us how to get here." Then she froze. "Grief of the hand," she repeated. "What does that mean?"

Egbert shook his head. "It does not make sense." Then his face cleared, and he snapped his fingers. "There is another clue!" he said, his face alight. "Remember what it said on the cobblestones, just before we reached this place? 'Magic will lead the way.'" He gave an exaggerated bow to Kjell and waved him forward. "I do believe we need a mage. Kjell, will you practice a wee bit of magic on this door, and we'll see what it does?"

Kjell had been standing at the back of the group with his back to the door, watching for Followers. Hearing Egbert's announcement, he turned with his happy smile in place. "Do you want me to burn the door?" he asked.

Cwenhild tossed her blond braid over her shoulder. "I'm not sure it would burn," she answered. "But maybe instead of flames, you could use your magic the way you do when you're juggling the stones. What if you try to steer," she wiggled her hands like a bird in flight, "your way into the lock?"

Kjell bounced on his toes as he eyed the door. A blur of light, the disc made no noise. After a moment, he glanced over his shoulder. "I have no idea what I am doing," he said. "So, you may want to stand back."

With a rumble of agreement, they backed off, leaving Kjell alone. For a long moment, he simply stared at the door and then he closed his eyes. A bead of sweat run down his tight face. His smile was gone.

Suddenly, the light in the center of the disc began to glow even more brightly, making it impossible to look at. Everyone turned away, shielding their eyes. Without warning, a flash of energy and heat erupted, knocking Kjell to his knees.

The ground shook under Flint's feet and he lost his balance, tumbling behind a boulder. By the time he poked his head up for a look, Kjell was climbing slowly to his feet. His jaw was hanging open and the door was gone.

CHAPTER SEVENTEEN

Underground City

KUNNEGARDE OPENED HIS EYES. SOMEONE had entered the city. It had been so long. So very long. What could it mean?

Sitting up, he pushed aside the lid of his sarcophagus and climbed out. His sword and staff still leaned against the tomb where he had set them before he lay down. Picking them up, he examined them for damage. They were fine. Time had done them no harm.

Too bad he could not say the same for himself. Standing upright for the first time in over a millennium, he made a couple of cautious swipes with the sword before sheathing it. Then he focused his attention on the staff. A jolt of energy flew from the tip and burst against the far wall causing a small pile of rubble to tumble to the floor.

A smile of pure pleasure lit his face and without further preparation, he strode forward. Let the intruder come. He was ready.

"I say we draw straws to see who stays behind," said Gode. "We all want to see what's inside, but it makes sense to leave a guard out here."

Hovering near the entrance, Flint could see nothing in the dark cave. More than anything, he wanted to get inside and look around. Nonetheless, Gode was right. Someone had to stay on guard. At least if they drew straws, they all had an equal chance of being chosen.

"Good idea," he said. "I'll get them." Bending, he plucked twelve pieces of the stunted grass that grew above the treeline. Then, with a glance at Urravon, he discarded one. The elf would be no use on watch.

After, tearing off the ends of two of the straws, Flint arranged them so that only the tops were visible above his thumbs. Holding out his hands, he asked, "Who wants to go first?"

Everyone pushed forward and tugged a piece free before stepping back.

Hackett sighed and held up a short piece. "I don't mind," he said, sinking down to rest his back against the rock wall. I'm sure you can tell me all about it when you get back."

Hulda's face twisted as she held up her short straw. "At least, the view is beautiful," she said, settling down on the other side of the door. She gave a sideways glance at Hackett's missing arm. "I know we're good, especially Hackett, with that sword of his, but I'm not certain that the two of us will be able to hold off a whole army of Followers. We should stay in touch in case we need assistance."

Hackett's mouth twisted. "We should be able to see them early and provide plenty of warning," he said. "How about you shout out every minute or two and we'll answer. If the Followers show up, we'll yell extra loud, and you can come running."

"Sounds like a plan," agreed Gode. "We have no idea what

we're walking into, so it might be a good idea to have a strategy for in there as well."

"In all likelihood," said Egbert, "we are entering an ancient dwarven city. It may even date back to the time when the gods lived in the world. Who knows what we might find beyond this entrance?"

Flint's stomach clenched and his enthusiasm for the adventure waned. The Fifteenth Hammer had been well-guarded, and he would prefer to avoid facing more ghosts. Nevertheless, as a scout, he felt he should lead the party. "Kjell, can you make that light again?" he asked.

Kjell held out his hand, palm up and a ball of fire appeared.

"Perhaps we should go in with weapons drawn?" Flint suggested. "We have no idea what we are going to run into." Without waiting for their agreement, he drew Rising Star in a hiss of steal.

Around him, weapons appeared in everyone's hands. Then they stepped through the entranceway together.

Flint imagined that the small ball of firelight would provide only the tiniest illumination, but the light was magnified as it bounced off hundreds of reflective surfaces. Kjell let his fireball fade out and they all watched in amazement. Instead of getting dark, the room continued to glow with light coming from within the stones themselves.

The room was immense. And beautiful. The polished rock walls did not create a perfectly square room. Instead, Flint imagined it was like being inside a jewel.

Cwenhild stepped up beside Flint and let out a low whistle. "I wish my mother could see this," she said. "It is a place of real magic."

Egbert's voice was hushed. "There are tales of this place," he murmured as he gazed around. "I never imagined it could be true."

Gode strode toward the center of the room. "We may not

have much time," he said. "Let's explore as much as we can, in case the Followers show up." Raising his voice, he called, "All clear, Hackett?"

Hackett answered immediately in a voice so loud it started echoes in the hall, "All clear."

Gode chuckled. "All right, then, let's move along." With Flint and Kjell at his side, he cut through the hall. Everyone followed amidst exclamations of wonder as the light illuminated more wonders carved into the polished red walls.

Egbert wandered away from the others. "I want to stop and study these panels," he said. "I am sure I recognize some of the stories of origin that my father taught me."

Without slowing, Gode said, "Perhaps later there'll be time to examine everything more closely. Right now, let's just try to get the lay of the land. There has to be something here that can help us in our search for the God Sword."

"Maybe it's here," Fleta said with a little skip that left tracks in the thick layer of dust. "Maybe this is where the blade has been hidden all these years." She dragged a foot through her tracks. "No one has been here for ages."

Small openings perforated the exterior of the room and Gode led them to the largest of them. When he arrived, he turned and bellowed, "Hello, Hulda. Can you hear me?"

Everyone jumped and Flint's sword jerked upward.

Hulda's answer returned in a somewhat quieter voice. "All's clear."

Gode looked around at everyone again and his gaze lingered on Urravon. The elf had been even quieter than usual since they left the main road to follow the cobblestones. Flint noticed the hesitation and wondered what the spy would tell his leader the next time they were in contact. There could be few secrets with him along.

"Any guesses about what we'll find through here?" Gode asked.

"Rather than guessing," said Cwenhild. "I suggest we go look." Grasping her machete more tightly, she stepped through the opening. Kjell went with her.

"All clear," she said. "This is interesting."

The others crowded into the short hallway to see what had caught her attention. Cwenhild and Kjell stepped aside to let the others through.

The space was a much smaller version of the large entry room with its multifaceted walls. However, it was clearly a living space with everything made from rock. Cut into one wall, a hearth showed traces of black where smoke had stained the red rock. Benches surrounded a table that rose from the middle of the floor, while raised beds filled in the remaining space along the walls.

"This is probably a family dwelling," said Fleta. "It's beautiful, but do you notice that there are no windows anywhere?"

Dell examined the fireplace with interest. "It looks like they burned wood. The smoke must have travelled up this narrow chimney to the surface. Can you imagine how horrible it would have been when a fire was smoky?"

Gode stuck his head out of the room and yelled, "Hello, Hackett. Still there?"

The answer boomed back. "Still here. Still waiting."

"Let us check the next room," Egbert said. He made his way out of the family quarters back through the short twisting hallway.

Fleta ran a finger along the wall of the narrow passage. "It looks as if the only door in the whole place was the one at the main entrance," she said.

Flint followed them through the next opening and found an identical room.

Egbert gazed around. "The tales tell of a mountain city that housed all of the dwarves when they lived with Dworgunul," he said. "Each family must have had one room."

They had begun to relax and almost everyone had sheathed their weapons. The place appeared to have been deserted for ages. Gode stood in the grand room studying the doorways leading out from it. "It will take far too long to check every room unless we split up," he announced. "Take a partner. Stay alert. Let's see if we can find something more interesting than family quarters."

Flint and Fleta paired up and she said, "Let's head to the opposite side and check over there." Together they jogged across the room, crossing the trail of footprints.

The first entrance they chose led to a room the same as the others. On the way out, Fleta stopped to study the carvings that surrounded the doorway. "We may be able to save time if we can figure out a pattern in the carvings," she said, lightly touching the grooves in the wall. "Look. Did you notice that all the entrances we already went through had this mark? I'll bet that tells us it's a living quarter. And see this mark? It's different on every entrance. Maybe it's the family name."

"Or a number," suggested Flint.

"Hello, Hulda?" Gode's shout interrupted them.

"All clear!" answered Hulda immediately.

Flint was struck with the need to hurry. Followers could arrive at any minute. They either had to set up a defense or find an escape route.

Confident they had identified a pattern, Flint and Fleta hurried past the entryways with the living quarter mark.

Thirteen entrances later, Fleta exclaimed, "Look! This one's different."

The carving was more ornate than the ones for the living quarters and jewels were embedded into the rock. Clearly, it was not another family home.

Flint drew Rising Star while Fleta rested a hand on a dagger as they crept through the entrance. The short passageway was wider than anything they had seen so far. A dozen or more people could pass through together. Finally, it opened into a space almost as large as the first hall. An enormous amphitheatre had been carved into the stone with a wide stage many levels below them. The only other visible exit led off from the stage.

Fleta whistled, and said, "Get the others."

Shallak's shoulders slumped and he slowed from trot to walk before finally stopping. Beside him, Korgun busied himself with the nearly empty bag of fine red sand, preparing to leave another pile for the others to find.

Shallak knocked the bag aside, spilling some of the precious powder. "What are you doing, idiot?" he demanded. "We've lost them. There's been no sign anywhere along this road. Not since yesterday. They must have turned off somewhere."

He turned in a circle, studying the ground and muttered, "Gadrith will not be pleased."

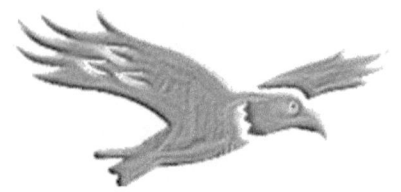

CHAPTER EIGHTEEN

The Sentry

FLINT STUCK HIS HEAD INTO the main hall and let out a whoop.

Immediately, Hulda answered, "All clear."

Strangling a laugh, he called, "We've found something!"

Hawks appeared from doorways around the great room and headed toward Flint. Egbert arrived first.

Indicating the carvings around the entrances, Flint asked, "Can you read this, Egbert?"

Fleta tossed her dark braid over her shoulder. "We found a pattern in the carvings outside all the family quarters. But look here," she said, rubbing her fingers over the gems. "This one is far more decorated. What does it mean?"

Egbert studied the markings for a moment, and then pressed his lips together and shook his head. "I cannot believe I ignored all this as decoration. They are signposts." Running his finger over the words, he said, "This is 'The Gathering

Place'. Perhaps it is where they met to speak with Dworgunul. Imagine religious ceremonies where the god was actually present."

They headed through the entranceway. At the top row of the amphitheatre, they stopped and stared down at the rows of carved seats.

Cwenhild murmured, "Do you think Dworgunul was really here? This whole place seems utterly impossible. I'm not sure I ever believed the gods walked here in our world."

A long silence followed her words as a sense of peace descended.

Finally, Gode pointed to the single exit at the back of the stage. "I think that door should be our next target. Let's just check on our guards." Without warning, he raised his voice and shouted, "All clear?"

"All clear!" Hackett's answer was easily heard in the echoing stone chambers.

Satisfied, Gode said, "Let's go."

Before he could start down the stairs, Urravon said, "We should pray." With that, he dropped to his knees and raised his hands, palms up, in the manner of the Worshippers of Dreff.

For a long moment, no one moved and then, Egbert drawled, "Young Urravon, I believe I understand your thinking, but perhaps, in this room, dedicated to Dworgunul, you best save your prayers for him. You do know that Dreff and Dworgunul were not the best of friends?"

Urravon opened his eyes and looked up at Egbert, his brow furrowed. As understanding dawned, he scrambled to his feet, blushing furiously.

Without another word, Gode clattered down the stairs, and one by one, the others followed. When he reached the platform at the bottom, Gode yelled, "Hello, Hackett?" The rising stone amplified his voice, and it reverberated around the huge space.

Hackett's voice returned like a distant echo. "All clear!"

Igon rubbed a hand across his stubbled face. "Perhaps someone should stay here at this entrance to relay messages," he said. "We may be getting out of range." At Flint's look of dismay, he added, "I'll stay. I don't mind."

Dagur grimaced. "Me too," he said. "I think, I'd rather stay a little closer to the surface. It feels like we're climbing down to the center of the world." Settling himself onto one of the stone benches meant for the audience, he stretched out and crossed his legs at the ankles.

Hackett joined him. "Just keep calling out every few minutes," he said with a jaunty wave before leaning back on his elbows.

"It's a good idea, Igon," said Cwenhild, gripping his shoulder briefly and tapping Dagur on the head before skipping down the last few steps to the platform. She lifted a hand and waved. "We'll see you in a bit." At the exit, she studied the carvings. "Egbert," she called, "what does this say?"

Egbert moved past Flint and Fleta to peer closely at the carvings. "I believe is says 'The Burial Place'," he said softly. "This might be interesting."

When he spotted Korgun and Shallak, Gadrith slowed to a walk. The Hawks must be near. He felt wobbly with relief. Already it had taken far longer to catch up with them than he had imagined.

After his initial frustration at the way the ambush had turned out, his optimism had returned. The Hawks were not invincible. They had run away from the ambush but he would not permit that a second time.

He stopped to allow the runners to approach. Behind him, the other Followers of Martokallu halted as well. He had been pushing the pace, determined to demonstrate his usefulness to Martokallu. A pair of injured Followers had been too incapacitated to keep up and he had been forced to kill them, rather than delay further.

The moment he saw Shallak's face, Gadrith knew something else had gone wrong. He checked an impulse to kill the two scouts immediately. He needed their information first.

Once again, he cursed Martokallu for not making him a General. If he could communicate with the Master, he would not be working in the dark. Immediately, he cast the idea away. Martokallu did not make mistakes. If Gadrith hoped to earn the position of General, he would have to prove his usefulness to the Master.

Shallak and Korgun stopped just beyond sword range and bowed their heads. "We lost them," Shallak rasped.

Gadrith clamped down on a rush of rage. Their incompetence was unacceptable. The Master would see their bumbling. He would blame Gadrith for their mistakes. He glowered at Shallak and took a step forward.

Shallak licked his lips and swallowed.

Ordinarily, Gadrith would have relished his fear. At this point, however, he needed solutions.

Korgun held up his hands. "We followed for two days and never let them out of our sight. Only once did they get ahead."

Pushing in front of his partner, Shallak said in a rush, 'We know where they turned off the main road."

While Egbert studied the carvings on the exterior of the room, Flint and Fleta slid past him into the passageway. It widened into yet another great room with multi-faceted walls. Arranged in neat rows, stone tombs filled the entire space. The great stone coffins came up to Flint's waist and as the others entered the Burial Place, he edged down a row.

All at once, the hair on the back of his neck stood up.

Trusting an instinct that told him someone was watching him, he drew Rising Star and whirled around.

A man stood beside a sarcophagus that was longer than any of the others. Flint's breath caught in his chest. Behind him, the others drew their weapons and spread out through the tombs.

Tall, thin, and unquestionably human, the man peered back through a polished silver mask. The circular eye-holes glared out above a perfectly symmetrical scowl, making Flint think of Dell. The frown would suit him far better than the delirious smile he always wore. A third eye was carved in the middle of the forehead, with a red jewel in place of an iris. It gave Flint the creeps.

Beside the man, a coffin lid tilted precariously against its base and footprints showed in the dusty floor around it. The chest of his tattered old robe was embroidered with a faded image of the Defenders of the God Sword's palm tattoos. Had he just crawled out of his grave?

While the man gave every appearance of frailty, he did not lean on the long staff of blackened metal that he gripped in his emaciated right hand. A perfectly spherical blue jewel topped its shaft. Banding it was a silver ring from which five points protruded. Four smaller spikes created a square while the fifth—shaped like a flash of lightning—rose from the middle of the gem.

Tension filled the room as the man studied the group. Finally, in a surprisingly strong voice, he said, "I am Kunnegarde." Twice, he thumped his staff on the stone floor, sending echoes to bounce around them. "I am the Sentry." He drew a wheezy breath. "I knoweth wherefore thou art here, and I knoweth thee hast a mage amongst thee. Otherwise, thee couldst not pass through the outer door. Since thou hadst the key, Gan hast judged thee worthy. Now, 'tis mine own turn."

He stepped away from his sarcophagus and stood with his

feet braced and the staff gripped tightly before him. "Cometh forward, mage. We shall battle with the power of our minds. Only then canst I judge thy worthiness."

Without hesitation, Kjell moved closer. He gave Kunnegarde his happy smile and said, "I am Kjell."

Relief washed over Shallak when he finally spotted the place where the Hawks had left the road. Seeing it from the new angle, he could not imagine how they had missed the trail. The Hawks had tried to camouflage it, but the evidence was unmistakable. Thick brush had been slashed away to clear a path into the forest.

Without a word, Shallak led the Followers of Martokallu off the main road and onto the narrow track. Broken branches plainly marked the Hawks' passage for the first hundred yards. Then he stepped out of the undergrowth onto cobblestones. From there it was clear sailing.

Shoving him aside, Gadrith took the lead and picked up the pace. Shallak smiled as the knot of worry lifted from his chest. They would catch their quarry and end the chase.

The instant Kunnegarde plunged into his mind, Kjell was thrown back to his time under Martokallu's control. He shuddered at the invasion as his vision blurred and colours blended together.

He went rigid, fighting the invasion. He would not stand for it again. Even as his mind clouded over, he forced himself to think.

Unlike the day two centuries earlier when Hain had burrowed into him with Martokallu's power, Kjell had access to magic of his own. He closed his eyes and focused on the strand of energy he recognized as Kunnegarde's attack. It felt as though his mind were held on a string and that Kunnegarde could cut it at any moment.

Suddenly, anger flooded through Kjell. It was not like the rage that had ruled his life during his time under Martokallu. It was honest and decent. It was clean and worthy. He did not have to allow anyone to control him again. The choice of how to live was his alone.

Instinctively, he knew that anger could never defeat the terrible twist of energy boring into his mind. Anger was weak. Anger would always hold the taste of corruption.

With an effort of will, he banished the fear and fury. Reaching deeply, he thought of the wonderful things in the world. He pictured beauty. And joy. Then he spun that energy into a ball and hurled it back at Kunnegarde.

Kjell threw everything he had into the attack. Would it be enough? Kunnegarde's power continued to tighten around his mind. In another moment, he would be lost.

All at once, Kunnegarde released him. Kjell staggered at the relief, gasping for breath as his eyes snapped open.

Kunnegarde stood easily with his staff resting at his side. "Thou hast lost our battle of minds," he said, tilting his head to the side as he studied Kjell. "Mayhap, thou hast also won. I feel thy potential. Thou art inexperienced and young."

Kjell felt the urge to laugh aloud. Stifling it, he raised his eyebrows and returned Kunnegarde's stare.

The old man sucked in a wheezy breath. It was difficult to believe that such a feeble body was capable of the force Kjell had just experienced.

"Thou shalt continueth to learn and continueth to gain power," Kunnegarde said. He pushed back his hood and removed his mask, revealing a face with skin stretched so tightly over the bones that it was little more than a skull. A wispy beard covered his chin and thin white hair straggled down his back.

Only a pair of blazing blue eyes showed no sign of his great age. They settled calmly on Kjell. "I bequeath this mask to thee," he said in a voice that shook the stone walls. Unceremoniously, Kunnegarde stepped toward Kjell and shoved the shiny silver relic at him. "It serveth to focus and to magnify thy mind-control powers. Be canny with it."

Then he passed over his staff. "Taketh this as well, for thou art in need of it. 'Tis a formidable weapon. Mayhap, more importantly, 'tis the key."

Rooted to the spot, Kjell reached out instinctively to receive the gifts, but Kunnegarde's words did not make sense. Only moments earlier, he had known a complete invasion of his mind. He had all but given up when the fiery prod withdrew and was still struggling to regain his equilibrium.

Kunnegarde surveyed Kjell and gave him a light shove. "Pulleth thyself together, lad," he said, amusement lighting his eyes. "Thou art fine. Thou didst prove thy worth."

Turning his attention to the remaining Hawks, he asked, "Who art the leader hither?"

Egbert cleared his throat and bowed formally. "I am Egbert Martell, son of Adler, Forty-Second Hammer of Dworgunul. It is an honour to meet you, Lord Kunnegarde."

Kunnegarde's scraggly eyebrows rose. "Forty-second?' he muttered. "How long hast I lain hither?" He looked Egbert up and down. "Thou art tall for a dwarf." Then he shrugged and returned the bow. "I am pleased to meet thee, Egbert, son of Adler." Reaching inside his robes, he withdrew a roll of parchment. "Taketh this, for 'tis thine," he said, handing it over.

Egbert received the ancient roll with the same dazed confusion Kjell had shown. "We thank you, Kunnegarde. We will strive to be worthy," he said.

Kunnegarde grunted. "Of course, thou shalt. I knowst thy minds and hearts." Under his breath, he added, "I shalt not have given it to thee otherwise." Turning back to Kjell, he said, "Holdth. One last thing." He grasped the ring he wore on his left hand and with an appalling crunch, wrenched it free from a shrunken finger. Baring his teeth, he examined the damage done by the ring's removal. The skin had torn free, leaving dry bone exposed.

With a shrug, he dismissed the injury and handed the ring to Kjell. "Taketh good care of it."

At the sound of running footsteps, everyone wheeled toward the entrance.

Dagur and Igon rushed into the room, wide-eyed and breathless.

"The Followers are here!" cried Dagur.

CHAPTER NINETEEN

Flight

"THEY'RE COMING!" CRIED IGON. "FOLLOWERS are right behind us!"

He and Dagur raced over to stand with the other Hawks as they drew their weapons.

His cutlass ready, Dagur said, "They got Hulda and Hackett." He shook his head and wiped away a trickle of sweat with the back of his hand. "They shouted for help, and we ran but before we made it to the main room, the Followers charged in."

As if to confirm his story, Gadrith hurtled through the entrance, skidding to a halt at the sight of the Hawks' raised weapons.

While the two sides assessed each other in silence, Kunnegarde cut his eyes sideways and said, "Doth not tarry hither. This is mine own battle." The air rang as he drew his sword.

Gode glanced at him and frowned. "We would not leave you, old man," he said.

Irritation flickered across Kunnegarde's face. "Who art thee calling old?" he muttered. He flicked his head toward an entrance at the far end of the burial place. "Go. I am the Sentry. I alone shalt fight. Taketh the side passage. Thou shalt findth the mountaintop."

Gode looked at Egbert. Then, in silent agreement, they turned and ran with the others an instant behind.

The sight of his prey escaping again angered Gadrith almost to the point of recklessness. But he held onto his temper. Nothing more could go wrong. Tempted as he was to push past the old man to continue the chase, he forced himself to stop and face him.

Studying the skeletal figure, he bit back a bitter laugh. How long would it take to cut him in half? "You would challenge me?" he demanded. "You dare to challenge a Follower of Martokallu?"

"I doth not need mine own Mask of Truth to see thee doth harbour evil in thine soul," answered the old man. "Martokallu, thou sayest? I hadst once a brother by that name." Shrugging, he added, "But millennia have passed since we lived in this world together."

Gadrith felt a prickle of fear as he realized why the challenger looked so familiar. He was the Master's fabled brother, Kunnegarde. His fear faded. Martokallu would be eternally grateful to him if he delivered his brother to him. In his gratitude, Martokallu would make him a General.

"Your brother lives yet," Gadrith said. "He is the most powerful mage in the land. Soon, he will rule over all of Abbarkon."

Kunnegarde stepped back in astonishment. "Mine own brother doth live? What sorcery is this?"

"The strongest sort of sorcery," answered Gadrith. "Martokallu not only lives, he also commands an army of Followers who have strength far beyond what humans can muster."

Kunnegarde's blue eyes narrowed. "And thou art one of his Followers?" he demanded. "He hath set himself up as a god?" Distaste rippled across his face.

"The gods are gone," Gadrith said. "The humans need a leader who is strong. Join us."

"Joineth thee?" sputtered Kunnegarde. He raised his sword to waist height and stepped forward. "Joineth thee?" He bit off a laugh. "Martokallu steppeth beyond the bounds of goodness."

Jerking back as if struck, Gadrith forced himself to wait. What would the apparition do? A brother of Martokallu was not to be underestimated. Who knew what power hid within his shrunken figure?

His squadron of nineteen Followers shifted into position. With weapons drawn, they awaited his orders.

Gadrith checked an impulse to rush to attack. He had offered an alternate solution. It would be far better if Kunnegarde elected to join them. Imagine the Master's pleasure at having his brother back at his side.

Kunnegarde did not take long to decide. He raised his left hand and instantly, blue flame enveloped his fingers. With a shout, he hurled a fireball directly at Gadrith.

Caught off-guard, Gadrith wrenched his sword around in time to deflect the fiery missile but not before the heat of the flames seared his face.

In quick succession, Kunnegarde hurled five more fireballs at the Followers. Two of the flaming projectiles were knocked aside and exploded against the stone wall in a spray of rock. However, three Followers fell to the ground screeching in pain as the magical fire consumed their skin.

Realizing he could not wait while the mage destroyed his soldiers from a distance, Gadrith roared, "Charge!"

Kunnegarde waited, unmoving as they rushed at him. At the last moment, he threw his arms wide and shouted, "Earth and Air!"

Gadrith stumbled as the smooth rock floor beneath his feet turned to sand that pulled at his boots. In the same instant, two of his soldiers flew upwards. Their helmets crunched against the stone ceiling before they tumbled back to the sand and lay senseless beside him.

Regaining his balance, Gadrith dragged himself free of the clinging sand. As he neared Kunnegarde, he raised his sword in an overhand attack. Kunnegarde extended his own blade, and then turning neatly on his left foot, he executed a spinning slash that sent Gadrith's strike wide.

The old man continued in his circle, blue lightning shooting from the pommel of his sword as he spun. The force of the magical jolt caught Gadrith in the chest and knocked him flat on his back. He lay stunned, unable to draw a breath.

Then Kunnegarde sent a blast of wind to slow the other Followers. He followed it with a barrage of fireballs and two more Followers ignited.

Kunnegarde's speed bought him a moment to look around. Gasping, Gadrith saw him note the prisoner they had taken when they first arrived at the fortress. The woman would make a fine new Follower. They just needed to get to a General who could make the change for her.

Taking advantage of Kunnegarde's distraction, Gadrith rolled over and crept closer to the man whose powers were as vast as Martokallu's. Even knowing he was the Master's brother, Gadrith did not hesitate. Kunnegarde had made his choice.

He kept his motions so slow as to be undetectable until he was close enough. Then, using the speed with which

Martokallu had endowed him, Gadrith leapt up and swung his sword in a wide arc.

Kunnegarde's inattention cost him. He danced aside at the last moment, but Gadrith's sword caught him on the wrist. As his sword clattered to the floor, Kunnegarde grabbed Gadrith's sword arm.

Unable to stop it, Gadrith watched helplessly as Kunnegarde pulled a stream of images from his mind. For an instant, the conduit ran both ways and he saw Martokallu through Kunnegarde's eyes. Instead of his respected and worshipped Master, he saw a good man, a kind and thoughtful older brother, twisted into a monster, ensnared by his own quest for power.

In a booming voice that echoed around the stone chamber, Kunnegarde cried, "MINE OWN BROTHER SHALT NOT WIN!"

Gadrith felt his arm go hot, then cold. When he glanced down at Kunnegarde's bony fingers where they gripped his arm, he saw frost gathering on his sleeve. In horror, he watched as the cracks on his grey skin widened. Without warning, his arm shattered like a vase thrown onto a tile floor.

He had time to see triumph in Kunnegarde's eyes before Shallak raised his sword and sliced through the skeletal neck.

Flint and Cwenhild surged to the lead. Behind them, Dell and Gode kept pace with Dagur and Igon while Egbert huffed along near the back of the group with Fleta hauling on his arm to keep him moving. Kjell and Urravon took up the rear with the scrawny elf suffering almost as much as Egbert. Winding higher and higher, the passage led steeply upward and darkness descended as they left the cavernous rooms behind.

"Kjell," called Dell. "Make a light."

Leaving his position at the rear, Kjell sprinted toward the front of their procession. When he lifted his hand to create a ball of firelight, the jewel in Kunnegarde's ring released a burst of blue light. Blinded by a dark even deeper after the brief flash of light, he ran on. Lifting his hand, he squinted at the ring, trying to see the light again.

"Kjell?" barked Dell. "We need to see where we're going."

"Of course," Kjell replied, dismissing the mystery of the ring. A ball of fire appeared on his palm. But it was hard to hold his hand steady as he ran. Without thinking, he tossed the ball forward and sent it to float above his head. To his surprise the ghostly light stayed just in front, leading them through the twisting cavern. How far was it to the surface? He could feel the strain of maintaining the light.

Suddenly the passage ended, and they skidded to a stop in front of a solid wall of rock.

Egbert bent over, resting his hands on his knees as he gasped for air. Sweat streamed down his face and soaked his beard. "Use—magic—Kjell—S," he wheezed.

Eyeing the rock doubtfully, Kjell gripped his new staff and mask more tightly. There was no sign of an opening.

"I can't hear anyone coming," muttered Dell.

Egbert straightened, looking a little recovered. "Lord Kunnegarde was fabled to be a most fearsome warrior," he said. "Perhaps, he will defeat the Followers."

"Stand back," said Kjell, resting the staff on the floor as Kunnegarde had done. He sent a probing finger of magic at the wall. Stronger than anything he had felt before, the blue line flew towards a narrow channel of stone and swirled around.

Suddenly, the rock vanished and sunlight streamed through an opening wide enough to allow them passage.

Fleta whistled. "Well done, Kjell," she said.

"We don't have time to admire his work," Dell said. "Move!" He dove through and they scrambled after him.

Far above the original entrance, the clearing where they had met the Worshippers of Dreff was visible far in the distance.

Dell leaned into the opening and listened. "Still no one coming," he said. "Can you close this up again in case Kunnegarde is overrun?"

"I can try," said Kjell. Again, he grounded the staff and sent a probing lick of magic toward the opening. This time, he was ready for the surge of power. It flowed easily around the perimeter of the hole, but nothing caught. Stepping back, Kjell shook his head. "I don't know how to close it. We'll have to leave it."

"In that case, we should get a move on," said Dell. "Egbert, have you had a chance to look at that map? Do you have a plan?"

"And when would I have had time to look at the map?" Egbert snapped. "Not only was I running for my life, but it was as dark as the inside of tomb in that passageway." He pulled the map case from inside his tunic.

"We don't have time to study it now," said Gode. "Let's just get out of here."

But Egbert had already unrolled Kunnegarde's gift. Holding the map close to his nose, he said, "It is difficult to be certain, but it appears we will have to head back to the Chain of Thollcrawnow." He glanced over his shoulder at the hole. "Right now, we need to put some distance between us and those Followers." Wincing, he added, "I hate to admit it, but we need the horses. Fleta, would you and Flint run ahead?"

Fleta scrubbed at her face, wiping away tears as she raced down the switch-backing path. At her side, Flint swivelled his head, trying to see in all directions at once. He felt exposed on the mountaintop. Every rock and outcropping could hide an archer waiting to pick them off.

"How did they do it?" Fleta asked. Her tears had stopped, but her voice was thick with emotion.

Flint did not need to ask what she meant. "I don't know," he answered. "They shouldn't have been able to sneak up on Hulda and Hackett without them raising an alarm."

"I can't believe they're gone," she gasped. There was nothing more to be said and they ran on in silence.

It was a somber group who straggled down the mountain. Everyone was thinking about the two Hawks no longer with them.

Egbert could not help noticing the elaborate precautions the others took as they descended the mountain. He knew they were trying to help him so they could move more quickly but it was humiliating. Still, he could not force himself to walk any faster.

As soon as he was comfortably seated in a saddle, he would have a nice leisurely look at the map. Sucking in a breath, he shook his head at the thought. Never in his wildest dreams had he imagined a time when he would look forward to mounting a horse.

Concentrating on putting one foot in front of another, he thought about Hackett and Hulda. He had known them since they joined the Hawks ten years earlier.

He would miss Hackett terribly. The big, one-armed warrior always had a tale ready. He had such a great mind for details. On the trip south, he had been Egbert's closest confidant and friend.

Always more reserved, Hulda tended to keep people at a distance, but he would miss her too. When she first arrived in Halklyen, she had been barely sixteen years old, and she had just watched her mother die. Egbert guessed that some of the grief she felt about her mother's death was rooted in guilt. Dell had told him how the woman had fought and died to save Hulda when the Followers came after them.

The early training Hulda received from her warrior mother

quickly earned her the position as leader of the Vultures. Thinking about it, Egbert could not get over the idea that she had been defeated so easily. How had the Followers got close enough? She was so good with her bow. It was difficult to imagine her allowing them to get inside her range.

When he finally spotted the horses coming up the trail, Egbert could have wept with relief. Fleta rode in the lead with the horses tied in a line behind her, while Flint took up the rear.

As soon as she got close enough, Fleta called, "We found Hackett but there's no sign of Hulda anywhere."

Somehow, they had managed to load Hackett's heavy body onto his horse. The anguish in Fleta's eyes made Egbert want to comfort his little girl, but he knew she would not welcome his attentions right now.

Flint frowned. "We didn't want to hang around waiting for the Followers to figure out that we'd be back for the horses." He twisted around to look at Hackett. "We need to bury him."

Igon moved up beside Hackett. "Dell, give me a hand."

Together, they lifted the body down, staggering under his weight. As gently as possible, they set him on the ground, arranging him on his back with his hands folded neatly across his stomach. In this position, the vicious wounds on his body were visible. He had not died easily.

A tear ran down Cwenhild's cheek, as she knelt and covered him with a blanket.

The Hawks gathered around in silence and Egbert felt a tight ball form in his throat. It was not fair. Neither Hackett nor Hulda had deserved to die. Somehow it was even worse to know they had not found Hulda's body.

Finally, Gode said, "Go to Abbarkov, Hackett. You will be missed." With that, he picked up a stone in each hand. Weighing them thoughtfully for a long moment, he bent to place them on the blanket.

One by one, the Hawks followed his example, each whispering a farewell when he or she stepped close. They continued to add to the pile until Hackett's body was covered and safe from scavengers.

Looking over her shoulder to check that the Followers had not found them, Cwenhild started a second pile of stones nearby.

"For Hulda," she murmured. "You will never be forgotten." Pushing herself to her feet, she turned her back on the others and stared down the mountain.

CHAPTER TWENTY

Doubt

AS THEY STARTED DOWN THE mountain, Dell asked again, "Do we know where we're going?"

Egbert looped his reins around the saddle horn and pulled the map case out from inside his cloak. After carefully sliding the map from its leather tube, he unrolled it.

Nudging his horse closer, Flint looked over Egbert's shoulder. The irregularly -shaped vellum map must have been very old if Kunnegarde had been looking after it for as long as they believed. But the colours were still vivid.

Egbert studied it, squinting to read the fine print. "It looks like we are heading to the eastern end of the Chain of Thollcrawnow," he said, gazing into the distance as he tugged on a beard braid. It had lost its little tie that held it together and was coming loose. "Perhaps we should stop to see the Worshippers of Dreff along the way." He looked at Urravon, who did not show any reaction to this proposal. "We might need their help to get past the Protectors of the God Sword. Also," he tapped a thick finger on the map before looking around, "it is rather close to Martokallu's fortress. They might be of use there too."

Cwenhild shook her head. "I don't trust Radomil," she said.

Egbert snorted. "I do not believe there is any reason to trust him, but be that as it may, he might have answers we need. And he certainly has the soldiers."

"We have a plan then," said Gode. "Let's put a little distance between us and those Followers before we rest for the night."

Gadrith could not tear his eyes away from the stump of his arm. It did not look like a fresh wound. There was no sign of blood and it had scarred over already. He must have lost consciousness because he had no idea how much time had passed since the battle. He was lying in the same spot he had fallen when Kunnegarde shattered his arm.

Raising his head from the rocky floor, he came face to face with Kunnegarde's skull. With a groan he closed his eyes. So, the old man was dead. Had anyone survived? Rolling over, he climbed to his feet.

Vision swimming, he swayed for an instant before things came into focus. One of the other Followers must have taken charge. Seven bodies lay neatly in front of a tomb. Seven! That meant they were down to only a dozen soldiers to finish the mission.

At least they had collected a prisoner earlier. She would make a fine replacement. Unfortunately, they had no one along who could perform the transformation.

Again, he cursed Martokallu's decision to send him so far away without first raising him up to be a General. It was bad enough trying to function without the information that Martokallu's mind-link could provide. How was he supposed to deal with losses if he could not replace his soldiers?

Spotting his sword on the ground beside the pile of dust that had once been his right hand, Gadrith bent to pick it up. The weight was awkward in his left hand and he pressed his lips together as he forced himself through a rudimentary drill.

The toe of his boot knocked against Kunnegarde's blade and he stopped his exercise to stare at it. The weapon was far superior to the one he had been issued as a young man.

Setting aside the sword he had carried for centuries, Gadrith picked up Kunnegarde's weapon and swept it experimentally through the air. He grimaced at his clumsiness. Could things get any worse? Martokallu would never raise him to General. He was a complete failure.

He glanced at the remains of his army. Shallak had survived. He hovered nearby, watching Gadrith with veiled eyes. Had he organized the dead bodies? No doubt he would be angling for a promotion of his own. But he would not get the opportunity to prove his worth on this trip. Gadrith hated to admit it, but it was time to go home.

As they rode, Kjell experimented with the staff that Kunnegarde had given him. Having no idea as to its purpose, he tried pointing it at different things and whispering commands. Nothing worked. Or at least, Flint had not seen anything happen.

The sun was high before Kjell gave up trying to discover the staff's secrets. He tied it to his saddle and pulled out the shiny silver mask. If what Kunnegarde had said was true, Kjell would be able to see into the heart and mind of anyone he looked at through the mask.

Flint was grateful to be riding behind Kjell. He did not want the mage peering inside his head. Who knew what he might find there? Kjell must have had the same thought because after sliding the leather strap over his head and gazing around for a few minutes, he took it off and put it away.

Flint edged his horse over to Fleta. She had ridden beside Egbert for the past two days. He could see how worried she was about the older man. He looked ready to drop out of his saddle.

"We should be there pretty soon," Flint said. Looking over at Egbert, he asked, "Do we have a plan for when we arrive?"

Dell moved in closer as well.

After a furtive glance at Urravon, Flint whispered, "Did you see Urravon disappear last night? The elves probably know all about the map already."

Dell muttered, "Let's hope that's all he told them." In a louder voice, he suggested, "Egbert, you look wiped. Why don't you take it easy when we get there? I'll go make the report to Radomil and show him the map."

Not looking at Egbert, Fleta answered for him, "I think that sounds like a great idea. I have to admit, I'm looking forward to getting out of this saddle and having a comfortable sleep."

Kjell nudged his horse into the conversation, his customary smile missing. He too cut his eyes toward Urravon. "Don't trust the elf," he murmured. "I have not yet mastered the way of the mask, but I get a strange feeling when I look at him. We should be careful when we go into their camp."

Flint almost laughed aloud. He had not trusted Urravon since the first moment he met him on the day of King Sebastien's coronation.

Dell, however, appeared to think about it. Stretching his arms above his head, he said, "We're all tired. Perhaps the best thing to do would be to make camp and rest before we meet with the Worshippers."

Fleta immediately agreed, "It would be better to face them when we're fresh." She cut her eyes to Urravon and snapped her mouth shut.

"If I remember correctly," said Flint, "there was a nice

campsite just ahead—good water and plenty of grass for the horses."

Showing a flash of energy, Egbert raised his head and said, "I am a wee bit tired. A rest would be most welcome."

The sun had dropped near the horizon so that it shone directly into their eyes when Dagur turned in his saddle and called, "Someone beat us to the campsite. It looks like the Worshippers of Dreff."

Flint caught the anxious look Fleta threw him and suddenly felt guilty that he had not scouted ahead. He would never forgive himself if they had ridden into a trap. Trying to sound confident, he said, "It may be nothing more than their deciding to change sites. They're a big group. It looked like they had been at their last location for a while."

He and Fleta dug in their heels and trotted up beside Dagur. Gode and Dell followed with Kjell.

Gode spoke quickly, keeping his voice low so Urravon could not overhear. "We're going to have to brazen this out. I know we're tired, but we need to be prepared in case this is more than a simple meeting. If they are allies, we could use their help. If they aren't, well then—" He raised his eyebrows significantly and Flint felt a shiver run down his spine.

"Stay on guard," said Kjell. "Radomil uses his magic to pull you under his influence. I should be the one to visit him. I could tell him about the map and ask for his help."

Gode and Dell exchanged a glance. Kunnegarde may have judged him worthy, but Flint knew they still doubted Kjell's loyalty.

After a pause, Dell answered, "Perhaps it would be best if you stayed with the group while I speak with Radomil. Thanks to you, I know how to avoid his influence."

The time for planning ended as six sentries appeared out of nowhere. Their hoods made it difficult to be certain, but Flint thought the largest one was Talagon.

Sure enough, when the elf spoke, his rumbling voice was easily recognizable. "Welcome Hawks," he said. "You have had a quick journey. Did you meet success?" His words of greeting were contradicted by the malicious gleam in his single eye.

Dell said, "Success? Well, we shall see. Radomil may be interested in hearing our tale. I don't mind meeting with him right now but I think the rest of us would prefer to skip the talk and take a nap instead. It's been a hard few days."

Flint recognized Dell's tone as one he used for his tumbling act. It was far more cheerful and enthusiastic than his usual voice.

Igon, stepped forward and said, "I'll come to the meeting too, Dell."

Dell nodded curtly without taking his eyes off Talagon.

The big elf turned to one of his subordinates. "Take them to the guest tents," he ordered. "Have someone care for their horses."

Before the sentry could respond, Gode said, "We'll tend to our horses ourselves."

Talagon's eyes narrowed, but he agreed, "As you wish."

Everything was laid out the same as the first camp they had visited. The big canvas tents formed neat rows with wide alleyways. Downstream from the cooking tents, the horses were tethered on ropes strung between trees along the creek. There was no sign of praying people this time. Instead many of the Worshippers of Dreff in their white robes and shiny plate armour stood stiffly at attention outside their tents.

With one more glance at Talagon, the sentry led the Hawks away. Dell and Igon remained mounted as they watched the others leave. When Flint rode past Dell, the masked man winked at him, and he felt a surge of anticipation. They may have walked into a trap, but they would not be caught unaware.

Flint checked a desire to draw his sword. The need to appear relaxed outweighed his need for its reassuring touch. By pretending to trust the Worshippers of Dreff, the Hawks would find out if they were truly allies.

For a moment, Dell doubted the wisdom of sending Kjell away. What if he was not as immune to Radomil's powers of persuasion as he hoped? Nonetheless, he cleared his throat and asked, "I assume Radomil is available to see us now?" He snapped the bladed fingers of his gauntlet while doing nothing to soften his customary tone. To his delight, Talagon stiffened at the rudeness.

"Follow me," the tall elf said. Ramrod straight, he spun on his heel and marched through the camp.

Dell and Igon followed his glistening armour to the largest tent. At the doorway, Radomil swept the canvas aside and fixed the two Hawks with an unwelcoming stare.

Dismounting, they looped their reins around a small tree. Dell took his time, knowing it would drive the elf crazy.

When they were ready, Talagon narrowed his eyes before ducking into the tent.

Igon cocked his head at Dell and waved for him to go first. When Dell slipped under the canvas, Radomil rose smoothly from a cushioned seat on the floor.

Seizing Dell's hand in both of his, he said, "Dell, it is a true pleasure to welcome you back among us." Turning to Igon, he grasped his hand as well. "And Igon. I am very pleased to see you again." He looked back at the canvas door and let his shoulders drop in a pantomime of dismay. "Will the others not be joining us? I do hope everyone is well."

Warned against Radomil's magic, Dell easily felt how it worked at the edges of his consciousness. It was a powerful pull, and it took an enormous effort to push it away. Breathing deeply, he struggled to stay focused. "It was not an easy mission," he said, staring at the centre post to avoid looking at Radomil. "We lost two of our people." Behind his mask, his face tightened as he fended off Radomil's probing tendrils. He needed to get far away from the man. Soon. "The Followers of Martokallu are after us," he said without fanfare. "They caught up twice. Once we held them off and escaped, but the second time, we were not so lucky. Hulda and Hackett are gone."

"Oh, that is dreadful," Radomil said. "There is nothing worse than losing a friend." The corners of his mouth pulled down and tears gathered in the corners of his eyes.

Once again, Dell found himself fighting against the pull of the magic. In a moment of clarity, he realized that Radomil's power was linked to his words.

Forcing himself to interrupt, Dell continued the story. "We found the Four Fingers Mountain. A door led inside the mountain. I'm sure you've heard the stories of Kunnegarde? The human who helped to protect the God Sword?" Dell knew he was babbling but he did not want to allow a second of silence. He rushed through the story, so Radomil was forced to listen without interrupting. Congratulating himself at staying free of Radomil's grip, he concluded, "He decided he would trust us with a map. We finally know where to go."

Dell was caught. There was risk in continuing to talk but he needed to hear Radomil's response to the bait of the map. Closing his mouth, he clamped down on the edges of his mind. A quick glance at Igon told him the big man had already lost the battle. He was completely under the power of the Cheveralian.

"A map?" Radomil repeated, his face creased with a delighted smile. "How marvellous. Did you bring it along to show me?"

CHAPTER TWENTY-ONE

Betrayal

BEFORE DELL HAD A CHANCE to consider the wisdom of his action, he reached inside his armour and pulled out the map that Egbert had handed over earlier. Fully aware that he might be reacting to Radomil's charms, he forced himself to maintain a grip on the vellum even while Radomil greedily studied the painted outlines.

With a satisfied chuckle, Radomil muttered, "Yes, yes. This will do nicely." He continued to stare at the map until, without warning, he tugged the vellum from Dell's unresisting fingers.

When Dell tried to fight back, he found himself pinned to the floor, unable to move while Radomil strode across the tent to the door where Talagon stood at attention.

Before ducking through the entrance, Radomil said, "Talagon, my dear friend, you may now do with him as you wish."

Even as Dell struggled against the invisible bonds holding

him, he knew he would be too slow. Talagon gave him no time. The instant the tent flap fell back in place, he drew his cutlass. Whirling, he lifted the blade and sliced off Igon's head.

Shock galvanized Dell into action. He reached down to draw a dagger. However, before his hand could find the blade, the two soldiers who had been in the tent when he first entered, seized him. Twisting his arms behind his back, they forced him to his knees.

Talagon stood in front of his captive and slowly drew on a metal-spiked gauntlet. Almost too quietly for Dell to hear, he murmured, "I have been admiring your lovely gauntlet. Perhaps you would appreciate a closer view of mine."

With his left hand, Talagon tugged off his hood, revealing a scarred face with a black leather eye patch. Frozen, Dell had no choice but to stare into his single working eye. At the sight, a spike of hatred drove up through his chest.

When Talagon drew back his fist, Dell forced himself to close his eyes and relax. The expected blow landed with a detonation of pain and his wooden mask cracked while Dell twisted furiously against the hands holding him.

His eyes popped open just as Talagon prepared for a second punch. This time, he kept his eyes open. Timing his move carefully, he pulled his head back while twisting away from the soldiers' hands. His mask split down the side on impact and Dell felt the wood cut into his face.

Reeling back from the punch, he again wrestled with the restraining hands. The soldier grasping his left hand struggled to maintain a grip on his wrist without injuring himself on Dell's bladed gauntlet.

On the third punch, Dell's mask disintegrated. The metal of Talagon's gauntlet tore into his skin. With the protection gone, Dell knew he would not survive another blow. Desperate, he wrenched his left hand free from the restraining soldier. Reaching up, he grasped the man's neck and gave it a vicious tug. A great chunk of his throat tore free and blood erupted from the wound. With a snarl, Dell tossed the limp body aside.

The sudden attack caused the second guard to loosen his grip. Dell wrenched his other hand free in time to grasp a dagger from his bandolier. Twisting, he plunged it into the elf's chest.

Talagon reared back in surprise at having his prey fight back. Then, a slow smile spread across his face. "Yes, we shall have a real battle," he said. Raising his cutlass, he beckoned with his gauntleted hand.

Dell smiled back. Exposed for the first time since he donned the mask twelve years ago, his scarred face dripped blood. Not waiting for a second invitation, he struck in a flash. His bladed gauntlet erased Talagon's grin, catching him in the corner of his mouth, slicing up through his cheek, and stopping short of his single eyeball. The elf collapsed, clutching his face and screeching.

Dell stood over him. "What's the matter?" he asked. "I thought you enjoyed pain." His face twisted. "I should kill you, but maybe it's better to let you live. How will you explain this?" He landed a solid kick in Radomil's ribs and the man stopped yelling. "That's better. I wouldn't want everyone to think it was me making all the noise."

By lying on their stomachs and working carefully, the Hawks had loosened the tent pegs. Kjell had the best view of Radomil's tent. Barely five minutes after Dell and Igon entered, the leader had exited, carrying Kunnegarde's vellum map. There was no way Dell had handed it over willingly.

He bit his lip. He should never have allowed them to go without him.

The elf leader waved to a group of soldiers who were waiting nearby. They immediately drew their weapons and started toward the Hawk's tent.

Rising to a crouch, Gode whispered, "We go under the tent walls." He gripped the bottom of the canvas and swept a gaze around at the others. "Watch your back. Let's go!"

Pushing the fabric aside, he dove through the opening and came to his feet in a roll.

In the middle of a sneak attack, the sudden appearance of the armed Hawks surprised the Worshippers of Dreff. During the first rush, five soldiers dropped to the ground as Cwenhild and Fleta fired arrows.

Flint took on two elves at once. He danced between the two, knocking their attacks aside. Plainly, he would be no match for them with only his single blade.

Rather than reaching for his bow to help, Kjell raised his hands. On a whim, he created a stream of fire that followed his target. The result was devastating. The soldiers screeched and threw themselves to the ground where they rolled to smother the flames.

Flint raised Rising Star in salute before throwing himself at another opponent. In the meantime, Egbert had battled an elf to his knees, but he was tiring. Rushing to his side, Kjell yelled, "Egbert, get behind me."

As the smith staggered to his feet, Kjell sent a stream of fire at the elf. He shrieked and flopped onto his back.

At that moment, Dell emerged from Radomil's tent, blinking in the sunlight. Or perhaps it was not Dell. The man's bloody face was bare. Kjell realized he had no idea what Dell looked like under his jester mask.

Nonetheless, Dell's weapons, armour and even the way he moved were easily recognizable. There was no doubt that Dell had escaped whatever fate had been planned for him.

As Kjell turned his flames on another pair of Worshippers, Dell started toward the fray. Then, he wheeled away and snatched up the reins of both his own horse and Igon's.

Throwing himself into the saddle, he let out a piercing whistle.

The sound distracted Kjell and suddenly, his flames sputtered to a stop. He struggled to reach the magic again, but nothing happened.

A scolding voice said, "Cometh, boy. Thou canst do better than that."

Kjell spun around to look at Egbert, but it was not the smith's voice he had heard.

"Concentrate!" the voice urged.

At that moment, Dell drove his horse into the center of the Hawks' line and shouted, "Hawks! Retreat."

Fleta paused in the middle of loosing an arrow and stared up at Dell's damaged face. Seeing the danger, Dell whipped out a dagger and flung it at her target. Then he tossed the reins of Igon's horse to her and called, "Help me get the other horses." At once, he kicked his horse to a gallop. As he passed his victim, he leaned low in his saddle and plucked up his blade.

Fleta leapt into Igon's big saddle. Bending over the horse's neck, she sped toward Flint. The horse crashed into his opponent and sent him flying, head over heels.

Stretching out a hand, Fleta cried, "Get on!"

Flint caught a hold and threw a leg over, clasping her around the waist as she kicked the mount to a gallop.

In the meantime, Dell's whistle caused two of the Hawks' horses to break loose from their tethers. They raced wildly through the camp toward him. Gode snatched at the reins of one and tugged him to a stop. Mounting, he reached down, grasped Egbert's arm, and hauled him up as well.

Dell directed his horse straight at Cwenhild's adversary, knocking him to the ground before pulling her up in front of him. Dagur caught the final horse and hoisted himself aboard.

Somehow, Kjell got his flames shooting again, but the distraction of having the Hawks move into his target area caused the stream to sputter to a stop. It was like the first time he had tried to juggle with his mind. Every little thing distracted him and he could not find the centre of his power.

Dagur raced toward him and, abandoning his magic, Kjell threw himself up behind the saddle. "We'll need more horses," he cried.

"I'm on it," shouted Dagur as he pulled the horse's nose in the direction of the picket lines.

Kjell focused on the knots that held the horses and as he and Dagur drew near, every rope suddenly came undone. All at once, nervous horses began to dash in every direction.

At the same time, a Worshipper of Dreff appeared beside Dagur and Kjell's horse. He swung his sword in a low arc aimed at the horse's foreleg. Kjell tried to parry the blow, but he knew before he started that he was too slow.

All at once, Kunnegarde's ring flared blue, and the soldier's blade stopped as if it had hit an invisible wall.

Dagur did not give the surprised Worshipper a chance to recover. Reaching out with his cutlass, he slit the elf's throat.

Unable to conceal his anger, Radomil bared his teeth as he watched the Hawks gallop away. Turning to survey the carnage they had left behind, he sucked in a noisy breath and kicked the body of one of his fallen soldiers. To his disgust, the man's burned flesh left a mark on his polished boots.

Panicked horses stampeded through the tents, leaving devastation in their wake. It would take hours to catch them all. By then pursuit would be far more difficult.

How could this have happened? There were only nine of them. Nine easily manipulated humans. They should have died without fighting back. Months of planning was ruined. The Hawks would know the elves were not their allies, and they would not allow the Worshippers to get close again.

Radomil scowled. Had he acted too soon? But no, he had

the map. And they did not.

Suddenly, he felt better. His face relaxed into its normal cheerful expression. There was no hurry. The Worshippers of Dreff would pack up in the morning. Thanks to the Hawks, he would soon hold the God Sword in his hand.

And the power would be his.

CHAPTER TWENTY-TWO

Bloodbath

"FOLLOWERS!" GASPED THE SCOUT AS he tumbled through the door into the library. "Followers are right behind us."

Four other King's Guards raced in behind him. The first one shouted, "There are at least forty of them."

From the table he had set up in the main area outside the room that housed the library, Halvor leapt up and drew a pair of daggers. "How long?" he demanded.

Around him, the off-duty King's Guards bounded up from whatever corners they had claimed. There were only three Hawks still at the library, but King Sebastien had sent fifty King's Guards along to ensure the safety of the books.

Martokallu was right to fear the knowledge held within the remote library. He had successfully kept three generations in the dark, but that time was over. Already he had gleaned valuable lessons from the volumes he had been studying.

The scout opened his mouth to answer but only a choking

cough came out. The tip of a rusted blade thrust through his back and protruded just below his Adam's apple. As he toppled forward, a Follower of Martokallu with green glowing eyes came into view.

The monster hurled himself at the next King's Guard who met him with an upraised sword. Behind him, Followers poured into the room.

Halvor made good use of his six serrated throwing blades. In quick succession, he disabled five Followers before finding himself in a battle with only one short dagger left for defense. Darting in, he aimed a slash at a Follower's neck but caught him across the face instead. Bright blue blood boiled out and dripped off his chin as he bared his teeth in an ugly grin.

Lunging close again, Halvor stabbed upward, but the Follower caught his blade on his sword and pushed back. Halvor could smell his foul breath as they grappled. Why had he thrown his fifth dagger? The rule was to always maintain one for each hand.

Gulner slashed through his opponent's neck with a whirling backhand blow and twirled over to Halvor's side. The Hawks' newest recruit was perhaps the only sword fighter faster than Gytha. She had found him on her recent tour of the country where, for the past several months, she had been inspecting every town in Abbarkon. Gytha was King Sebastien's secret weapon. Her task was to ensure that only honest people held positions of power. It meant that she had removed several Followers from their roles as advisors to city rulers.

In Derflanag, where Flint grew up, Gytha had discovered a great deal of corruption. And it was there that she first saw Gulner. He had been skirmishing with a troop of King's Guards. Although heavily outnumbered, he easily disarmed them one after another.

When Gulner told the story of how Gytha saved his life, he did not dwell on how many guards he had taken down, instead, he stood up to his full height, and hollered, "In the name of the King, halt!"

The way he told it, the startled fighters froze and stared up at the tall blonde woman who spoke with such authority. Gulner mimicked her regal walk as she leapt off her horse and marched up to the highest ranking of the King's Guard. "What is the reason for this brawling?" he demanded in a voice very close to Gytha's own.

Then he took the part of the guard, and pompously announced, "This man was caught stealing from the duke's food supply. An order has been passed for his execution."

Switching back to Gytha's voice, he resumed her posture and declared, "The duke has more than enough food for everyone."

The guard had not been one to give up easily. "No matter," Gulner would say, drawing the corners of his mouth down in a self-important frown. "This man has been sentenced to death and the sentence will be carried out."

Barely taking a breath, he would switch to Gytha again and proclaim, "No, it won't. I am taking him into custody in the name of King Sebastien."

The story was always good for a laugh and Halvor had come to appreciate Gulner for his quick wit. He could appreciate his quick blade as well. Gulner slammed into Halvor's assailant, sending him off-balance. As the Follower lurched sideways, Gulner whipped his blade around and stabbed him through the heart.

Halvor had no chance to thank his rescuer before the man flew at another Follower. Ducking to retrieve three of his blades, Halvor regretted for the first time that he did not carry a larger weapon. He stuck the extra two blades in his belt and, feeling better with a dagger in each hand, surveyed the room.

The place was a bloodbath. Too many King's Guards were falling under the Followers' blades. Something would have to be done to increase the level of training the soldiers received. In the meantime, Gytha and Gulner flew around supporting the guards and dismembering Followers. It was a dance of death.

Halvor had seen Followers in action before. They were good. But two of the attackers struck him as exceptional fighters. They were bigger than the others as well. One huge monster towered over everyone. When their eyes met across the room, Halvor imagined that Hain had returned to life. Tales of Martokallu's General had been told around evening fires for hundreds of years. They said he could communicate directly with Martokallu and that his strength and size were rewards for his years of obedience to his Master.

Nonetheless, Halvor knew it could not be Hain. Hain was dead. Dell had killed him by tearing his spinal cord from his body. Nobody survived that. Not even a Follower of Martokallu.

The Follower was not Hain. If anything, he was taller. Horns grew out of his forehead like a spiky helmet and instead of the two long swords that Hain had carried, this monster wielded a sword in one hand and a ball and chain in the other. Each swing caused devastating damage. Halvor winced as the ball caught a young King's Guard in the head and dashed him up against the stone wall.

Amid the chaos, a beautiful young woman walked alone and untouched through the battle. Her hair fell in dark waves and her purple eyes caught Halvor's. Riveted by her beauty, he watched her lift a long slender staff. A curving blade extended beyond its tip, but it was the base that she aimed at him. He caught the glint of a purple jewel.

She smiled at him and his heart stopped. She was the most beautiful woman he had ever seen. Then Gulner slammed into his side and sent him sprawling onto the bloodied body of one of the dead Followers.

A burst of purple energy crackled over Halvor's head where he had been a moment earlier and one of the King's Guards standing behind him gave a strangled gasp before his flesh crumpled in on itself in a horrible reversal of life.

Halvor gaped, his stomach twisting, until nothing remained of the man but a pile of dust. Scrambling to his feet, he resisted looking in the woman's direction and bolted from the cavern. One small part of his mind knew he should stop and face his fear. He should not leave the battle. But he could not stop himself. The woman had sent him into an absolute panic.

The moment he staggered outside, Halvor's thinking calmed. The terror faded and with it the desire to scream. As his breathing calmed, he realized they could never win against such power.

The only way anyone could survive was to run. He thrust his head through the door and bellowed, "Hawks! King's Guards! Run!"

His blades ready, Halvor stepped back, gulping for air as he waited.

Gulner was the first one through the door. "Let's ride!" he shouted, barrelling for the horses that the scouts had abandoned.

Gytha was a step behind. "We're the only ones left," she cried. "Let's go."

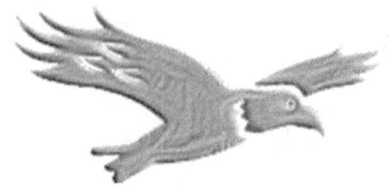

CHAPTER TWENTY-THREE

A Trap

STEPPING BACK FROM THE MIRROR, Velte smiled at the effect of her new dress. It was perfect. The purple silk clung to her slender young body and the full skirt swept the floor. It would draw attention, but only that of the right sort. Her usual purple and black robes were modeled on Martokallu's. They were fine for most occasions, but today, she needed to blend in with the townspeople.

Picking up her staff, she flourished it in a succession of elaborate twirls. The short, curved blade on the end glinted in the light. It had been a long time since she used the staff as an actual weapon. Over the years, it had become a tool to focus her power. Energy hummed from her fingertips down through the polished wood into the amethyst on its tip, making it glow purple.

Velte struck a pose and studied her reflection. She really was gorgeous. Pursing her lips, she blew a kiss before lifting the staff again to study it. She could not carry it openly on the streets of Tsarval, but neither could she leave it behind in the unguarded room of an inn.

With a smile that lit her purple eyes, she lifted the staff high and spoke the words under her breath. Purple light flashed from the gemstone and the reflection changed to show an elegantly dressed woman holding a parasol over her shoulder.

The weapon was gone.

She looked lovely. It was time to get down to business.

Martokallu wanted her to locate the Hawks and report back to him. Something was not right. He could not see them. It was as if they had vanished off the face of the world.

She pouted prettily, still watching the mirror. The Master should never have sent Gadrith to chase down the Hawks. The healer always was an incompetent fool. Besides, he was not a General and therefore incapable of communicating directly with Martokallu.

The Master had watched the events in Tsaralvia, but without a General, there had been nothing he could do to intervene. That was why he had sent her. His last clear vision of the Hawks had shown a brief clash outside the ancient Dwarvish stronghold of Four Fingers. Gadrith had killed one man and taken a woman prisoner before leading his troop into the fortress entrance.

Since then, there had been only scattered images of Gadrith, and nothing of the Hawks. It would be nice to think they were all dead, but the few glimpses that did come through indicated that Gadrith was still on their trail.

Martokallu suspected magic was hiding them from him. With a shudder, Velte recalled the Master's rage when he learned of the Hawks' first defiant use of magic. A cloak had hidden them from his sight for fifteen long years while they worked their rebellion.

More recently, she had been on the receiving end of his

anger when she, Thrall and Wout were sent to capture the library at Oruk. They had failed to kill every guard, though they had reclaimed the fortress. Unfortunately, word of the attack would get back to the king and cause further disruption.

The corner of her lips tightened. Martokallu had no reason for concern. The puny humans could never triumph over Followers of Martokallu. They may have won a few battles, but in the end, the war would not go their way.

She wished she had been at the battle where so many Followers had died. She knew she would have made the difference in turning the fight to their advantage. Hain had allowed himself to grow weak. When was the last time he had left the fortress? But they would not be caught off-guard again. Not if she had anything to do with it.

When Martokallu elevated her to General, he had bestowed upon her the ultimate powers. She could share his visions and spoke directly with his mind. It was an honour and she would be worthy of his trust.

This would be an easy mission. A simple spell had permitted her to travel instantly to a spot just outside the city of Tsarval. The Hawks had visited the Hammer of Dworgunul once and judging by the little they knew of Gadrith's route, they would make a stop on their return.

Velte had only to wait for them to arrive. When she killed them all, Martokallu's vision would be restored to him and she would have proved her true value.

The eight remaining Hawks approached the gates of Tsarval. The last time they passed through the portal, they had been running from the Protectors of the God Sword. That day, there had been eleven of them. Twelve, if you counted the spy, Urravon.

Fleta wondered how they would be received on this second visit. Would the guards recognize the bedraggled riders lined up with the other early morning arrivals? Would they have them arrested? It was impossible to know. Almost everyone had argued in favour of going around the city, but Egbert was determined to speak with his uncle.

Harbert's help with the translation of the verse on the disc had been invaluable. They could only hope that he would have more information to share. More importantly, he had a collection of maps that Egbert wanted to look at. He had studied the map Kunnegarde gave him before Radomil stole it but he wanted to compare his memory with a map of the Chain of Thollcrawnow.

The problem was they did not know whether they could trust Harbert. In all likelihood, he had set the Protectors of the God Sword on them. And why had he not told them exactly how to find the four finger rocks? Surely that nugget of information had to be in the records.

Glancing at Flint's grim face, Fleta leaned close and whispered, "Even if Egbert doesn't get to look at the maps, maybe we can still have a bath."

In the process of scanning the crowd, Flint sputtered with laughter. "You would say that," he said, raising an eyebrow. "But it's not a bad thought."

Dell turned to look in their direction and almost immediately averted his gaze. Without his mask, he had lost a little of his usual swagger. Bruises and cuts covered his face, almost hiding the shiny burn scars. Only his eyes had avoided injury in the fire that had set him on the path to vengeance.

In bits and pieces, he had told them what happened inside Radomil's tent. He blamed himself for being arrogant and believing himself immune to Radomil's magic. Igon's mistake was in trusting him. Whether or not it was true, Dell took full responsibility for Igon's death.

Struck by a sudden idea, Fleta edged over to Dell and murmured, "Did you tell Radomil about the mask or the staff?

Or," she gestured to Kjell's finger, "the ring?"

Dell's lips flattened into a thin white line. "He didn't ask. As soon as he had the map, he handed Igon and me off to that snake, Talagon."

Suddenly, a commotion inside the gates sprang up. Straining to see, Fleta glimpsed armed soldiers. She sat bolt upright, and looked over her shoulder to meet Flint's eyes. He tried to appear confident, but the effort made him look rather ill.

In an undertone, Gode said, "Keep your calm. We don't know they're here for us."

Fleta forced her hand away from her throwing knives and noticed Cwenhild release the tension on her bow.

The people in front of them moved through the gate.

As Gode nudged his horse forward, Fleta recognized Niviit, Harbert's head guard. He sat rigidly in his saddle staring directly at the Hawks.

As Gode met his gaze, Niviit snapped an order in Tsaralvian. At once, the gate guards came to attention and saluted. When he rattled off another command, they turned back to the Hawks and waved them through without asking a single question.

Gode glanced around at the others and murmured, "Here we go. Stay calm."

He led them through the gate and Niviit said, "Welcome Hawks." His words matched neither his tone nor his dark expression. "Harbert bids you join him in his palace." Without another word, he turned his horse onto the broad avenue.

Dell looked ready to argue, but Egbert muttered. "Just do it. This what we wanted."

His brown eyes flashing, Dell nodded sharply and fell in behind Egbert. Niviit's soldiers closed in on either side of the Hawks, riding uncomfortably close with their swords held across their laps.

Had they ridden into another trap? Again, Fleta's fingers twitched toward her daggers. She would be far more comfortable with one or two in her hands but a glance at the soldier on her right made her decide to wait.

CHAPTER TWENTY-FOUR

Welcome

NIVIIT TAPPED ON THE LIBRARY door before swinging it open to reveal Harbert. The Hammer of Dworgunul was stretched out in a padded chair that was set to catch the light pouring in through a tall window. With an air of distraction, he looked up from the thick book that filled his lap.

Niviit snapped to attention and announced, "The Hawks." With a stiff bow, he stepped aside to allow Egbert into the room. Gode, Cwenhild, Fleta, Flint and Kjell followed.

Dell had refused to surrender his weapons so Niviit had told him to remain outside. Dagur elected to stay with him. It was probably a wise move. The number of betrayals they had suffered in Tsarval gave them more than enough reasons to be wary. Flint had considered staying outside as well, but with a rueful smile to himself, he acknowledged that he hated to miss out on anything.

Harbert closed his book and stood up, beaming. "Greetings

of the day, Egbert. It is good to see you looking so well," he said, reaching out his hand as he stepped forward.

Egbert grasped the offered hand, and answered, "Greetings of the day to you, uncle. We have had many adventures since last we visited." He cocked his head and studied his uncle. "Perhaps, you have heard about them?"

Harbert had better control over his facial expressions than the first time they met. It was impossible to tell if he had any information about the Hawks' journey. "All I have heard so far," Harbert said with a slow blink, "is that you were spotted approaching the city gates. Niviit felt it best if he accompanied you here. I do admit I am most interested in learning what has happened since you left."

Stepping back, he set his book on the nearby desk. When he raised his head again, he had a twinkle in his eye. "I spoke with Tul after you hurried away. You impressed him with your blade skills." His eyes rested on Kjell, and his eyebrows rose as he noted the new staff. "He was particularly impressed with your magic."

Kjell lit up with a smile and bowed from the waist.

Gode stepped past Egbert and asked, "Tul? He wouldn't be the powerful dwarf who fights with a mace?" He waved a vague hand over his face. "Shiny helmet? And you can only see his beard?"

Harbert tilted his head to the side. "I suspect you have a very good reason for wishing to know more about Tul," he said. Turning, he strode to the corner of the room where he reached behind a chair and pulled out Gode's battle-axe. With a grin, he said, "Whatever your excuse for leaving this behind, I am sure young Egbert would appreciate if you took better care of the weapons he makes for you."

"You found her!" Gode exclaimed, hurrying toward Harbert with outstretched arms.

But Niviit moved even more quickly. Thrusting himself

between Gode and the Hammer, his sword flashed out and stopped at Gode's throat.

His eyes wide, Gode raised his hands.

With an apologetic smile, Harbert handed the axe to Niviit, and said, "Please see that our visitor gets this at a convenient time."

Niviit let his sword drop and came to attention. "This will be returned to you later," he said, bowing to Gode before stepping back to his position against the wall.

Harbert shrugged and gestured toward the comfortable chairs in front of the wide fireplace. "Please, I am forgetting my manners. Sit down. I want to hear all about your adventures."

He settled himself in the chair closest to the hearth and waited while the others joined him. "But first, perhaps I should tell you. A woman has been asking around Tsarval about you." He glanced at Niviit. "I understand she is very beautiful. Should we send word that you are here?"

Feeling much refreshed after a bath and a good night's sleep in a comfortable bed, Fleta led the way through the streets of Tsarval. The dwarves on the sidewalks eyed them with curiosity and she suddenly wished her cloak did not look quite so shabby. After more than a month on the road, it was grubby and threadbare.

"A beautiful woman with long black hair," mused Gode. "Who could it be?" He held the haft of his axe across his knees. Thrilled to get it back, it had hardly left his hands since Niviit returned it to him. He and Egbert had checked it closely for damage. To their delight, not even dropping it on cobblestones could damage the blade and it was pronounced flawless.

Flint was happy too. When Gode returned his second sword to him, he had sheathed it in his baldric with a delighted smile. As she watched, his hand crept back to grasp the hilt, checking that the sword was ready for action.

"Maybe it's Hulda," said Fleta. Hope flooded her at the thought. It was entirely possible that the woman had survived the Follower attack and escaped to Tsarval. They had never found her body.

The corner of Gode's mouth lifted in a wistful smile. "That would be lovely," he said. But she knew he did not believe it.

Fleta's hope fluttered away too. But it was nice to bring Hulda back to life even for a moment. She had been Fleta's teacher and idol for as long as she could remember. It was going to be hard getting used to the idea that she was gone.

Squaring her shoulders, Fleta glanced around at the others. Kjell rode with Kunnegarde's staff held upright in front of him. He was staring at the blue jewel that was set in the middle of the five prongs, his brow creased in concentration. The previous evening, he had visited Harbert to ask the Hammer if he knew anything about Kunnegarde's staff. What had he discovered?

Her eye stopped on Dell. Very early that morning, he had visited the old smith who taught Egbert's father. When he appeared for breakfast, he had a new mask. She did not like it. Since Radomil broke the wooden one with its manic smile, Fleta had grown used to seeing Dell's scars. The gleaming new face did not feel right.

She re-read the directions Niviit had written in careful penmanship. The inn was directly ahead. Catching Gode's eye, she gestured toward the magnificent four-story building. Built of the same white stone as the other buildings in Tsarval, it was one of the more elaborately decorated ones with grinning gargoyles sculpted along its roofline.

"We'll go into the public room," Gode said. "We can send a message to let her know we're there." A dwarf at the grand entrance was staring at them with his mouth slightly agape.

Gode smiled at him and said, "Greetings of the day, sir."

The man's mouth snapped shut and he mumbled something before hurrying away.

Dell snorted. "Let's not walk into another trap, shall we?" he muttered. "We've done that too many times already. Check your weapons now, everyone, and be ready." His voice sounded strangely distant behind the metal mask. "I'm staying by the door to keep watch. Egbert, you'll probably have to do the talking. Kjell, I want to see you ready with that new staff of yours. Try out your mask too. It would be good to know her intentions." He cocked his head to the side. "Don't worry, people pretend not to notice when someone is wearing a strange mask."

For a moment, Fleta caught a glint of humour through Dell's eye-holes when he turned to her.

"Flint, Fleta, take up positions beside Egbert. Gode, Dagur, and Cwenhild, I want you to cover the perimeter of the room. Watch everyone. Suspect everyone."

Velte felt Martokallu's mind bump against hers. *Have you found them yet?* he demanded. *I see nothing.*

For a moment, she could not respond as fear clenched her stomach. Forcing her concern aside, she kept her tone light as she replied, *No sign of them yet, Master. They will come to me soon. I sent out invitations and they are a curious lot.*

You have prepared everything? he asked.

To her relief, he was not angry. *Just as you planned, Master. Your Followers wait outside the city with Gadrith. When I know for certain the Hawks are within the walls, I will send word and Gadrith will unleash his forces on them. They will not escape us again.* Velte did not try to hide her excitement as she imagined the coming battle. She would redeem herself after the missed opportunity at the Oruk Library.

See that it is, came the answer in her head.

My mages also wait outside the wall, Velte added. *They will ensure the success of the plan.* She waited, hoping for praise, but he was gone.

Hardly seeing her reflection, she stared into her mirror. The Hawks could not arrive soon enough for her. A knock at the door roused her from her deliberations.

Giving her hair a quick pat, she called, "Come."

The door swung inward to reveal a young boy. His eyes flashed towards her for a moment before dropping to the floor. "Excuse me, miss," he said. "There's someone downstairs asking for you."

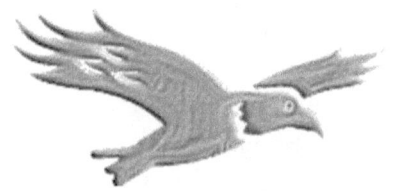

CHAPTER TWENTY-FIVE

Plans

FROM HIS TABLE IN THE corner, Egbert watched a beautiful young woman stroll into the public room. Nearby, Flint and Fleta nursed steins of ale. They looked as if they had hardly tasted it. Egbert's ale was half gone already. It was delicious. Lifting it to his lips again, he watched the woman try to decide who had sent the message. Her eyes slid past his before continuing around the room.

Finally, she leaned down to speak to the young boy. Egbert had paid him a bronze coin to carry his message. In response, the boy lifted a skinny finger to point at Egbert who raised his stein in salute.

The woman flashed a dazzling smile and started toward him. As she sauntered between the tables, every man and most of the women in the room followed her with their eyes. Taking no notice of them, she kept her attention riveted on Egbert.

Her unusual purple eyes held him pinned in place. He

forced himself to breath and took another sip of his ale. When she drew near, he struggled to his feet, finding himself tongue-tied. What could he possibly say to such a woman?

She saved him by speaking first. "You must be Egbert," she murmured in a warm voice. "It is such a pleasure to meet you." Stretching out one delicate hand, she waited in the manner of someone expecting to have it kissed.

Flustered, Egbert took the proffered hand, drew his heels together in a click and brought his lips near the porcelain skin. As he rose, he found his voice. "Greetings of the day, madam." He thought he had detected an Abbarkonian accent in her speech, nevertheless, she had begun in Tsaralvian, so he continued in the same language. "Egbert Martell at your service. And you are?" He pulled out a chair for her.

The entire room watched as she perched on the edge of the seat, her plum gown falling to the floor in perfect lines. She waited until he had settled in front of his ale again and the buzz of conversation rose up around them.

"My name is Velte Lugusin," she said, tilting her head to the side and blinking at him. "As you may have guessed, I grew up in Abbarkon although I have spent many years in Tsaralvia. I just made a trip back home to visit family."

Egbert smiled and said, "I thought I heard a trace of an accent."

Velte beamed. "You are so clever," she said. "I have heard wonderful stories about you. Your name first came up when I was in Kallcunarth. You are a big hero." She leaned forward and smiled into his eyes. "I hoped I might meet you one day."

With a bashful wave, Egbert muttered, "Do not believe everything you hear."

"And modest too," she said. One slender hand reached out and settled her parasol more securely against the table.

Egbert relaxed as she began to talk about her family in Abbarkon, until with a start, he recalled how Radomil had charmed them. Sitting bolt upright in his chair, he glanced around at the Hawks who stood watch. They all pretended to ignore him. Forcing himself to interrupt her chatter, he asked, "Is there something I can do for you?"

Briefly, her flirtatious look disappeared, replaced by something more dangerous. Almost immediately, her smile was back in place. She fluttered a hand gracefully and said, "I am not here to ask for assistance, but rather, to provide it. However," she let her gaze rove over the room and leaned forward to whisper, "not here. There are too many ears. Meet me tomorrow morning by the main gates just as the clocks chime eleven. I have information that could help your search." She raised her voice again. "It has been so nice to meet you, Egbert Martell. Thank you for coming to see me."

Dismissed, Egbert stood while she gathered her parasol. As he pulled back her chair, he eyed her long black hair. Who was she? He still had no idea what she wanted. What did she know of their quest?

Turning, she smiled at him and his knees almost buckled. It was all he could do to bow over her proffered hand before she pirouetted and began her stroll through the tavern.

Back inside her room, Velte reached out with her mind. *Master? I met with the Hawks. Can you see them now?*

The voice roared back inside her head. *No, I cannot see them. Are you certain you found the right people?*

Her throat tightened. Had she been mistaken? But no, it was them. *I spoke with only one man, but around the room, seven others kept close watch.*

The volume in her mind increased and she pressed a hand to her forehead. *I cannot sense anything blocking me,* Martokallu shrieked. *Their mage must be cloaking their presence again.*

Clinging to control, Velte answered, *I have set the bait. They will die tonight. We will destroy them, Master.*

See that you do, he grated before both the voice and the pain vanished.

Realizing she could not depend upon Martokallu's vision, Velte raced to the window, hoping she was not too late. There they were, moseying through the square. She waited to see which exit they took and then turned to the mirror.

The purple-eyed beauty was gone, replaced by a middle-aged housemaid who kept her purple eyes demurely lowered.

It would do.

She hurried from the room. Without Martokallu to guide her, she would have to find out for herself where the Hawks were staying.

Fleta snorted. "Of course, you trust Velte." she exclaimed. "You're a man and she's beautiful! But what sort of credential is that?" She swung her legs to the floor and sat up on the long couch. The discussion had been going round and round since they returned to their suite in Harbert's house.

Cwenhild smiled at Fleta's disgust. "Besides her pretty story and her fluttering eyelashes, we have no reason to believe her," she agreed. "I say we make the meeting, but let's take every precaution. Everyone except Egbert will be in place at least one hour before eleven. We'll scout the area for traps."

Kjell cleared his throat. "Just to be clear, I know I said I couldn't get a good read from her with the mask, but that doesn't mean I believe we should trust her. In fact, my sense is just the opposite. There is something decidedly strange about her."

"I'll say," agreed Cwenhild.

Fleta choked off a laugh at Cwenhild's deadpan delivery and several of the others grinned as well, grateful for the break in tension.

Gode cleared his throat. "If that's settled, let's talk about the progress we're making with the maps," he said. "Egbert, you had a long meeting with Harbert last night. Did you learn anything useful?"

Egbert smiled, relieved to be off the subject of the mysterious woman. He had told them everything she said and had put up with a great deal of teasing about her flirting.

"Harbert has many beautiful maps," Egbert replied. "But none are so old as Kunnegarde's. Nonetheless, I believe I found the spot on one of them." His brow wrinkled. "It is odd how little of the territory through the Chain of Thollcrawnow is mapped. It is a no-man's land." Pounding a meaty fist on his thigh, he scowled. "I cannot believe we had the map in our hands and then lost it."

Dell's head drooped. On entering the suite, he had removed his new mask and Fleta looked at the puckered skin of his cheek. The cuts and bruises from the beating Talagon had given him looked worse if anything. His whole face was a mess of purple and yellow.

"I take full responsibility for that," Dell said. "Maybe I should go and steal it back from Radomil." His head came up and he gazed around at the others with a wicked smile. "Or maybe, I don't have to go looking for him. No doubt he's heading in that direction right now. I can stop him on his way."

Gode's mouth twisted. "I like the way you're thinking, my friend," he said. "We could perform a valuable assassination in the process."

Dell's sinister smile stretched. Struck, Fleta stared. For as long as she had known him, she had only ever seen his painted jester smile.

"As far as I'm concerned," Dell said, "there is no good reason for Radomil to live."

Kjell had contributed nothing to the discussion. Suddenly, he sat bolt upright in his chair. Someone was talking to him.

Boy, tellest them to stop all this blathering. I knowst thee lost the map. The disapproval was clear. *Although, I suppose thou art not to blame for that. Thou placed your trust where none was earned. And, in the end, thou didst escape.* The voice seemed to be talking to himself. *Nonetheless, a map is unnecessary. I shall lead thee to the God Sword. Thou and thy friends continueth to prove thy hearts and minds are true.*

Kjell twisted his head around, hoping to see someone behind him. But no one was there. Perhaps he was going mad. The voice was coming from inside his head. "Who are you?" he demanded, ignoring the other Hawks who turned to gape at him.

I am Kunnegarde, of course. I am in the ring. Didst thou think I died? The sound of a cheerful chuckle rang out. *Thou art a young fool.*

Kjell lifted his hand and stared at Kunnegarde's blue ring. It blazed with light. Then as he watched, it faded.

Falling back in his chair, he gazed around at the open-mouthed Hawks. His smile returned and he said, "We don't have to worry about finding a map."

CHAPTER TWENTY-SIX

Alliances

HOBBLING LIKE AN OLD WOMAN, Velte left Tsarval through the main city gates. No one gave her a second glance. She was just one more poor farmer making her way home after selling her wares in the market.

Martokallu had shown her where to find Gadrith. He and the few soldiers remaining to him were hidden in a hollow a short distance from the city. It was an annoying but necessary trip since Gadrith had no other way of communicating with either her or Martokallu. She shuddered to think how infuriating it would be to have no means of speaking with the Master. She treasured her connection. Although it was worrying that Martokallu could not see the Hawks. How were they hiding themselves?

As she stepped off the road into the woods, she took a moment to adjust her appearance. Looking once more like a beautiful young woman, she sauntered into the Followers' hideaway.

Gadrith was sitting on a rock beside a tent in the middle of the well-ordered camp. His head hung down and he had lost an arm. No wonder Martokallu was so angry with him.

A half-empty bottle of wine dangled from his fingers. No guards were set and there was no sign of the other Followers. She shook her head at the lack of discipline. No wonder Gadrith had not succeeded in crushing the Hawks.

Giving him no time to question her arrival, she said, "Gadrith, how lovely to see you. The Master sent me to see what aid I might offer. You know how important he considers this mission."

Looking up at the sound of her velvety voice, Gadrith's jaw dropped.

She flashed a smile and said, "I know it has been so difficult working without access to the Master's vision. I am here to help with that."

His eyes flared, and he lurched up from his seat.

Before he could launch into one of his tedious monologues, she purred, "I have good news. The Hawks are within the walls of Tsarval, lodged at the home of the Hammer of Dworgunul. I have arranged a meeting for tomorrow morning. They believe I have important news to share." She smiled coquettishly. "However, they will not be expecting anything tonight."

Gadrith sat up straight. "We'll go over the walls at midnight," he said. "We'll find them in their beds." He looked down at the stump of his arm. "They will not escape us again."

Velte's smile dimmed. She saw no need to cozen him further. He was too dense to figure it out on his own. She would have to take charge. "Do you wish to fight the entire city?" she asked. "Because, if not, I would suggest we consider a stealthier entrance."

Gadrith stiffened at her tone.

Velte ignored his resentment. It may have started out as his mission, but the instant he failed, he lost all credibility. "Martokallu has been watching the city," she said. "I know where the guards are stationed and when the changes occur. We will do what is necessary to put an end to the Hawks, and we will do it without instigating a citywide fight. I brought twelve mages with me. What are your numbers?" She already knew the answer from the visions Martokallu had shared, but she preferred to allow the illusion that she needed his help.

"I have twenty-two. None are mages, but they will fight." Gadrith's frown deepened. She imagined he was remembering that his Followers had twice failed to kill the Hawks. "We took a prisoner. Could you see her now and help her make the change?"

The corners of Velte's lips turned up as she glanced at the setting sun. "We have time," she said. "Bring her to me." They would have to wait until full dark before they could begin the attack anyway. Except for the mages who could control their appearances, the Followers were far too hideous to arrive unnoticed. Turning up at the gates while there was enough light to see them would create needless panic.

Gadrith gulped a mouthful of wine, swallowed hard and shouted, "Shallak!"

At once, a Follower emerged from a nearby tent. He gave a slight bow to Gadrith and then a deeper one to Velte. "My lady," he said.

Gadrith waved his hand dismissively. "Bring the woman," he ordered.

With another bow, Shallak turned and ambled down the alley formed by the tents.

Gadrith watched him go before taking another swig of wine. Wordlessly, he offered the bottle to Velte who shook her head.

Scowling, he tipped the bottle back and drained it.

Velte permitted herself a satisfied smile. Although she took no pleasure in Gadrith's failure, there was joy to be had in seeing his remorse. He had been sent to do a simple job and from what she had seen, there had been ample opportunity to do it. But at every turn, he had allowed himself to be defeated. She would change that tonight.

At a shriek of protest, she turned to see Shallak hauling a struggling woman toward her. Her pale skin was mottled with rage and as she fought to free herself from Shallak's grip, her black hair swung aside to reveal a missing ear. In other circumstances, she would be pretty, perhaps even beautiful. And she was young. Truly young. There was no magic in her glamour. Velte felt a momentary reluctance to bring such a rival into the Followers.

Then, she dismissed the thought. This was no mage. She too would age, and that flawless skin would wrinkle and waste away while Velte remained smooth and unblemished.

Gadrith stepped to the entranceway of his tent and raised the flap so Shallak could drag the woman inside. She did not make it easy, twisting and fighting every step of the way.

Velte looked to the sky and smiled. She would enjoy this.

As Shallak wrestled her into the tent, Hulda spotted a beautiful woman. For an instant, hope sparked within her. Had she come to free her?

She was tempted to abandon her protests and listen to what they had to say, but Hulda knew she could not give up. It did not matter that she was exhausted or that her head throbbed. The instant she surrendered, it would all be over. Every time the Followers tired of her protests, one of them thumped her on the head hard enough to knock her unconscious. And every time she woke up, she started to fight again.

No matter what she did though, she could not break free from any of them. Even when they were not paying attention, Followers moved more quickly that she imagined possible.

And without her blades, she was next to helpless.

The beautiful woman ducked into the tent behind Hulda. "Tie her there," she said, indicating the heavy center pole.

Hulda's heart sank and she wrenched against Shallak's grip, causing her shoulders to strain in their sockets and her eyes to water at the pain.

The woman clicked her tongue reprovingly. "I suggest you take every care to avoid bringing this tent down on our heads," she said. Her purple eyes held Hulda pinned to the spot.

Hardly able to breathe, Hulda froze as Shallak tied her to the pole.

With a smile, the woman circled Hulda. "That's better, isn't it? I am Velte. It is a pleasure to meet you."

The voice was smooth and welcoming, but Hulda was not fooled. She had no reason to trust someone who had just ordered her trussed to a pole. Shallak had accomplished the task with great efficiency, binding her wrists tightly behind her back and around the polished pole.

Hulda dropped her head for a moment and dug deeply into her reserves of energy. When she straightened up, she glared at Velte and said, "Nice to meet you too, I'm sure." Almost at once though, she dropped her gaze. There was power in those purple eyes. She could feel it. "You've hauled me all this way. What are your plans?"

Velte did not react to Hulda's anger. Her voice remained gentle as she said, "We wish to know if you are worthy."

When Hulda glanced unwillingly in her direction, she saw a gentle, welcoming smile.

Hulda felt that spark of hope again. Perhaps she could trust Velte. She was so beautiful. What harm would she wish on Hulda?

Then, Hulda stiffened. Velte was pushing at the edges of her consciousness. It was as if the woman was trying to crawl inside her mind. Hulda scrunched up her face, trying to resist the invasion into her thoughts. At the same time, she got a sense of Velte's mind. It was horrifying and desperately evil—nothing like the lovely woman with the friendly face.

Hulda's whole being rebelled against the darkness. She fought to find a light to hold onto as every corner of her mind was ruthlessly probed. She knew that to remain true to herself, she had to fight back.

Remembering how Kjell had talked about using his joy to create magic, she focused her attention on the wonderful parts of her life. She thought of her mother, of the time spent training by her side, of the stories she told, of how hard she had fought to save Hulda. She thought of her new family, the Hawks, of Dell and his tough exterior that hid a caring heart, of Gode and his happy ease with the world.

"You want to play hard to get," murmured Velte and suddenly, Hulda felt the pressure in her head disappear.

She looked up to find Velte's friendly smile gone. Her face was pinched, and she tapped her toe impatiently. Glancing at Gadrith, she said, "This will take more time than I imagined. We should go." As she turned back to Hulda, she let her face soften. "I'll be back to see you later. You will join us." With that, she swept from the tent.

Gadrith looked at Shallak and ordered, "Watch her." After a final angry glare for Hulda, he ducked under the tent flap, following Velte out into the night.

Gadrith would have preferred to make a bold attack on the city. He relished the idea of an all-out fight. With the added strength of the mages, the Followers of Martokallu were invincible. He could do with a win.

However, Velte had argued for stealth, and he was in no position to defy her authority. Taking advantage of the moonless night, he led them up to the walls of Tsarval.

His sword was in his left hand. No matter that he had

practiced with the blade every day since Kunnegarde turned his other arm to dust, it still felt awkward. His left hand was his staff hand. Nonetheless, he could handle the blade well enough to cause plenty of damage. He missed the easy access to his staff though. It was strapped to his back and if he needed to perform a healing, he would have to work it free.

No alarms were raised as they approached the city gate and Gadrith's confidence soared. He could smell success. Velte appeared at his side and her perfume filled his nostrils. She slid past him and placed her hand against the thick metal gates. Without a sound, they opened wide enough for two people to squeeze through together.

Standing aside, she waved her mages through the gap. Gadrith followed with his men. Velte was the last to enter the city and with a touch, she secured the gate behind her.

Gadrith's rage boiled up again as he recalled how Martokallu had sent him out on the mission with neither a mage nor a seer. Had the Master hoped he would fail? Setting his jaw, he dismissed the traitorous idea. Tonight would be a success. Tonight, the Hawks would die.

Hulda leaned back against the tent's center pole and closed her eyes. Shallak would lose interest in guarding her if she put up no protest. He was not smart enough to worry when she was quiet. She had to work hard at staying awake as she maintained her relaxed position. It had been a difficult week since they captured her.

Every minute of the day she thought about how she had allowed the Followers to creep up on her and Hackett. If she had only paid better attention, he would not be dead.

It was that silly game she had been playing with Gode. Calling out every few minutes, she had allowed herself to become distracted.

A shudder shook her as she recalled how Hackett had

thrown himself in front of her when a Follower broke through her defense. It was her fault he was dead.

Her eyes shot open. Across the tent, Shallak gave a rumbling snore and settled himself more comfortably.

Trying to remain perfectly silent, Hulda twisted against the rope that bound her hands. There was a little play in the knots. With time and patience, she would get loose and escape whatever plans that horrible woman had for her.

Gadrith followed the shadowy figures of the mages through the streets to the Hawks' lodgings. It made such a difference knowing where they were going. Again, he cursed Martokallu for sending him out without access to his vision. The Hawks would not know what hit them. Killing them in their sleep would not be as satisfying as a battle, but in the end, it got the same results.

Perhaps Velte was right about making a stealthy entrance. They would be in and out without anyone the wiser.

Then, he heard a metallic scrape behind him, and a guard called, "Who goes there?"

Instantly, one of the mages turned and fired a bolt of energy. Without another sound, the guard collapsed.

It was too late though. The penetrating note of a ram's horn sounded an alarm and light poured into the square as prepared torches were ignited. All at once, guards converged from every direction.

Caught in the illumination, the Followers were easy targets for the dwarven crossbows. The mages turned most of the arrows aside, but a few lodged in the Followers' tattered armour. Fortunately, none of them struck hard enough to cause serious damage.

A jolt of pure delight ran up Gadrith's spine as he bounded toward the wall. Crossbows took time to reload. Landing lightly beside an open-mouthed dwarf, he slashed at the archer's unprotected neck. Left hand or right hand, it made no difference. Nothing beat the pure joy of killing.

Blood splashed across him, and he turned to find another target.

CHAPTER TWENTY-SEVEN

Midnight Raid

KJELL WOKE WITH A START. He had slept on a couch in Harbert's guest suite. Staring around the dark room, he listened to the steady breathing of Gode and Dell. What had disturbed him?

Pushing aside his blanket, he went to the window. The quiet street was lit by a pair of streetlights. Then a horn sounded low and long in the distance. As if in response, Kunnegarde's ring lit up.

The Followers have found thee again, Kunnegarde said inside his head. *Thee must defend thyselves. Doth not permit them a victory.*

Spinning away from the window, Kjell shouted, "Hawks! Wake up! Followers are here!"

In all his time as Captain of the Elite City Guard, Vavrinec had never heard the ram's horn blown except during drills. A normal evening passed with him and his troop patrolling the streets of Tsarval with nary a thing to disturb the peace.

Occasionally, they broke up a fight outside a tavern or escorted a drunken dwarf to his door, but this was his first midnight summoning in almost five years on patrol.

He raised his own ram's horn to his lips and answered the call with a long blast. In the next instant, he was running with his contingent of fifteen men at his heels. Each had been chosen from the regular ranks after demonstrating particularly strong skills. To further ensure they were in top fighting form, at the end of every shift, the Elites spent an extra two hours honing their techniques and fitness before going off duty.

When they reached the main gate, a dart of fear pierced through him. The bodies of regular guards littered the square. Some were slashed to pieces while others had been burned alive. It was horrifying.

Pressing his lips together, Vavrinec reviewed their training. They were ready. He raised his clenched fist. At once, the Elites stopped and shifted into two offset rows of eight. No commands were necessary as they settled their tower shields on the cobblestones to create a shield wall.

It was difficult to tell amid the chaos, but Vavrinec guessed there were at least forty attackers. They were too tall to be dwarves. Some were taller even than the few humans he had met. As he watched, the invaders slaughtered the last of the regular guard.

Then, at a shouted command, a dozen of them whirled toward Vavrinec and his Elites. In an undisciplined horde, they dashed across the square, arriving with impossible speed.

Even as he braced for their arrival, Vavrinec had time to note two things. First, over half of the attackers did not join the assault and second, eight newcomers had just appeared. The light reflected off their chainmail. Where had they come from? They were not dwarven reinforcements but humans.

That was all the time Vavrinec had to wonder before a

heavy weight crashed against his shield. Popping up from behind its shelter, he hammered his war axe against the tall soldier's neck. Bright orange blood sprayed across his face, and he ducked into cover once more. On either side of him, his Elites were equally successful, and the attackers fell back in a disordered muddle.

"Advance two!" Vavrinec shouted and they pushed forward two steps, forcing the attackers off-balance.

A woman cried, "Gadrith, you fool, get out of our way!"

On the other side of the barrier, Vavrinec heard a muttered curse and the pressure against the shields vanished.

There was only a moment to celebrate before another blow struck his shield. Instinctively, he ducked behind it, but when he stepped out to meet the attack, no one was there.

A flash illuminated the square so brightly that when it faded, the torches appeared dim. Beside him, a polished shield reflected a wave of blue light. Instantly, he understood. "Mages!" he shouted.

His squad dove behind their shields. They had rehearsed this drill only occasionally. He had never truly believed they would need it. The first row of men rested the tops of their shields on the shields behind them, creating a lean-to shelter. They then reached for the crossbows they wore slung across their backs. The men behind handed their bows through to the front so that each shooter had two loaded bows.

As soon as everyone was ready, Vavrinec risked a peek. The row of mages had turned their attention to the second group of warriors. Seeing their distraction, he yelled, "Fire!"

Eight bolts shot through the air and four mages dropped to the ground. Barely allowing time to swap bows, he again cried, "Fire!"

Warned, the mages were ready for them this time. The second volley of arrows bounced harmlessly against an invisible shield.

Vavrinec cursed under his breath and shouted, "Crossbows away." There was no point wasting ammunition. They would have to attack.

When he rounded the corner into the square, Kjell skidded to a halt. Followers were everywhere. He recognized several of them as members of Velte's special squadron of mages. How had he never come to her attention? Surely, she should have known he had magic even if he did not. She would be nearby. But where? He swept his gaze around the square and spotted her at the back, where she could direct the fight.

He studied her through the eyeholes of Kunnegarde's mask and his vision wavered. As he fought a surge of dizziness, he realized she was wearing a glamour. Suddenly, he understood. She was the woman they had met earlier at the hotel. How had he not seen it earlier? The spell had broken when he thought her name. She was horrifying. Ravaged skin covered the emaciated body of a corpse.

Kjell smiled to himself and aimed a burst of fire in her direction. The flames did not touch her, but Velte swivelled to stare at him. In the fire-lit square, her face registered astonishment. No doubt, she had heard the reports of his death. He supposed she might be startled by his abilities as well. No one had suspected him of harbouring magic.

Gadrith looked around at his perfect battle and bit down on a scream. It was supposed to have been simple and straight forward. The Hawks were supposed to die.

Instead, while it had started out well enough, with the city guards presenting very little challenge, everything changed when a squadron of reinforcements arrived. And somehow, the Hawks had been warned. Impossibly, they had shown up just a few moments behind the reinforcements.

While Velte kept her mages pounding away at the line of

reserves who were better trained than the first squad of city guards, Gadrith turned his attention to the Hawks. Their mage sent streams of fire into his Followers. Briefly, he considered asking Velte for assistance, but with a grunt, he dismissed the idea. He would take care of the problem himself. Screaming a battle cry, he raised his sword above his head and charged.

He did not reach the mage though. Instead, a young warrior, who Gadrith recognized from the fight in the canyon, confronted him. From what he recalled, the boy had not been much of a threat. In fact, he had been among the first to flee.

However, a flurry of sword blows informed him that he might have underestimated the young fighter's abilities. How had he not noticed how well he used his two blades? As Gadrith struggled to bring his left hand around, he lost his balance and left his stomach exposed.

Flint slid Rising Star past the Follower's tattered robes and thrust it through to the hilt. Gritting his teeth, he stared into the monster's glowing green eyes. When they went blank, he wrenched his blade free and kicked the limp body off the blade.

Stepping away from the grotesque body with its unnatural blood, he swept his gaze over the battlefield. The fighting had almost come to a standstill.

Alone in the center of the square, Dagur was taking tiny, uncertain steps toward the woman they had met in the public house. Somehow, she was drawing him to her.

Flint shouted, "Dagur, no!"

But Dagur walked on until he came to a halt in front of the woman.

With a glorious smile, she reached out and touched his elbow, which caused Dagur to grin like a fool. Then, she drew back her staff, touched its curved blade to Dagur's chest, and plunged it into his heart.

As she held him upright, her eyes began to glow a brilliant purple. Dagur hung unresisting, his eyes glued to hers. Until abruptly, she pulled her blade free and in a burst of gore, Dagur's head exploded.

CHAPTER TWENTY-EIGHT

Defeat

GADRITH GLOWERED AT VELTE'S BACK as he staggered along behind her. She had ordered a retreat. A retreat! Followers did not retreat. It did not matter how many soldiers had fallen. They could still win. Especially with Velte's power and all her mages.

Clutching a poultice to his stomach, he wished he had even a glimmer of magic. The healing would take ages. The boy had shown no mercy when he shoved his blade in so deeply and sawed it around. Gadrith was a mess, and his strength was fading.

With a lurch, he caught himself on his staff as he stumbled off the road to follow Velte into the trees. She was furious. It had been the shock of seeing Kjell among the Hawks that had set her off. Everyone said he was dead. Maybe it was true that Followers never died. That was an interesting thought.

Gadrith did not recall hearing that Kjell had magic. His fire was spectacular. Even Velte had struggled to stand against it. Gadrith had been fortunate to escape unscathed by the flames. Others around him had gone up like dry tinder.

Grimacing, Gadrith almost wished Kjell had been able to set Velte alight. Despite the loss of her magic, it would have been something to celebrate. But he had seen how she turned the flames aside. She was never in any danger. What must it be like to have such power?

Gadrith stumbled again and he held his breath against the pain. He would have preferred to howl his agony, but Followers did not complain. His lips twisted. The boy who stabbed him would make a good Follower. He was a merciless killer.

Velte stalked along the road with the few mages who had survived the disastrous battle trailing behind. They would find a better to place kill the Hawks. Somewhere without all the interference. Somewhere she could get the jump on Kjell.

How had she never known of his power? He had been a General for two centuries. Why had she never sensed it? And how was he not dead? All the reports confirmed Martokallu's vision that showed Kjell lying dead in the road. That was something that would bear investigating when she caught up with him. She would let the traitor live long enough to satisfy her curiosity.

First, though, she would deal with the prisoner. If they were going to continue to lose fights, they needed to step up the recruiting. Reaching the hidden camp, she headed for the tent where the woman was tied up. When she slipped inside, Shallak jerked awake and stared around in bewilderment.

Meanwhile the prisoner's face went slack, and she slumped back against the centre pole.

Velte smiled. "My dear, don't look so disappointed. I am about to grant you the greatest gift of your life." She sauntered around to the rear of the tent and struck Shallak with her staff. "Get out," she said.

Then, turning, she saw that the woman had rubbed her wrists bloody trying to get free. In fact, she had almost accomplished it. A few moments longer, and she would have been gone. For the first time since the battle turned against them, Velte felt a glow of victory. This one would be hers.

Hulda shrank back as Velte knelt in front of her and placed a hand on her cheek.

"There is nothing to worry about, my dear," Velte murmured, stroking the smooth skin. "You will thank me for this." She did not waste time. Earlier she had tried to explore Hulda's mind. That was her favourite way to help someone make the change. Hulda, however, had resisted too strongly.

No matter. There were other methods. Curling her hands into claws, she set them on Hulda's chest. With a quick twist, her fingers penetrated the skin and bone until she held the beating heart in the palm of her hand.

Staring into Hulda's horrified eyes, she recited the words that began the life of every Follower. "Your heart belongs to Martokallu. Everything you do is done in the service of the Master."

Then she let go. Sitting back, she watched Hulda's mind drown in the rush of power. Velte could see it in her eyes. All thought of escape vanished. She was a Follower.

For the first time in over two thousand years, Martokallu felt helpless. From his quiet throne room, he had been unable to see most of battle in Tsarval. Occasional flashes came through Velte's eyes, but even so, his view of the Hawks was always obscured. They appeared as little more than smoky smudges.

With a growl, he thought of Gadrith who had fallen to the blade of a faceless warrior. The fighting style looked like that of the boy who had stabbed him in the stomach. His hand tightened into a fist as he recalled the wound he had taken from a boy so young he did not need to shave.

Watching now, he saw Gadrith scuttle away. The man had been a disappointment since the beginning of the mission. Martokallu had thought to test his abilities with a small task. His failure was obvious. He could never be worthy of the rank of General.

In a flash, Martokallu understood that he could not afford to continue to send small groups out to fight the battles. He needed an army big enough to assure a win. How though? Leaning back in his throne, he stared up at the distant ceiling.

It had never been necessary to recruit more than a few new Followers a year. Because they were such a drain on his own power, he could maintain only three Generals capable of helping recruits make the change. Increasing numbers in the usual fashion would be a slow and ponderous process.

Sitting up straight, he reached for his wine and froze with the glass half-way to his mouth. Suddenly, the answer was clear. He already had a huge slave force working in the halls and chambers of his fortress. They had worked hard to realize his dream of an excavation equal to the ancient dwarven cities.

The repairs to the southern entrance were all but complete. Soon the workers would be unnecessary. A smile spread across the misty remains of Martokallu's face. He would have Thrall take control of the slaves. He could form them into a battering ram that would break the Hawks and bring the people of Abbarkon into line.

Seated behind his desk, King Sebastien worked steadily through the pile of correspondence that came in night and day from every corner of the kingdom. Most of it was good news. All across Abbarkon, almost every leader who had been enthralled by Martokallu had been replaced by a carefully selected ambassador.

Since the day he took the throne, Sebastien had worked tirelessly to restore the kingdom to glory. During all that time, Supreme Commander of the Guards, Hrefna, had rarely left his side. A tall, plain-spoken woman, she had been reluctant to don the ostentatious armour that had marked her predecessor, Supreme Commander Paal.

It was too flashy for her taste. Both the breastplate and the kite shield were emblazoned with the King's Insignia. As well, every ridge of the plate metal was trimmed in gold. The armour maker had insisted that such ostentation was important. It brought pride to the King's Guards.

In the end, she had allowed herself to be convinced. Because of her height, very few modifications to Paal's armour were necessary, but the dented helmet required a complete overhaul. She had asked for extra reinforcement above the temples. She had also insisted on carrying her own sword.

It pleased King Sebastien that since taking up her post, Hrefna had found no cause to make use of either the armour or the sword. However, it was reassuring that she found time to train every day. He was well-versed in the danger of assassins. It was impossible to keep everyone happy.

Hearing a commotion in the hallway, King Sebastien looked up from his papers. Hrefna stepped between him and the door, sending him a warning look and drawing her sword.

Four quick knocks followed by two slow ones indicated that the door guards had determined there was a good reason to interrupt the king.

Hrefna glanced at Sebastien. At his nod, she called, "Come."

The door burst open and Halvor entered, followed closely by Gytha and Gulner. Their clothes were grubby and dusty, and they had dark circles under their eyes. When they crossed the threshold, all three immediately dropped to one knee.

As King Sebastien stepped from behind his desk, Halvor

leapt to his feet. "Your Highness," he said, his brown eyes filled with remorse.

King Sebastien laid a hand on his shoulder. With a sinking heart, he said, "Tell me."

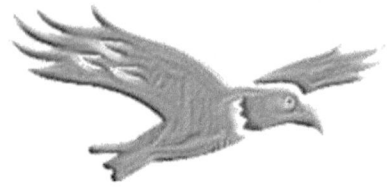

CHAPTER TWENTY-NINE

Plots

HALVOR WAS RIGHT. IT WAS crucial that they reclaim Oruk Library as soon as possible. Given enough time, Martokallu might order the destruction of the precious books.

King Sebastien winced at the notion of sending his people up against Followers again. He had vowed to be a good king. When he made that pledge, he had intended it to mean an end to war. For people to live good and happy lives, peace was essential. The idea of continuing to fight did not sit well with him.

Rocking back on his chair, he stared up at the ceiling. He had to consider the option. Regardless of how reluctant he was to lead his people into danger, it would be weak to sit back and allow such a wealth of knowledge to be lost.

Before leaving for the mission in Tsaralvia, Gode had urged Sebastien to institute a more rigorous training regimen for the entire King's Guard. In the sixteen years since he left the service to start the Hawks, routines had become lax, and training was slipshod at best. He had argued that a well-trained military force was critical to peace.

Despite his unwillingness to send soldiers to die, King Sebastien allowed himself to be convinced. To that end, he had charged Gytha with the task of improving training. She had set up the routines before leaving her daughter Asdis in charge while she set out to visit the towns of the kingdom. Asdis had turned out to be a particularly good drill sergeant.

King Sebastien smiled. Fleta would have said it was because of all the practice she got from bossing her and Flint around

According to the routines that Gytha had set up, each soldier was required to put in two hours of training at the end of every shift. As a result, the King's Guards were a far fitter and more skilled group than had guarded King Abelard. They carried their new skills with pride.

Asdis had organized several tournaments with boasting rights as the only prize. King Sebastien regularly reviewed the contests and was interested to see that no single warrior stood out above the others. With the constant training, they had all come up to a common level of excellence.

As part of her diplomatic mission, Gytha set up similar training programs in every town and city she visited. They too were experiencing a great deal of success with the program.

That meant it was possible to send a large fighting force against the Followers at Oruk. He could recruit from all over the kingdom. He would talk to Orma to see if she could set up a shield so that Martokallu would not see their approach.

Letting the legs of his chair hit the floor with a thunk, King Sebastien reached for his quill. He would send a letter to the leaders of every outlying town. The more soldiers he could muster, the better.

As the final Follower slithered out through the gate, Gode

rushed to Dagur's side. He was identifiable only by his armour since his skull had been shattered by the woman's magic.

"Flint, get the drawbar!" Gode shouted as he hoisted Dagur up and slung him across his shoulders.

Flint grabbed Fleta's arm, grateful to see she was unharmed. "Give me a hand," he said.

She shot him a wide-eyed glance and they sprinted to the gate. Flint slammed the gates closed with his shoulder, while she picked up the heavy steel bar.

"How did they get this off?" Fleta grunted as she strained against the weight.

Flint grabbed the other end and pushed it toward the crossbars. With a clang, it slid into place. "I'll bet it was magic," he said as he turned to survey the corpse-littered courtyard. Already a medical team had arrived, and they crouched over the bodies.

"Should we help?" asked Fleta. "This is our fault. The Followers wouldn't have attacked if we hadn't been here."

"They're better off with the medics," Flint said. "The others are leaving. Let's go."

They hurried after Gode and his grizzly burden. "What are we going to do?" asked Flint as he caught up.

Gode grimaced. "We'll take Dagur to Harbert," he said. "And then, we're leaving." He spoke quietly, but his anger was evident. "We have the staff. We have Kunnegarde's guidance. Let's go get the God Sword. It's time to end this." He took one last look around the bloody square, then turned and strode off through the narrow streets.

With Niviit at his side, Harbert met them at the door of his home. Seeing Dagur's lifeless body, the Hammer said, "Bring him through here." He led them toward the dining room and gestured to the long table. "Lay him out."

Dagur's chainmail rattled against the wooden surface as Gode arranged his long legs.

Biting her lip, Cwenhild pulled his hood up to hide his missing head, and murmured, "This isn't right. What an ugly way to die. Especially since she used her magic to draw him in before she killed him."

Swallowing against a sudden nausea, Flint agreed. The results of fighting with magic were worse than with blades. He closed his eyes and tried to block out the image. He would miss Dagur. The man had always known how to have fun.

"You will want to have a funeral for him," Harbert said.

Egbert put a hand on his uncle's shoulder. "We will make our farewells now, and then we must ride. It is time to end this. Can we ask you to perform the ceremony in our stead?"

"I would be honoured," answered Harbert.

One by one, the Hawks stepped up to take Dagur's hand and say their goodbyes. When it was Flint's turn, he found his eyes clouded by tears as he remembered the friends they had lost. It had started with Cadmon's death at Martokallu's hands, and then, Hackett, Igon and Hulda. "Let Dagur be the final sacrifice," he whispered as he turned away.

At the suite in Harbert's home, they scooped up their gear and headed to the stables. By the time the horses were saddled, Harbert and Egbert had completed their goodbyes. Without another wasted moment, the Hawks headed out of Tsarval despite the inky black sky.

Flint ran a hand across his face. He was tired. After the excitement of the battle and the rush to leave, a wave of exhaustion hit him and he wavered in his saddle.

Fleta leaned close and muttered, "I'm going to watch the back trail." Jerking a thumb toward Kjell who rode at the front of the procession with his eyes closed, she added, "Keep an eye on him."

As she dropped back, Flint nudged his horse up beside Kjell. Studying the mage, he tried to guess whether he was asleep. Then Kunnegarde's ring glowed blue and Kjell sat up straight.

When the light faded away, Kjell said, "We have time. They are not yet following."

"Kjell is one of the nicest people I know," Fleta said as she and Flint settled down outside the circle of light cast by the small cooking fire.

Flint grunted. "He is very nice," he agreed. "What's that got to do with anything?" They had volunteered for first watch. After nearly twenty hours in the saddle, he had passed beyond exhaustion. Perhaps he would never need to sleep again. He peered out into the darkness. Did Followers make noise when they walked?

"I've been thinking about this all day," Fleta said. "It's hard to imagine that he was a Follower. We want to believe they're all evil—that it's all right to kill them—that they are our real enemy. But it's not true. They were once normal, everyday people. Not evil, just human." She paused and drew a dagger. "The evil must come from Martokallu."

Flint rubbed a hand across the stubble on his chin. He would have to shave one of these days. "I'm not sure I have the energy to think about that right now," he said.

"You're probably right," Fleta said. "But maybe it will keep you awake."

They lapsed into silence as he pondered her words. Two hours later, he was still trying to wrap his head around the ethics of killing Followers when the constellation outlining Abbarkov's Chalice changed its angle sufficiently to indicate the end of their watch.

Climbing stiffly to his feet, Flint reached down a hand for Fleta. "I don't know about you," he said, "but if a Follower jumped out of the trees right now, I wouldn't hesitate to split him right down the middle."

Martokallu spent a long morning watching the elven army move into place. Busy trying to see what was going on in Cheveral, he had almost missed the enormous gathering on his doorstep. There were thousands of them. He could not imagine what they were doing in the Chain of Thollcrawnow.

He had been watching Velte battle the Hawks. She said she would take care of them, but again they had proven too slippery. Disgusted with her failure, he had let his vision spiral up to the skies. That was when he had spotted the horde marching past Tsarval. They had avoided the city, so he knew they did not want to be seen.

Martokallu hated elves. Dwarves he could put up with, but the sight of the elves roused his old prejudice. It had been years—perhaps centuries—since he gave them more than a passing thought. It put him in mind of his brother.

Lately, he had been thinking more and more of Kunnegarde. It was the search for the God Sword that had brought him to mind. His brother had always been so different from him. He had no difficulty making friends. Friends with humans. Friends with dwarves. Friends with elves. It did not matter. Everyone was the same as far as he was concerned. And everyone liked him.

Unlike him, Kunnegarde had never cared about rank or advancement. His army career proved that. Martokallu had made it to the top—General before he was thirty. His brother never made it past Brigadier. And, for the last part of the war, he had not even been around. Who knew what he had been up to.

Martokallu felt a flash of that old anger when he remembered the alliance that had formed between his brother and the elven prisoner. What was he thinking? It had been a righteous war. The elves had been the enemy. Kunnegarde had no business besmirching the family name with his carelessness.

Martokallu could never understand how his brother naively

discounted the differences between the races. Humans were so obviously superior. Dreff's loss in the war of the gods made that very clear.

Even more upsetting had been the approval Kunnegarde received from both Abbarkov and Dworgunul for his traitorous friendship. How could the gods welcome such an unholy alliance?

Martokallu's attention returned to the army filing into a wide valley on the eastern side of the mountain range. His catalogue of questions continued to grow as he watched them set up a perimeter guard. He even felt a moment of grudging approval when he saw how orderly the elves went about doing it. Order and organization were important. Perhaps this leader was an elf he could respect.

Radomil wanted to dance. He wanted to sing. He had done it! Soon he would hold the God Sword in his hand, and he would have the power to accomplish anything. Anything and everything!

Nonetheless, he kept a tight rein on his excitement. He had not confided his real hopes for the blade to anyone. Stepping back from the polished stone door, he studied it for weaknesses. There was no sign of either a lock or a handle. The outline of the door was clearly visible but there was nothing to indicate that it had ever moved.

His satisfaction began to slide away. How did the door open? He unrolled the map for another look. There had to be instructions. It did not make sense to get them so close and not provide an answer. However, the ancient vellum, offered no hints.

Radomil's shoulders slumped and then noticing Talagon hovering behind him, he hitched himself to his full height. The man was always sticking his nose in where it did not belong. His nose and his ugly face. The slashes that Dell had left him with were puckered and red. It hurt to look at him.

"We could not expect them to make it too easy," Radomil said with a laugh he hoped did not sound forced.

"No sir," responded Talagon. His single eye roved over the polished surface and his face tightened.

Not wanting to feel the guard's judgment, Radomil said, "Set up a perimeter guard before you order prayers. We do not wish to be surprised."

Talagon dropped his gaze, and answered, "Yes, sir."

Radomil enjoyed Talagon's discomfort. The man had begged to be allowed to fall on his sword after the disaster with the Hawks. But Radomil had refused to give him permission to take the coward's way out. Talagon had been found lacking. As punishment, he would have to live with his mistake.

CHAPTER THIRTY

Preparation

FROM THE EDGE OF THE clearing, Velte watched the Followers pack up their camp. It was taking too long. She wanted to be moving.

Suddenly, she grabbed her head in pain as Martokallu blasted his anger at her. *Two mages lost. Nine Followers. What is going on there? Why are the Hawks still alive?* He did not wait for an answer. *Am I correct in assuming that they continue to live? My vision is still faulty when I try to see what they are doing. All I really know is that you did not kill enough of the defenders.*

My Lord, she answered. *I killed one of the Hawks and we have changed another. Only seven remain now.*

Do not fool yourself. Each word hit her with the precision of a hammer. *Seven Hawks are more than enough to cause us trouble. Stop them. Now.* The pain disappeared along with the voice.

With all the dignity she could muster, Velte straightened from her crouch. She looked around to see if anyone had witnessed her punishment and caught Gadrith staring at her. Raising her head defiantly, she stalked across the clearing toward him.

"The Master is angry at yet another failure," she said. She enjoyed watching Gadrith wince at the reminder. "We are ordered to pursue them and finish this mission."

Suddenly, she realized there was another problem. She and her mages would not be able to travel in their normal fashion, flashing from one location to the next. Without Martokallu's guidance, they would have to follow their prey on foot.

Fixing her gaze over his shoulder, she drew in a deep calming breath. Refreshed she turned on her smile and said, "No doubt, the Hawks will be preparing to leave town—if they have not already gone. I will go and ask some questions."

Glancing at the bandage strapped to his stomach, she lifted an eyebrow and said, "I assume you will be prepared to travel when I return?"

Sitting watch in the dim light of the early morning, Kjell studied his blue ring. It began to glow again. Since Kunnegarde awakened him in Harbert's palace to inform him that the Followers were attacking the city, it had been flashing to life on an irregular basis.

In all that time, Kunnegarde had spoken to him only once. Just as they left Harbert's home, he had told Kjell to lead the Hawks to the northern side of Vaarndal.

Now that they had arrived, he was rather surprised that Kunnegarde had not interrupted his sleep again. Perhaps he was waiting for morning. As if responding to his thoughts, he heard the resonant tones in his head.

Good morning. Thou hast made excellent time getting hither.

Kjell wanted to answer but he felt uncomfortable speaking aloud.

There shall be trouble ahead. Dost thee recall Radomil, to whom thou gaveth the map?

Kjell wanted to argue that they had not exactly given the map to Radomil, but Kunnegarde did not give him an opportunity to reply.

Of course, I doth not understand why thou wouldst hand it over to anyone, especially after I expressly made it thine. Kunnegarde easily took both sides of the conversation as he continued. *Be prepared, for Radomil hath beaten thee to the Sword.* The voice took on a musing tone. *Though, he canst not open the door, so mayhap he hath not truly beaten thee to the Sword, but he hath beaten thee to the door.*

Without a break, Kunnegarde continued in his usual resonant voice. *Payeth attention today. I shall guide thee carefully.* Then he muttered, *Though, I suppose if any of thou art worth his salt as a tracker, thou shalt not need my help. Followeth the army into the mountains.*

Silence followed. After a long moment, Kjell nudged Egbert who sat guard beside him. "It's time to go," he said. "It looks like it's going to be a long day. The Worshippers of Dreff beat us to the God Sword."

Egbert lifted an eyebrow and studied him. Finally, he grunted and said, "I will wake the others. You can start breakfast."

Thrilled by the success of the experiment, Thrall reviewed his new army. Faster than he would have believed possible, he had executed Martokallu's orders to prepare the slaves for immediate attack.

Of course, they were not an army of warriors. Nonetheless, they would be dressed in armour and armed with axes or swords. They would march. They would fight. They would look like an army. Therefore, they were an army. They were his army.

When the time came, Thrall would exert his will upon them,

and they would kill. From there it would be easy. They would feel no pain so nothing except a deathblow would stop them from the directive he put upon them.

And too, he reassured himself, he did have a reserve force of elite soldiers. Real soldiers. Followers.

Wout had been working hard to train his sixteen assassins. The Hawks had made fools of them for the last time. There would be no more underestimating the opponent or overestimating their own preparation for war. Modelling the training techniques on the ones used in Kallcunarth had turned out to be an excellent decision. Martokallu's observations had been very helpful. The new training regimens had turned the Followers into an unbeatable force.

Thrall did not expect Wout's assassins would be necessary during the attack. There were too few of them to make much difference in a direct battle. They would find a better way to deploy them.

It had to work. He wished there was time to wait for Velte and her mages to return. Even that bumbling fool, Gadrith would be welcome.

Thrall did not understand Martokallu's sudden urgency. Why had he waited for so long and then jumped into action with so little planning? For centuries, Martokallu had played the long game, moving everything into place in readiness for taking over Abbarkon. People in power were enthralled. Influence and authority was gathered like the reins of a team of horses.

Now, just when all those meticulous designs were in ruins, Martokallu insisted that the time for action had arrived. To Thrall, it seemed a recipe for disaster.

At least, they would have Martokallu's vision to guide the fight. Thrall and Wout would serve as Generals so they would have direct links to everything Martokallu could see.

The advantage such information gave them was

indispensable. No matter what defense the enemy put up, Thrall could target their weak spots. That was always the best battle strategy. King Sebastien would not be expecting an attack either. Another advantage. Victory was guaranteed.

Thou art close enough. Keep thy heads down and thy eyes up. O'er that crest, lies an army at rest, said Kunnegarde.

At once, Kjell reined in his horse and the others stopped behind him. "Kunnegarde says we're close enough," he relayed.

Flint said, "Let me scout ahead. We need to know what it looks like before we can make a plan."

"Good idea," agreed Fleta, nudging her horse through to the front. "I'll come with you."

The moment Flint and Fleta came into sight, Egbert pounced. "What did you see?" he demanded. "Is there a way into the canyon?"

Flint looked at the older man and saw new lines on his face. The trip had been hard on him. After weeks of relentless riding, most of his belly was gone. He was not exactly skinny, but there was a new hard and lean look about him.

"There's a way," Fleta said. "Let's talk."

When the others gathered around the tiny cooking fire, Flint gazed at the anxious faces.

"It doesn't look good," he said. "The entire force of Worshippers of Dreff is there. Talagon has guards stationed at six-foot intervals. A gong is sounded every two minutes and they shift to the left. At the end of the line, up against the cliff face, they rotate off-duty until their time comes up again. There are probably fifty soldiers who just hang out around the center of the clearing, waiting for their turn to rotate back on duty."

Gode grimaced and scowled at Fleta. "I thought you said

there was a way in."

Fleta grinned. "Flint skipped the good news," she said. "There's a door carved into the mountain. It could be the entrance to whatever the map was leading to. And—" she wiggled her eyebrows, "—no one stationed above the door."

Cwenhild snorted. "Above the door? Are you crazy? What are we supposed to do? Fly down while they watch us?" She shook her head and scowled. "That's your good news?" When Fleta's smile grew broader, she stopped talking, and put her hands on her hips. "You have an idea," she said softly.

Turning to Dell, Flint asked, "Tell me you brought the Cloak of Nothing." At Dell's nod, he clapped him on the back and turned to Cwenhild. "And you brought your climbing gear, right?"

Looking interested, she leaned back on one foot. "Yes, I did," she answered, with the beginnings of a smile.

Egbert tugged on his beard braids. "I see where this is going," he said. "Of course, it would have to be done under the cover of darkness."

Gode added, "A distraction might be a good idea too. We don't want the whole camp of Worshippers to see the door open."

Flint looked at Egbert. "Would it be possible to rig a system where we could get down without having to scrabble about on the rock?"

Fleta elbowed Flint aside and demanded, "What do you mean? We? Nothing has been decided about who's going in."

Flint's smile disappeared. Whichever way this plan went, it was risky. Cocking his head to the side, he said, "I was thinking that Cwenhild, Dell, Kjell and I could slide down the cliff face to the door and try to get inside. Fleta—" he turned pleading eyes on her, "—you could stay at the top with your bow and help Egbert with whatever needs to be done to get us down, and—" he added, almost as an afterthought, "—up again."

"It makes sense," said Egbert. He patted his new crossbow. It had been a parting gift from Nulebar, the dwarf who had trained his father at the forge. "I might get a chance to put this beauty to use as well."

Turning to Gode, Flint said, "I hoped you would create a diversion." He glanced at Dell. "Maybe a small explosion or two?"

Dell, who had taken to removing his mask around camp, smiled at that suggestion. When they stayed with Harbert, he had replenished his supply of explosive powder and Egbert had forged several new grenades filled with nasty bits of sharpened metal.

Fleta crossed her arms across her chest. "Cwenhild is a better shot with a bow," she said.

"But Cwenhild has climbing experience that you do not," said Gode. "Flint's right. You'd be most useful above. Now we need to work on the details." He glanced at the sun where it sat high in the sky. "I suggest we take a nap and then, when it's dark, we'll move into position."

CHAPTER THIRTY-ONE

Secrets

TUL NEEDED TO THINK. HE needed a plan. Leaving his chair, he paced the length of the long room. Never in his two thousand years of guarding the God Sword had anyone come so close to discovering the entrance to the fortress. His scouts reported that there were two separate groups in the area.

His first impulse had been to send out a force and eliminate the intruders. But, when he heard how large the army was, he realized it might be wiser to remain inside and wait for them to wear out their patience trying to break through the door.

The second group was another matter. They were the ones who called themselves the Hawks. Already, his comrades, Gan and Kunnegarde had judged them worthy. Likewise, his two encounters with the young humans had given him hope that they might be worthy of the sword. He sensed the world needed a new defender. Perhaps his time was coming to an end.

Tul would not mind passing off his duties to someone younger. He had not had the privilege of sleeping away the last two thousand years as Kunnegarde and Gan had done. Despite Dworgunul's gift of immortality, he was tired.

Having settled in his mind that he would wait and see who came through the door, Tul continued through the corridors until he reached the chamber where the God Sword was hidden.

He reassured himself that the blade was safe. Stepping past the pair of dwarves who were part of a two-thousand-year succession of guards, he ran his hand over the stone door that shielded the God Sword from the world. Without the key, the door remained impenetrable.

Satisfied, Tul returned to his waiting room. Settling himself into the chair he had built specially for this purpose, he prepared to wait. How often had he sat there over the centuries? But never before had he anticipated the arrival of a potential successor.

He would see who entered, and he would test the strength of the challenger. Only if the person proved worthy would he have to decide what to do next.

There was no way past the huge slab of rock. As Radomil inspected it for the hundredth time, he realized that beyond a vague outline, there was nothing to indicate it really was a door. Maybe it was a marker. What if the sword was buried nearby?

Even as he studied the cliff face, Radomil wondered what had made him believe it was a door. The symmetrical arch could be there just to bring balance to the carving beneath it. Chiseled in the exact center of the polished stone was an intricate, circular design. Hidden within that deeply carved pattern were five small holes.

Radomil's first thought had been that those holes might

conceal a release for the door. He had ordered his blacksmith to report to him with his tools. The man had spent several hours trying different methods of inserting wires into the holes. They had even gone so far as to build a temporary forge so that he could create a five-pronged implement that allowed them to press into all five holes at the same time.

Nothing worked.

As the daylight faded, Radomil decided it could wait until morning. He would have the army maintain its vigil, but he would go to bed. Perhaps sleep would inspire him.

The Hawks had already left town. Velte knew which gate they departed from and the direction they had headed. It had been a simple matter to persuade one of the city guards to tell her everything he remembered about the group that left after the midnight attack. The beautiful woman only had to ask.

As she jogged north along the road to Vaarndal, Velte renewed her vow to catch the Hawks. And when she had them in her sights, she would destroy them. Nothing would distract her from eliminating each and every one.

Turning to the newest recruit, she asked, "How far would you expect them to go tonight?"

Without a break in her stride, Hulda replied, "They will ride all night and sleep briefly during the day. They must have received important information that they are putting into action."

Velte cursed Gadrith. If it had not been for his injuries, they would have been on the road far earlier. As it was, the Hawks had a lead of at least ten hours. If the Followers did not step up the pace, it was likely they would get even further behind.

Orma dropped stiffly to one knee as she entered the brightly lit throne room.

King Sebastien hurried forward and clasped her hands,

drawing her to her feet. "There is no need for that, Orma," he said. "We're old friends here."

He led her to a chair and seated himself across from her, leaning forward with his elbows on his knees.

She settled onto the cushions and said, "You look well, Your Majesty. This job suits you."

Sebastien closed his eyes and pinched the bridge of his nose before meeting her gaze again. "There are aspects of the job that I enjoy," he said, "but the thing I have brought you here to discuss today is not one of them."

Orma folded her hands in her lap and waited.

"You heard what happened at the Oruk Library?" King Sebastien asked.

"I heard," answered Orma.

Sebastien sighed and looked up at the corner of the room. "Halvor has convinced me that I must send a force to reclaim it." He slapped his thighs and rose. "The last thing I want as king is to order my people off to battle," he declared as he paced the length of the room. "I do not want them to die in my name. I want the citizens of Abbarkon to live long and happy lives."

Orma stood too and stepped in his path, placing a hand on his sleeve. "Sometimes, we can only bring order to the land by fighting back against the things that are not right," she murmured. Then she cleared her throat. "Cadmon understood that. He was very good at planning and fighting and killing. But it was not what he wanted to do. It was his belief that we must fight to make the world a better place. Turning a blind eye to what is happening can never be the answer."

She guided him to the window and pointed down at the people bustling about the street. "You are going to war for them," she said. "A weak king would ignore the problem and hope for it to go away. The people need a leader who is not afraid to see the evil and do something about it."

Sebastien's lips tightened. "I think I knew that, but I needed to hear it. Thank you, Orma." He turned to Hrefna who stood in her usual spot three steps from the door. "Would you give us a moment?" he asked. "I'll be safe in here with you outside the door and Orma in here to protect me."

Hrefna gave Orma a dubious look, before bowing her head and moving to the door. Giving two brisk knocks, she received an answering knock of two slow and three quick. After another doubtful glance over her shoulder, she drew her sword and swung the door open.

The hallway was empty except for the four guards assigned to be there. Sheathing her sword, she said, "Call if you need me. I'll be right outside."

As the door closed behind her, Orma said, "You have gained her loyalty. And not only hers. I believe you will find your people willing to stand behind you. They know you want to make Abbarkon a better place. Oruk Library is part of what will help us recover. Most people do not remember a time when books were freely available, but they can appreciate how life might be when they are."

Sebastien sighed. "I like that you say when and not if," he said. "I want to make books and learning a normal part of our lives. The theft of our knowledge is Martokallu's greatest crime."

He led her back to the chairs and sat down opposite her once more. "I appreciate the philosophical support. However, that is not why I asked you here." He glanced at the door once again before leaning forward to murmur, "Cadmon once explained to me how Halklyen went unnoticed for all those years. I also heard from Fleta how exhausted you were after the battle at Fasnul."

One corner of Orma's mouth lifted. "It was draining. But worth every bit of effort."

Sebastien took a deep breath. "I do not want to ask you to

do something that would cause you harm." He searched her eyes.

"Go ahead and ask," she said. "I am stronger than I look."

King Sebastien cleared his throat and blurted, "Is there something you could do to conceal my plans from Martokallu?"

"There are things I can do," Orma answered. "But there will still be the risk of spies." She grimaced. "Secrecy was our best weapon in Halklyen. On at least one occasion, a careless word in front of an outsider cost lives."

Sebastien leaned close to Orma and murmured, "I want to assemble the largest army Abbarkon has ever seen, and I want to do it without Martokallu knowing. I have already sent out messages to every town and city in the country. Very shortly, we will begin to see groups of two or three people arriving from everywhere. I asked them not to travel in uniform or to reveal their weapons. Ideally, they will have a false reason for travelling." He sat back and grinned. "I want Martokallu to see nothing more than roads busy because of the returning trade."

Orma's eyebrows rose. "You've been part of the plans for the Hawks for a long time!" she whispered. "I thought all those wonderful ideas came from Cadmon, but this has a flavour too similar to ignore. It was you, wasn't it?"

King Sebastien grinned. "So, can you help?" he asked.

"I can help," Orma answered. "This could work."

CHAPTER THIRTY-TWO

Stealth

EGBERT WOKE UP THINKING ABOUT the block and tackle in his forge. He used it to move heavy pieces of iron and it was exactly what he needed. He glanced around the small, neat campsite. The sun was almost down and everyone except Gode was still rolled in their blankets.

Rising, he went quietly to Gode. "Why didn't you wake me?" he whispered. "Am I not supposed to sit the watch with you?"

Gode shifted aside to make room. "You looked like you could use the sleep. It's been quiet."

"I cannot say I do not appreciate it," Egbert said, biting down on a smile as he settled onto the log.

Gode studied him. "You've had an idea," he said.

"I think so," replied Egbert, staring blindly at the trees. "I need to find a log. Would you lend me your axe? I'll leave my hammer in exchange." He pulled his hammer from his belt and offered it.

Gode took the heavy hammer and hefted it experimentally. "I'm not sure I'd know what to do with it," he said absently as he drew his axe and held it out haft first.

"Swing hard," Egbert answered. "It makes an impact." Taking Gode's weapon, he pushed to his feet and headed into the woods.

He wanted a tree that had fallen recently. It had to be dry but with no rot and he wanted a length without any branches. There was plenty of windfall from which to choose. Testing each log with the axe, he listened hard for the sound of rot. Gode would worry about his precious blade but chopping wood would cause it no damage. A little honest work would be good for the steel.

It did not take long for Egbert to find what he needed. Setting to work, he hacked out a section about twice his height. The sun had already dropped below the horizon. He would need to hurry.

As he raised the axe above his head, he caught a rustle of movement and Fleta appeared.

"Greetings of the day, my girl," he called before smashing through the last few fibres and allowing his section to roll free. Straightening, he leaned on the axe as he caught his breath. "I hope I did not wake you. I have had a wonderful idea. We shall make a pulley so we can lift people up from below faster." He bent and lifted the log. "We haul this to the top of the cliff, anchor it behind some rocks and use it to haul on the rope."

Fleta's face lit up. "That's brilliant," she said. "We just have to polish it up to let the rope run."

"We may not have time to make it perfect," Egbert said. "But we can make it smooth enough to serve for tonight." He hoisted the length of wood onto his shoulder and carted it back to camp. Releasing it with a thump, he strode over to Gode.

"Thank you for the use of your blade, my friend," Egbert said, handing it back. "I must say the balance is near perfect."

Gode took it and ran a thumb along the edge. "It should be," he said. "The finest blacksmith I know made it for me." He grinned. "You can have your hammer back. I took a few swings with it. It might not cut but it would stop anyone who got in its way." Pulling out his whetstone from a pocket, he settled down to bring the axe's blade back to a razor edge.

Egbert rubbed his hands together. "Now, Fleta, my dear, if you would lend me one of your little blades, we will have this ready in no time."

Pulling two identical daggers from her belt, she offered them to Egbert. "Which one do you want?" she asked.

Egbert laughed. "This one will do nicely," he said, selecting the one in her left hand. "I thank you."

Together, they bent over the log, cutting the bark away to expose smooth yellow wood.

Fleta straightened, stretching her back as she wiped sweat from her face. The bark had resisted their efforts and Flint had joined in to help. In the moonlight, the newly exposed wood gleamed.

"How long should I cut the ropes?" Cwenhild asked.

Fleta stared off into the trees as she measured the distance in her mind. "The ledge is about fifteen feet above the ground," she said finally.

"That sounds about right," agreed Flint, handing back Fleta's dagger.

"We should have plenty of rope then," said Cwenhild. "We can easily get four lengths of thirty feet."

As she and Dell set about measuring it, Egbert also returned Fleta's dagger. "Our work here is finished," he said. "You may wish to run a whetstone over those edges when you have a moment. Right now, help me brace the log between this pair of trees. It is time to test the theory."

When they had it in place, Egbert looped one of the ropes twice around the log before handing one end to Fleta and one to Flint. "Go ahead and pull, Fleta. Flint, I want you to give her some resistance."

"Tug of war!" Fleta said. "My favourite."

"Tug of war while we're standing beside each other," said Flint. "This is weird." He leaned back on the rope and Fleta dug in her heels and hauled on the other end. Without too much effort, she pulled him along several feet.

Unexpectedly, she released the tension and Flint fell backwards. Laughing, he said, "It works!"

"Perfect timing," said Gode. "We should go now." He was heading out on his own. He would be providing the distraction.

Only a small sliver of moon shone through some wispy clouds. It would be a dark walk. "If you stay on that heading," Fleta said, indicating the constellation of Abbarkov's Chalice, you should end up in the right place."

Flint chuckled. "You can't miss them," he said. "You'll hear the Worshippers of Dreff long before you see them."

"You're going to be in place long before we're ready," Fleta said. "Wait until the Chalice is right above you. That should give us enough time."

"Will do," Gode answered. He rested a hand lightly on her shoulder. "Be careful out there."

"You too," she replied, a sudden knot clenching in her stomach.

As Gode slipped into the trees, Flint said, "Fleta, you lead. I'll help carry this log."

"I can take a turn carrying it," Fleta said.

"You just make sure you find the straightest route there," said Cwenhild. "I think Egbert found the heaviest piece of wood he could."

Dropping down, Fleta crawled toward the cliff edge. There was nothing to hear over the clang of the gong. Nerving herself up, she raised her head and peered down on the camp. Their luck was holding. Most of the armed force was nowhere near the door. In addition, it appeared even darker in the narrow valley. The lack of light would work to their advantage.

Their biggest problem lay right under her nose. The two soldiers stationed on either side of the door were not a part of the rotating guards. The whole time she watched, they did not move. She remained perfectly still for three soundings of the gong before lowering her head and inching backwards.

They had wedged the pulley between a tree and an immense rock. Flint, Cwenhild, Dell and Kjell were ready to go. They each had a length of rope tied securely around their waists while the ends were wrapped around the pulley log. All they had to do was to wait for the distraction to begin.

Running. Velte's lip curled. She could not believe she was running. Like an ordinary mortal. It had been centuries since she bothered even to walk any great distance.

To add insult to injury, they had no idea if they were going in the right direction. The only information they had to work from came from the gate guard in the dwarven city. It was too humiliating for words.

The images Martokallu had sent showed a huge force of elves moving along the road. Unfortunately, he could see nothing of the Hawks. To compound the problem, none of the Followers was a particularly good tracker. Nonetheless, each time they came to a crossroads, they had thoroughly examined the gravel surface for evidence of recent travel.

So far, there had been nothing to indicate that the Hawks had left the main road. Everyone who had passed this way in the last day had gone in the same direction as the army.

A shiver ran up Velte's spine as she remembered

Martokallu's anger when he showed her the army of elves. He had no idea what they were up to. His fury felt like a blow when he contacted her through the mind link.

But one good thing had come out of it. The scope of their mission had increased.

Not only were they to eliminate the Hawks, but they were also to discover the purpose of the elven army and do everything possible to disturb their plans.

An order like that sounded appealing. Disruption was always interesting.

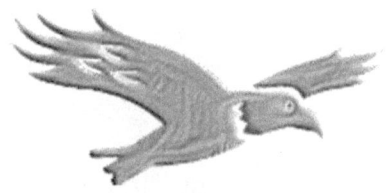

CHAPTER THIRTY-THREE

Revenge

GODE LAY ON HIS BACK watching the stars. When the constellation, Abbarkov's Chalice, moved directly overhead, he rolled to his feet and picked up the pack that contained fourteen exploding grenades. While waiting, he had tended the tinderbox, careful to keep the fire far from the explosives.

The idea was to lob the grenades into the line of guards. That would shake up their perfect line. It would also make everyone look toward the explosion, giving Kjell a chance to examine the door and figure out how to get past it.

Sliding through the dark woods, Gode found a spot where he could see several Worshippers of Dreff. He waited until the gong rang. Then, while the soldiers were in motion, he lit a grenade.

Wearing Kunnegarde's mask and the Cloak of Nothing, Kjell sat with his legs hanging over the edge of the cliff in clear sight of the elves. He was armed with only a knife in his belt and Kunnegarde's staff. His bow had gotten in the way of the rope harness, so he had left it with the horses. If he needed to, he could still shoot fire.

Suddenly, an explosion cracked the air. As tempting as it was to watch Gode's disruption, Kjell rolled onto his stomach.

On the other end of the rope, Fleta and Egbert leaned back and took up the slack. With one last glance at the soldiers below him, Kjell slid over the edge. To his amusement, the rope appeared to float above the cliff in the instant before he braced himself against the rock face. They let him down, the rope sliding smoothly around the improvised pulley and moments later, he settled on the ground.

Neither guard heard his arrival. They were straining to see what was happening at the other end of the camp.

As Kjell touched down, he drew his knife and sank it into the throat of the guard on his right. The elf slumped against him, and his partner turned in surprise.

Pushing the Worshipper of Dreff aside, Kjell lost his blade. With his bare hand, he caught the second guard by the throat. Grimly, he started to squeeze. It was not what he wanted to do, but Radomil and Talagon had proven it was impossible to have a calm and reasoned discussion with the elves.

To his surprise, his hand felt hot—almost too hot to maintain the grip. Horrified, Kjell stared as the man's face began to melt. His magic was causing the ghastly effect. Swallowing against his disgust, he held on doggedly. The dying elf made no noise, resisting only feebly. When he finally became an unresisting weight, Kjell let the body slide to the ground.

A quick inspection told him he was alone and he turned to the door. The circular design in its center was the first thing that caught his attention. He ran his fingers over the pattern as Flint landed silently at his side.

They did not speak, and Flint turned away to keep watch. Moments later, Cwenhild dropped down. Dell was the final arrival and he too faced away from the door.

When they were certain no one had witnessed their arrival, they untied the knots around their waists. Fleta must have been watching from above because the instant the ropes were free, she hauled them up.

Another explosion came from the other end of the camp. The army had completely lost its air of order. Soldiers ran everywhere and there were screams of pain as flying shrapnel caught in flesh. Captains shouted orders while the gong continued to ring out the changes.

Kjell ignored the commotion and concentrated on the door. His fingers found five indentations in the circular design. Immediately, he understood.

Kunnegarde had said the staff was the key. He swung it around and poked the prongs at the holes. As the metal skittered across the polished stone, he held his breath, willing it to work. Suddenly, the five prongs caught in the holes and the staff slid into place.

Nothing happened.

Remembering how he had pushed his magic into the lock on the door of the dwarven city, he sent a stream of power to the staff. Instantly, the sapphire lit up with a dazzling blue glow. He waited, expecting it to start spinning as the disc had done. But nothing.

Then he felt a low rumbling under his feet and the door creaked opened on rusted hinges. Cool air rushed past him, and he took a step into the black tunnel.

Behind him, a shout came from the line of tents.

"We've got trouble," Cwenhild muttered.

Kjell whirled and spotted Radomil stalking toward them. He wore his armour, but his robe hung unfastened, and his long black hair fell loose and dishevelled around his face.

Evidently, he had been awakened by the explosions and the opening of the door.

When he spotted the Hawks, his head jerked up and he shouted, "Talagon. To me!"

Waving the others through the door, Kjell cried, "Go!" With a yank, he freed his staff from the door and turned to face the tall elf.

Talagon appeared out of the darkness with twenty-five Worshippers on his heels. Seeing his master, he called, "Sir?"

Radomil kept his eyes on Kjell and barked, "Three Hawks just ran through that door. Deal with them."

"Yes, sir!" Talagon shouted and raced toward the hole in the mountain. Seconds later, darkness swallowed the squadron.

Kjell let them go. His attention never wavered from Radomil. What he had been unable to see earlier was utterly clear. The mask showed Radomil's heart and soul in all their twisted and shadowy ugliness. It was the bleakest thing he had ever seen.

As distasteful as it was, Kjell had accepted the necessity of killing the two guards. However, as he faced Radomil, he felt no repugnance at the thought of ending the elf's life. He would be doing the world a favour.

Radomil lunged at Kjell.

Dancing aside, Kjell released a bolt of orange fire. His aim went wide and with a lazy swipe of his hand, Radomil parried the attack. Then, raising his own staff, he sent a blast of black energy in return.

To Kjell, it appeared as if the bolt approached in slow motion. Stepping aside, he turned to see the stone behind him shudder under the impact. At that, a wave of anger hit him. Radomil did not care who got hurt. His own people had entered the mountain and he was willing to risk a cave-in with his carelessness. What sort of leader did that? Whirling back to Radomil, Kjell hurled a blast of magic. It was more than fire and meant to kill.

Radomil batted at it with his hand as he had with the flames. But instead of changing course, the energy shattered into a thousand deadly shards. One struck Radomil in the chest leaving a blackened spot on his shiny armour and stopping him in his tracks for a moment.

A horrible smile lit his face and he chuckled. "We're playing for keeps now," he sneered. With a flick of his staff, he shot an enormous ball of black energy.

Kjell seized his staff in two hands and swung hard as if it was a game. When it struck, the force of the blow slammed him against the mountain. His feet went out from under him, and he landed hard on the ground.

Not giving him a chance to recover, Radomil raised his staff and attacked. Kjell scrambled up but he was too slow. The staff caught him in the ribs, and he hit the ground with a gasp.

Gaping through the mask's eyeholes, he suddenly remembered how Martokallu manipulated his Followers. Meeting Radomil's hate-filled eyes, he struck. From that point on, no further blasts lit up the night. The two men were frozen—Radomil caught mid-lunge, and Kjell lying on his back, while the battle raged on inside their heads.

Kjell shot into the sickening maze of convoluted reasoning and justifications that filled Radomil's thinking. It was horrible. Wrenching himself free of the twisted logic, Kjell pressed down on Radomil's will.

When Radomil called out for his god, Dreff offered only silence and Kjell shoved his way in there as well. It was like trying to plug a leaky dam with his fingers. Thoughts shot off in all directions.

Then Radomil took a different tack. Rather than fighting back, he tried to shut down his own mind. But held immobile by Kjell's entry, he could not summon the necessary blankness.

Disgusted by how much Radomil's mind reminded him of his own bewitchment when he was under Martokallu's influence, Kjell fought a desire to escape. Not for an instant did he enjoy the sensation of being inside Radomil's head. Just when he knew he would have to bolt, he felt the spread of a shadow.

Radomil's grasp on consciousness began to fray. As much as he struggled to hold on, berating himself in his weakness, Kjell knew he had won. He listened to Radomil admonish himself to fight as his strength skittered away.

Straining to maintain control, Kjell sensed the instant when Radomil lost his grip on himself. He felt the other mage's mind break and knew it was over. It took a moment longer, but Radomil's body finally got the message and toppled to the ground.

Gasping for air, Kjell scrambled to his feet. One sweeping glance around the camp told him that no one had noticed either the battle or the open door. Surprised, yet grateful, he turned to follow his friends into the mountain.

But he froze at the sound Kunnegarde's voice. *Hold boy! Thou hast done masterfully. Let us not waste thy work.*

The blue stone of Kunnegarde's ring was glowing more brightly than it had ever done before. Heat built on Kjell's finger, and wincing against the pain, he thrust his hand under his tunic to conceal the light. Then he turned his body away from the camp of Worshippers because the shining blue pulse showed brilliantly through the cloth.

Breathless, Kjell stared at it. "What are you doing, Kunnegarde?" he muttered aloud.

As if in response, the gem shattered, showering fragments of stone in every direction.

Kjell felt the wrench of loss. *Kunnegarde!* he called inside his mind. When his only answer was silence, he swallowed heavily and turned to enter the mountain.

The clank of armour behind him made him whirl around and raise his staff.

His breath froze in his chest when Radomil climbed awkwardly to his feet. The elf teetered unsteadily for a moment before gaining his balance.

Then he turned his gaze on Kjell and grinned with such carefree abandon that Kjell faltered.

Holding back the blast of magic that had surged to his fingertips, he cocked his head to the side and said, "You were dead."

CHAPTER THIRTY-FOUR

A New Start

FLETA BIT HER LIP. DAWN was beginning to illuminate the sky. They only had a few more minutes before full light. What were they doing down there? Had they managed to open the door?

Gode's distraction was working. Worshippers of Dreff ran wildly in every direction. At that moment, another grenade detonated in a burst of ear-thumping noise and brilliant light.

They had tied off the ropes and Egbert held them ready to toss over the instant they heard Flint's whistle.

A few minutes earlier, a rumble had shuddered through the stone under her feet, and she had heard a few brief shouts. Since then, she and Egbert had waited in tense silence. It was killing her. Why did she have to be the one left behind?

Finally, she could stand it no longer. Dropping to her stomach, she crept to the edge of the cliff and peered down.

Gode had to quell his laughter as he flitted from tree to tree. The reaction of the Worshippers when he lobbed his first grenade had been hilarious. Light from the explosion lit up their baffled faces and instead of retreating behind barriers, they had run around in circles.

Many of them fell to their knees and prayed in loud, frantic voices. He did not understand the words, but he recognized their posture and the up-turned palms from the visit to the first camp of the Worshippers of Dreff. One officer strode angrily about, shouting and waving his arms, trying to bring order to the lines.

Gode timed his attacks carefully. Whenever the officer bullied the men back into formation, he lobbed a grenade into their midst. The man was having less success with every blast.

Gode watched while the officer struggled to calm the soldiers once more. The injured and dead lay unheeded on the ground while the defenders stared blindly into the trees. Gode made himself wait. He was running low on grenades. His best bet was to get rid of the officer. One organized man could destroy their whole plan.

When the officer stepped into his range, he slid the fuse into the tinderbox, careful to allow no trace of the glowing coals to show. Then, still shielding the orange tip of the fuse, he counted slowly to ten and tossed it right beside the officer.

"Easy, boy. Dost thou not know me? 'Tis I, Kunnegarde."

Kjell froze. The words came from Radomil's lips, yet they sounded just like Kunnegarde's voice inside his head.

Kjell stepped back and raised his hands ready to launch an attack. At the same time, Radomil held his hands out to his sides, in a show of capitulation. The handsome face wore the same cheerful expression that had so beguiled the Hawks the first time they met. Through the eye-holes of his mask, Kjell looked beyond the smiling face into the soul that lay beneath the surface.

Everything had changed. The black shadows were gone. In their place were pockets of yellows and oranges, reds and purples. Kjell's head jerked back. How was it possible?

"'Tis a relief to be out of that blasted ring," Kunnegarde said. The voice no longer held Radomil's arrogance. "'Twas not natural. And—" He experimentally bent his arms and cavorted around. "'Tis a body in far better shape than my old one."

At that moment, one of Radomil's aids ran up from the other side of the tents. Dawn had lit the edges of the eastern mountains giving enough light to see. The soldier stopped short at the spectacle of his commander dancing.

"Sir?" he said.

Kunnegarde immediately snapped into a more dignified posture. "Report!" he barked.

Giving him an odd look, the soldier came to attention and said, "Sir, the officers are all dead. The men are—" He broke off as he searched for words. Trying again, he said, "There are no leaders, sir. What should we do?"

Kunnegarde regarded the soldier severely. "There is no help for it," he said. "We must leave this cursed country. Order a retreat from the fighting and begin preparations for withdrawal. We must return to Cheveral. We shall leave immediately."

The soldier's jaw dropped at this completely unexpected reversal in the plans. Kunnegarde did not give him a chance to think too long. "What are you waiting for?" he demanded. "Relay the orders and prepare to move out."

Dropping his eyes, the soldier stammered, "Y-yes sir!" Then he turned and bolted away.

Kunnegarde watched him go before breaking into gales of laughter. "Didst thou see his face?" he gasped, wiping tears from his eyes. "Oh my, I didst nail the accent!"

Flint was beginning to tire of underground constructions that went on and on forever. The dwarves had certainly perfected the art of tunneling, but it would be useful to know where each tunnel led. Like the stone city, countless rooms lined the corridors. The tunnels branched and twisted in upon themselves in some pattern known only to the designers.

Without Kjell, they had no way to illuminate their way. But it did not matter. Embedded in the walls were the same glowing jewels that Flint had first seen at the Oruk Library and then again in the stone city.

Maybe the God Sword would be easy to find. But it was going to take longer than they had initially thought.

"Should we split up?" suggested Cwenhild.

"I don't like that idea," replied Dell as he jogged at her side. "I'm already regretting leaving Kjell to handle Radomil on his own."

Flint knew what Dell was really saying. He did not trust any of them to handle anything alone. He would feel much more comfortable if he were working by himself.

Footsteps sounded behind them. It was more than one person and they were making no effort to be quiet. What had happened to Kjell?

Dell gestured them inside a passageway. But before they could take cover, Talagon raced around a corner and skidded to a halt. Behind him, a squadron of Worshippers stumbled, trying to avoid colliding with their leader.

Dell stepped closer to Talagon, separating himself from Flint and Cwenhild. "Talagon," he said, his voice stony with anger. "I am very pleased to see you, here." His emphasis on the word 'you' made his meaning clear.

Talagon sneered. "I see you have a new mask," he answered. "Just how ugly are you?"

His squadron moved into position on either side of him and the three Hawks found themselves facing twenty-six adversaries.

Dell snorted. "Calling me ugly is like the pot calling the kettle black. Have you looked in a mirror recently?"

The elven guard drew in a sharp breath but before he could reply, Dell said, "This is between us, Talagon. I will fight you—alone."

Talagon bit off a laugh. "I have all the advantages here," he said, gesturing to his soldiers with a broad sweep of his hand. "Why should I allow you to make any conditions?"

Dell tilted his head to the side and studied Talagon. "You are afraid to meet me in a fair fight," he said.

Rage flared in Talagon's eyes. He did not look away from Dell as he ordered, "Worshippers of Dreff, do not interfere. This is a battle of honour."

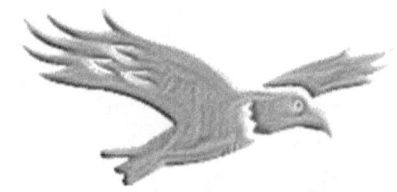

CHAPTER THIRTY-FIVE

Honour

As the sun rose over the mountain, Fleta stared at the camp in the canyon. All pretense of order had disappeared. Soldiers scurried around like ants in a disturbed anthill. Gode must have run out of grenades because there had been no explosions for the past ten minutes.

Lying on her stomach at the edge of the cliff, she had watched the battle between Kjell and Radomil. Tempted by Radomil's perfect stillness, she had considered using her bow. But unable to decide whether it might hurt Kjell, she had waited.

When the blue jewel shattered and Radomil climbed to his feet, she had been an instant away from firing. Fortunately, his first words made her hesitate. With a slow exhalation, she had loosened the tension on her bow.

She was about to call out as he capered about when the elven soldier approached. As Radomil ordered the

Worshippers of Dreff to withdraw, she ducked down and muffled her laughter in her sleeve.

By the time she lifted her head again, both Radomil—or rather Kunnegarde—and Kjell had disappeared into the tunnel.

Gesturing to Egbert, she waited while he crawled forward to join her at the edge of the cliff. When he lifted his head to peer over the rock, he gasped and whispered, "The Worshippers are leaving?"

Even as they watched, the last Worshipper of Dreff mounted his horse. He gave a final frantic look around before kicking his horse to a gallop.

Egbert and Fleta did not move until the dust had settled. Then Egbert stood and stretched. His mouth opened in a jaw-popping yawn as he stepped away from the cliff edge and walked back to the pulley where he had left his crossbow. "I never got to use this beauty," he said.

Fleta laughed. "Well, you may still get the chance. Shall we go find out what lies behind the door?"

"That sounds like a wonderful idea," said Gode, striding out of the trees.

Fleta whirled, barely managing to stop herself from launching the knife that she had drawn automatically.

Gode lifted his hands in surrender and smiled. "Good to see that you haven't let down your guard," he said.

Egbert too had turned at Gode's arrival. Letting out a breath, he lowered the crossbow and said, "It is good to see you, Gode." He gestured toward the ropes that he had just let down, "You are welcome to go first."

The latest visions from Martokallu were a complete mystery. Velte stared at a cave opening, trying to see past the veil of darkness. Giving up, she examined the Worshippers of Dreff camped outside it. As she watched, the army of elves erupted into chaos.

When she studied the image, searching for a reason for the sudden turmoil, she spotted an explosion on the outer edge of the circle of soldiers. The next image showed even greater commotion. What was going on?

She did not voice the question. It was always best to wait for the Master to speak first. When he projected another image, her hope rose. Perhaps it would explain the confusion. Sometimes he liked to feed the information slowly so that the final image was all the more dramatic for having to wait for it.

But the next image provided no further clarification. The soldiers, already milling about in panic, abruptly gave up any semblance of order. Grabbing anything within reach, they leapt on their horses and galloped away. She watched as they sped down a trail and guessed they would soon be passing by her and the other Followers.

It did not make sense. What would make the elves run? She wanted to demand answers from Martokallu, but he was strangely silent. Rather than risk his anger by asking questions, she would muddle through on her own.

First things first. It would be best to avoid a direct confrontation with the Worshippers "Clear the road," she shouted. "Take cover in the woods."

The Followers barely had time to scuttle off into the ditch before the first of the elves galloped past. Panicked, they looked neither right nor left as they hurtled along the road.

Velte narrowed her eyes at the elves' headlong flight. No one appeared to be in charge. All signs of the rigid order that Martokallu had so admired were gone. What could have happened to cause such a flight?

Long after the last of the elves passed by their hiding spot, Velte sat and considered the situation. Gadrith squirmed beside her but she ignored him and made no effort to explain.

Martokallu had ordered her to provide a disruption in the

elves' plans. Perhaps the exodus she had just witnessed would serve as well as anything she might muster. Should she turn and pursue the elves or continue down the road to see what had become of the Hawks? She bit her cheek as she considered the question. Why did Martokallu not speak? She would happily follow his directive.

Then she leapt to her feet. She knew where her priorities lay. Not bothering to enlighten Gadrith, she stepped out onto the road once more and turned in the direction from which the elves had just fled. It was time to destroy the Hawks.

The instant Talagon agreed to a battle of honour, Dell made a small shooing motion with his right hand. Reluctantly, Cwenhild and Flint backed down the corridor until they were out of sight.

Silently, they stared at each other. Then Flint screwed up his face and Cwenhild nodded. With one last glance over their shoulders, they turned and ran.

"He bought us some time," Flint panted as they sprinted past entrances and branches in the tunnel. "I just wish I knew where we were going." He did not doubt that Dell would defeat Talagon. However, he had no idea what would happen after that. Would Dell have to fight all the other elves in the squadron as well? They would not take the loss of their leader easily.

Guilt crept up Flint's spine. They should not have left Dell alone. But he knew the man well enough to understand that he had left them no choice.

"Hold up," said Cwenhild grabbing his arm and slowing to a walk. "You're right, he bought us some time, but we have to use it wisely." She glanced back at the intersection they had just charged past. "There must be some way to know which way to go."

Flint squinted into the darkness back the way they had

come. So far, there was no sound of pursuit. "I think we should stick to this tunnel," he said. "It's the largest. Let's see where it takes us. We'll either get extremely lost." He grinned. "Or if we're lucky, we'll find the God Sword."

Cwenhild laughed out loud. Starting off at a jog, she said, "I guess it's better than no plan at all."

Talagon's white robes glowed in the strange light of the underground tunnel while the highly polished steel of his chest plate reflected glittering shards that flashed as he moved. The resulting radiance made him appear large and threatening. An impatient gesture sent his soldiers hurrying out of his way.

Drawing his cutlass in a hiss of steel, he mocked, "Well, clown-face, let's see what sort of warrior you really are."

Dell said nothing but flexed the fingers of his bladed gauntlet and selected a dagger from his belt. Settling into a fighting crouch, he watched Talagon's approach.

Goaded by Dell's silence, Talagon continued to taunt. "I won't make the mistake of asking someone else to hold you this time," he said. Reaching up, he pulled back his hood to reveal four parallel scars that extended out from under his eye patch. The remaining eye glittered with anger as Talagon spat, "You tried to make me as ugly as you, but—"

Tired of the talking, the moment Talagon came within range, Dell pounced. Maintaining his grip on his dagger, he grasped a handful of Talagon's hair with his right hand. First, he forced the elf's head backwards, exposing his throat, and then he brought it forward onto his bladed gauntlet.

Blood gushed over his hand as he glowered into Talagon's stunned eye. Indifferent to the distress he saw there, Dell brought his right foot up and planted it hard in the middle of the blood-drenched breastplate.

Talagon flew backwards and landed heavily on the dusty floor. Two quick steps took Dell to his side. Reaching down, he thrust his serrated dagger deep into Talagon's open mouth, up into his brain.

Another rush of blood followed and ripping his blade free, Dell stepped back to glare at the stunned elven soldiers.

There were too many of them.

Before they could determine their best course of action, Dell whirled and bolted.

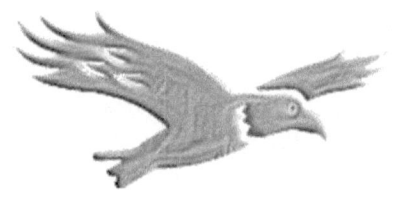

CHAPTER THIRTY-SIX

Understanding

CWENHILD WALKED WITH HER HAND wrapped tightly around the hilt of her machete. At her side, Flint kept twisting about as he tried to see in all directions at once. He had an overwhelming sense of being watched. With an inward shrug, he shook off the feeling. Except for the elves, they had seen no one.

That thought made him wince. They should not have left Dell to fight an entire squadron on his own. Talagon would not fight honourably. The man had no honour. Dell might be in trouble or worse—dead.

The problem was that it had always been Flint's policy to do whatever Dell told him. The man terrified him. He spun around, hoping to see Dell trotting toward them, but the tunnel remained empty.

Cwenhild cleared her throat. "I don't know why we left him," she said.

Flint swiped at his forehead. Under his chainmail, he was drenched in sweat. "It's as if whatever he says must be right," he said. Abruptly, he stopped walking. "We should go back."

Cwenhild's mouth set in a grim line as she shook her head. "If we were going to be of any help, we needed to stay then. By now, he has already won and is right behind us, or—" She did not need to finish the sentence.

Flint quickened his pace, fuelled by his fury with himself. The light remained steady if a little dim and, in its unchanging monotony, the corridor was endless. The longer they spent underground, the more Flint recognized the futility of his hope that they would miraculously locate the God Sword and escape before anything else happened.

Kjell strode beside Kunnegarde and tried to imagine what was running through the old man's head. He remembered all too well the feeling of waking up after Hulda's arrows severed the two-hundred-year connection with Martokallu. The world had seemed unutterably fresh and clean. In those first days, a sense of amazed wonder had engulfed him.

It would be different for Kunnegarde though. He had not spent the last two thousand years under the control of someone else's will. But it could not have been much of an existence lying in a sarcophagus, waiting for intruders.

As if in answer to Kjell's thoughts, Kunnegarde burst out, "'Tis marvellous to walk so easily. I hadst forgotten what a joy 'tis to move without magic. This body canst dance and run with nary an effort. Why 'tis as if the years have dropped away and I am a child once more." He capered a few steps along the tunnel. "Let us run," he called with an ecstatic leap and accelerated into a loping jog.

Kjell let out a whoop and joined him in a race through the corridors.

Side by side, they pounded along the corridor, until a

prickle of unease ran up Kjell's back. He grasped Kunnegarde's arm and tugged him to a stop.

"Hang on," Kjell said. "Something's wrong."

Lost in the joyous sense of running freely, Kunnegarde pulled away as his caution returned. "'Tis true," he said, shaking his head. "I feeleth it as well."

Suddenly alert, they proceeded more cautiously. A short distance later, they came across a corpse sprawled awkwardly across the dusty stone. Kjell stepped closer, wincing when he saw the torn face and neck.

"Dell did this," he said. "It's Talagon."

Kunnegarde straightened and moved away to examine the tracks in the dust. "Talagon hadst five and twenty soldiers with him. Where art they? And why didst they not protect their leader?"

Kjell's face twisted. He had no idea how Dell had managed to kill Radomil without suffering any injury to himself. He searched the floor for any indication that Dell had taken a wound but beyond the ugly pool where Radomil lay, there was no other sign of blood.

"Let's go," Kjell said. "We have to catch them. Flint, Cwenhild and Dell will have trouble holding off two dozen Worshippers of Dreff on their own."

With far more serious intent, they sped off in pursuit. It was difficult to see ahead because the tunnel bent in a long, gradual arc. Kunnegarde kept picking up the pace and before they knew it, they came up on the back of the elves who were proceeding at a restrained jog.

Kunnegarde turned a beaming face on Kjell and murmured, "Shall we?"

Returning the smile, Kjell sped up, and they raced to catch the Worshippers of Dreff. The noise of their footsteps attracted the attention of one of the trailing runners. When he turned to check, his mouth fell open in a comical display of surprise.

Not allowing him time to call out a warning, Kunnegarde released a wave of blue energy. The elf's head snapped back, and he dropped unconscious to the floor.

His loss did not go unnoticed. A shout from his partner alerted the other elves. They skidded to a halt and whirled with their swords raised. With trained discipline, they arranged themselves into four rows, but they did not immediately attack.

Kunnegarde raised his hands and whispered words of power. At his command, a giant piece of the floor lifted free. Giving it a violent shake, he sent the soldiers tumbling over one another.

"That was interesting," Kjell called. "But it won't stop them for long." Ignoring an impulse towards mercy, he sent a blast of fire. As much as he regretted it, they would have to slaughter the elves in order to save their friends.

The flames caught on the Worshippers' long white robes, and they writhed on the ground to extinguish the flames. Unable to watch, Kjell screwed his eyes closed.

Beside him, Kunnegarde muttered another spell and Kjell took a deep breath and opened his eyes.

His hands claws, Kunnegarde made an upward thrust with his fingers. Spikes of blue ice pushed up out of the floor A second gesture propelled the spikes forward like a swarm of knives. Most shattered when they hit the elves' plate armour, but one of the icicles found a target under the arm of an elf who raised his bow to aim at Kunnegarde. Blood spurted and he dropped like a stone.

With a shout of triumph, Kunnegarde released a blast of blue fire. Several of the elves shrieked as they threw themselves out of its path but two were caught in the flames. Unlike Kjell's fire, rolling on the ground did not extinguish it and the smell of roasting meat filled the air.

Filled with revulsion, Kjell turned away. But Kunnegarde

was caught up in the butchery. Only six men remained standing, and they lined up with their bows drawn. Before they could fire, Kunnegarde launched another barrage of icicles. In every case, the thin wedges of ice found their targets in the armholes of the breastplates.

When they fell, Kunnegarde laughed aloud. Then, he whipped the air into a howling wind that picked up the bodies of the dead and dying. Focusing the wind into a tight vortex, he made the loose-limbed corpses twirl dizzily around each other. Muttering one final spell, he opened a yawning black hole of nothingness, and the bodies were sucked into the void.

Kunnegarde let his hands drop and stepped back from the cracked rubble of the floor. When he saw Kjell's expression, his look of elation faded.

Instantly, his shoulders sagged and he dropped his head. "Kjell, my friend," he said. "I am sorry." Then, with resolution, he raised his chin and looked Kjell in the eye. "I lost control. 'Tis not something that will happen again."

Velte marched through the deserted camp. Tents stood where they had been abandoned in what had obviously been a mad rush to get away. Evidence of the haste was everywhere. None of the soldiers had stopped long enough to load anything onto their horses. Great stores of food appeared to be untouched. She still had no idea what had caused the panic. She wanted to ask Martokallu for visions of the Hawks, but he would have shared with her if he could see them at all.

Beyond the tents, she found the cave that Martokallu had shown her earlier. It looked like the entrance to Martokallu's Fortress. Except this door was far larger and the rock was highly polished. For his fortress, Martokallu had insisted that everything should remain as natural as possible.

Gadrith limped up beside her and her lip curled as she studied his bent figure. He had forced himself to run all day despite the open wound from which dark green blood continued to ooze. What must it be like to live with no magic? She would never be able to bear such inadequacy. She could have healed herself in an instant. She might even be able to help him. Not that she would.

He winced at her glare but stubbornly insisted on maintaining his illusion of command. "We must hurry," he said. "The last time I traced them to such a portal, they found a back entrance and evaded our force."

Velte smoothed her face and raised a delicate eyebrow. How did he always find time to state the obvious? Then she deliberately looked away, ignoring him and his revolting injury.

She sauntered up to the polished door, where she stood alone, testing the air, trying to figure out what had occurred. Then with a dramatic twirl that made her robe billow out around her, she turned to stare at the other mages who waited behind her.

"Can you taste it?" she demanded.

Muttered agreement rustled through them until one spoke in his gravelly voice. "There has been magic here, my lady. Powerful magic."

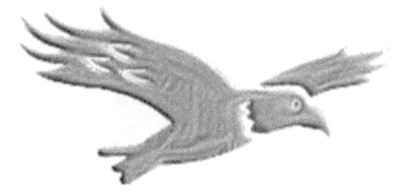

CHAPTER THIRTY-SEVEN

Pursuit

GASPING FOR BREATH, DELL SLOWED to a walk. He could not recall the last time he had run for any length of time. His heart and lungs were screaming. He tried to control his breathing so he could listen for the sound of pursuit. As far as he could tell, the elves had chosen not to chase him immediately. Left without a leader, they may have been unable to decide what to do.

He pushed himself to walk more quickly as his breathing slowed. A moment later, he heard a noise behind him. It did not seem loud enough to be the whole squadron of elves and he considered his options. He would not escape a second time by running away. Trying not to disturb the dust, he slid into one of the rooms as he passed.

From his hiding spot, he peered out. Almost immediately, Kjell and Radomil ran past.

Without even pausing to think, Dell stepped out into the

corridor and shouted, "Hold!"

Both Kjell and Radomil wheeled with their hands raised to cast a spell and found themselves face to face with Dell who held his weapons ready for attack.

The two mages grinned when they saw him.

"Dell!" cried Kjell, his hands dropping to his sides. "I'm so glad to see you. Where are Flint and Cwenhild?"

Dell did not relax. "What is this, Kjell?" he grated, circling away to the right. "Throwing in with the elves, now?"

Kjell's smile widened, and he said, "That is what it looks like, I suppose."

Careful to keep his hands visible, Radomil smiled as well and said, "'Tis true, I look as Radomil did. Though, Kjell hast killed him. I didst but take advantage of the recently vacated body. A short trip from the ring to the flesh. And—look!" he said as he capered about. "'Tis marvellous to dance like this."

Dell's eyes widened. Radomil would never choose to show himself in such an undignified manner. It must be true. His eyes shifted back and forth between Kunnegarde and Kjell until finally, he lowered his blades. "Well met, Kunnegarde," he said. "Welcome back."

Hearing the clatter of footsteps, Cwenhild and Flint spun around with their blades ready. When he recognized Dell, Flint relaxed and lowered his swords. At once, the ball of worry he had been carrying slipped away. Dell had won the battle with Talagon.

Kjell was at his side. What had happened back in the camp of the Followers of Dreff? He narrowed his eyes in the dim light. Who was the third man? As they drew closer and slowed to a stop, he suddenly recognized Radomil.

In that instant, both he and Cwenhild raised their blades.

Flint's eyes shifted to Dell, and he asked, "What's going on?"

But it was Radomil who answered. A happy smile broke out on his face, and he chuckled. "I am most joyous to seeth thee again. Well met, Mistress Cwenhild. Master Flint." He bowed from the waist toward each of them. "I suspect we shall become friends."

Without letting his blade waver, Flint said, "Friends? After you tried to have us all killed?" He checked his first impulse to attack since the elf had not drawn a weapon. But he remained wary, recalling how Radomil had charmed them the first time they met.

Kjell raised his hands, looking first at Cwenhild, and then Flint. "Hold Flint," he said. "This is not who you think it is. Do you recall the help Kunnegarde offered us as we searched for this fortress?"

Confused, Flint nodded reluctantly, but he did not allow Kjell to distract him from the threat. His worry returned with enough force to leave him nauseous. Radomil had already charmed Dell and even Kjell was a victim this time.

Flint took a step back and broadened his stance. If he had to battle all three of them, he would. His lips tightened as he considered the horrible consequences of such a battle. Swallowing hard, he said, "I also recall that Radomil intended to have us murdered in our beds."

The elf smiled into Flint's angry glare and said, "Mayhap, I dost resemble that surly dog, but truth be told, I am Kunnegarde."

Hearing this simple statement in words that so closely resembled the first thing Kunnegarde had said when they met in the stone city, Flint felt a thread of doubt. Was it possible?

Cwenhild lowered her machete but did not relax her guard. She studied Kjell's eyes through his silver mask. "How do we know you aren't bewitched?" she demanded.

Kjell held up his hands. "You are right to be suspicious," he said. "But remember, Radomil's charms had no effect on me. I was able to wake all of you from his spell." He gestured toward the tall elf. "If this truly was Radomil, would he know what was said in the underground city?"

"He might," retorted Cwenhild. "If you told him."

Kjell laughed. "True enough. You think of everything." Turning to Dell, he said, "I'm out of ideas. How do we convince her?"

Cwenhild stared at Dell. He gazed back, making no effort to argue the case. His mask hampered her efforts to read his face, but when he gave her a small nod without saying anything, Flint knew the story was true. That silent nod, so characteristic of Dell, was more reassuring than anything else he could have said or done. If he was bewitched, Radomil would have made him speak to convince them.

Cwenhild must have had the same thought. Letting out a deep breath, she stepped back and lowered her machete. "Welcome back Kunnegarde," she said. "Do you know which way we should go?"

Kunnegarde smiled. "If I recall correctly, thou art nearly to the throne room." He glanced around the stone corridor and studied an engraving that Flint had suspected might reveal their location if only he could read it. "I expect thou shalt find my friend Tul awaiting thy arrival."

It was the odd speech and the familiarity with the fortress that finally convinced Flint of Kunnegarde's identity.

"Dell," Flint said, "I am so glad to see you. We shouldn't have left you alone to fight Talagon."

Dell gave a small shrug.

"You fought Talagon alone?" Kjell asked. "How did you get away from the squadron of elves?"

"It was a fight of honour," Dell muttered. "Talagon was arrogant enough to accept the challenge, and—" Dell stopped and to everyone's surprise, barked out a laugh. "And when I beat him, I turned and ran as fast as I could." He faced Kjell and asked, "You didn't happen to encounter that same squadron of elves?"

Kjell dropped his gaze. "We met them." After a long pause, he added, "They are gone."

Flint wanted to ask what had happened, but Kjell looked as if he did not want to talk about it.

Kunnegarde must have felt the same way because he said, "Shall we continue, then? I senseth there art others who follow." He started down the corridor with Kjell at his side but abruptly swung back to look at Dell, Cwenhild and Flint who had hung back.

With a grin, Kunnegarde said, "When we didst leave the camp of the Worshippers of Dreff, the elves were departing. They wilt be well gone by now." Reaching up to scratch an ear, a look of surprise transformed into revulsion. For a long moment, he stood with one finger barely touching the tip of his pointy ear. His disgust was clearly visible. "I am an elf," he said.

"Yes, you are," answered Kjell.

"I do not like elves," Kunnegarde said, raising a second hand to touch the point of his other ear. "In all my years, I met only one elf who could be trusted."

Kjell said, "You will have to be the second exception to the rule."

Kunnegarde remained lost in memories until Flint asked, "What do you mean, the elves left?"

Dropping his hand, Kunnegarde bowed his head modestly and said, "The elves bethought me Radomil so when I didst order them return to Cheveral, they didst bolt from the field as if wolves snapped upon their tails."

"What about Fleta and Egbert and Gode?" demanded Cwenhild. "Where are they?"

"We're heading in the right direction," said Fleta as she stood over Talagon's body. "Dell was here."

Without looking too closely at the gruesome injuries, Egbert agreed. "There is no doubt about that."

Gode knelt and touched a finger to an undamaged section of the dead elf's cheek. "We are at least half an hour behind them," he said. "The body has begun to cool."

"Thirty minutes?" Egbert said. Striding forward, he called, "We may be able to catch them before they talk to Tul if we hurry. They are on the right path, and we are close to the throne room."

"How do you know?" asked Fleta, hurrying after him.

"I have been reading the signs," answered Egbert, pointing to the wall. "The engravings mark the distance to different locations."

Gode hurried after them and said, "Let's hustle."

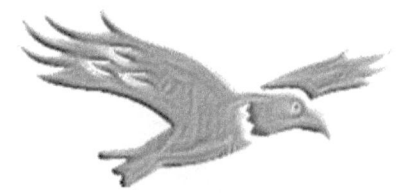

CHAPTER THIRTY-EIGHT

Judgment

Distracted by the tramp of so many feet, Velte walked with her head down, attempting to focus on the aftermath of magic that permeated the air. It was unlike anything she had ever encountered, yet at the same time, it felt vaguely familiar.

As they walked further down the corridor, the scent became fainter, and she briefly considered returning to the entrance of the cave just so she could study it further. However, she also felt a sense of urgency that made her feet keep moving away from the source.

Glancing up at the mages who walked in close formation around her, she demanded, "Does anyone recognize the taste of this magic?"

Gadrith, who walked ahead of her, surrounded by his own group of Followers, looked back when she spoke. He was about to answer when he abruptly snapped his mouth shut and turned around, picking up his pace.

At first, no one would meet her eyes and she pushed her black hair back in impatience. "Anyone?" she asked.

Finally, one of the mages ventured, "It reminds me of the Master."

Her head shot up and she sniffed again, tasting the air. For a moment, as she considered the idea, her careful glamour faded, and her monstrous face became visible. Noticing her lapse at once, she glared around at the other Followers, daring them to comment. They all averted their eyes and no one said anything.

"The Master?" she asked herself, rolling the idea around inside her head. Then, raising her chin, she gazed at the other mages. This time, her expression was cunning rather than angry and they looked back at her eagerly. "This is becoming interesting."

Ahead, the corridor made an abrupt turn. Flint slowed and muttered, "We can't see what's coming."

"You're right," whispered Cwenhild. "Let me check it out." Silently, she drew her machete with one hand and slid a dagger into the other. Keeping close to the inside wall, she crept up until she could see around the corner.

She stiffened and raised her eyebrows.

At that, Flint drew his swords while Dell tugged a dagger from his belt. The two mages tightened their grips on their staffs and stepped forward. Cwenhild raked her eyes over them and gestured sharply with her chin. Together, they rounded the corner in a rush.

Flint did not know what he expected but his tension drained away when he saw the solitary dwarf seated in a massive stone chair. It was positioned in the exact centre of a huge room with a ceiling so high the distant lights appeared as stars.

At their entrance, the dwarf looked up and set down his tankard. A heavy mace lay across the carved arms of his chair and one hand rested comfortably on its worn grip. His highly-polished steel armour glittered in the light and a shield decorated with the insignia of the Protectors of the God Sword leaned near his left hand.

Only his red beard, neatly tamed with a pair of side-braids, was visible beneath his helmet. "Do not fret yourselves," he growled. "You are here. Let us get on with it."

Flint stared around the room. There were no other Protectors of the God Sword to be seen but any number could be hidden nearby. He forced himself to slow his breathing and let his eyes run around the chamber once more. Was Tul truly alone?

The dwarf gripped his mace more securely and rose. Without taking his eyes off them, he picked up his shield. As he straightened, he said, "I am Tul." His piercing eyes lit on Flint. "You are Flint?"

Flint's jaw dropped open and he nodded. How did the dwarf know his name?

"He doesn't look like much," Tul muttered.

Flushing, Flint took a determined stride forward.

Tul waved him off. "I said, fret not, boy. You have passed your test already." With a flick of his eyes, he dismissed Flint and turned to study Kjell. His eyebrows rose when he noted his staff. "That looks familiar," he said. "And the mask too. You are Kjell then. The young mage."

Kjell rested his weight on one leg and cocked his head at Tul. "I have not been called young for two hundred years," he said, bowing.

"It's all in the perspective," replied Tul. He pursed his lips. "You too have passed your test."

Then he looked at Cwenhild. He studied her array of weapons, for she wore her bow on her back, a bandolier of daggers across her chest, and at her waist, the scabbard for her machete. After a long moment, he asked, "And you are the

Challenger? What is your name?"

Cwenhild hesitated, her eyes wide. Then, squaring her shoulders, she stepped away from her friends and said, "I am Cwenhild, daughter of Orma of Abbarkon."

Tul bowed in her direction and then without warning, leapt toward her. His mace whistled through the air directly at her head.

Ducking smoothly, Cwenhild danced out of the way of the spiked weapon and raised her machete. Barely taller than the dwarf, her longer reach gave her the smallest of advantages.

Flint tensed and looked for a way to join the fight, but Kunnegarde rested a hand on his shoulder and said, "Alloweth her to prove herself. Thou hadst thy chance."

Tul advanced on Cwenhild purposefully, sweeping his mace in deadly arcs. Cwenhild moved lightly, changing direction constantly, then ducking and weaving around. In a flash, she darted in and dealt a heavy blow on Tul's mace arm. The machete rebounded from his shiny armour, leaving no trace of the hit.

Tul did not even recognize the blow and continued to swing in unpredictable circles. All at once, Cwenhild's uncertainty disappeared. Flint saw it in her movements and knew she had been holding back because of the poisons in which she coated her weapons. When she realized he was fully protected by his armour, she began to fight in earnest.

Suddenly, Tul found himself the target of a rain of blows. Cwenhild moved in, struck like a snake, and danced back before Tul had time to get his heavy weapon moving.

On and on they fought with neither making any significant gains. The crash of steel on steel echoed painfully around the stone chamber.

Flint watched with every muscle clenched. If Cwenhild got in trouble, he was prepared to jump in despite Kunnegarde's warning.

Tul slowed. His strikes became less frequent, and he wavered on his feet after one of Cwenhild's harder hits. Abruptly, he let his mace drop to the floor and he bent over at the waist, heaving for air.

In confusion, Cwenhild lowered her own blade, but she stayed well out of Tul's reach.

With a grunt, Tul straightened and said, "I have seen enough. My comrades have judged truly. You are worthy." Drawing in a deep breath, he pronounced in a ringing voice, "Cwenhild, daughter of Orma of Abbarkon, you shall have the blade."

Kunnegarde moved past Cwenhild and stopped before Tul. He gazed down at the dwarf.

Tilting his head back, Tul stared up at him, but he did not raise his weapon.

"Well met my dwarven friend," Kunnegarde said. "Dost thou not recognize me? 'Tis thy old comrade-in-arms, Kunnegarde. Although," he added, reaching up to finger one pointed ear, "perhaps my disguise is too perfect. My wish is to visit Tul, my friend and brother."

Letting the handle of his mace clatter to the floor, Tul advanced on the tall elf in astonishment. Without doubt, he said, "It is you, old friend." Reaching out, he drew Kunnegarde down into a back-clapping embrace.

As if it was a signal, dozens of heavily-armed dwarves appeared from invisible niches all about the room. Flint's fingers twitched towards his sheathed swords, but the dwarves offered no threat as they strolled toward the stone throne. Most smiled in welcome.

As they arrived, they made a circle around Tul and the visitors. When the circle closed, they simultaneously dropped to one knee, drew their weapons, and raised them above their heads.

In response, Flint, Dell and Cwenhild drew their weapons

although they were hopelessly outnumbered.

Tul swept his eyes over them and lifted his mace above his head in an easy motion. "Cwenhild, daughter of Orma of Abbarkon, we salute you as the new Bearer of the God Sword."

Cwenhild's head snapped back and she gaped at the kneeling dwarves. For a long moment, she remained frozen, while her eyes darted around in alarm. And then as Tul's words sunk in, she relaxed. Lowering her blades, she closed her mouth and lifted her head.

"Protectors of the God Sword," she said and then paused to clear her throat. "I will do everything in my power to be worthy of your trust."

The dwarves watched solemnly, and self-consciously, she looked beyond them as if trying to decide what else she might say.

Flint caught the glint of alarm in her eye when her gaze skimmed past the entrance to the great room. Raising her machete slightly, she spoke just loudly enough for her listeners to hear.

"Protectors of the God Sword," she murmured. "Look to the entrance. We have visitors."

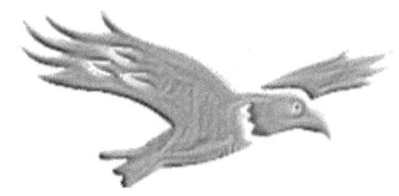

CHAPTER THIRTY-NINE

Tribute

A shout boomed from the hallway just outside the throne room. "Let them go!"

Flint recognized Gode's voice, but before he could react, Tul called, "Protectors, preserve the Bearer."

Immediately, the dwarves surrounded Cwenhild in a double circle. Facing outwards, they bristled with swords, axes, and maces.

With Cwenhild safe, Tul turned toward Kunnegarde and muttered, "Friend or foe?"

Kunnegarde gave him an ironic lift of his eyebrows before inclining his head toward Flint. "Thou had better be the one to invite them in," he said. "Mayhap, they wilt not know me."

Flint grinned back and jogged over to the entranceway. "Gode," he called. "You've arrived too late if you were hoping for a fight. Come in and meet the Protectors of the God Sword."

Holding his axe at his side, Gode edged around the corner. With narrowed eyes, he watched the dwarves over Flint's shoulder. "What's going on here?" he murmured. "Did Radomil bewitch you again?"

"No," answered Flint, holding out his hands, palm up. "I'm fine. Really."

Gode lifted his axe. "Prove it," he growled. "Who taught you everything you know about sword fighting?"

Instantly, Flint answered, "Cadmon. He was the father I never had."

At his answer, Fleta and Egbert sidled around the corner and Gode exhaled noisily.

"Flint!" Fleta said. "Gode thought you'd been charmed by Radomil but that's not Radomil is it?"

At the sight of her, Flint's muscles went weak. He had never liked the part of the plan that left her and Egbert alone in such an exposed position.

Cwenhild pushed her way out of the circle of Protectors. "I'm fine. I'm fine," she said as they tried to prevent her progress. "They're my friends." When they reluctantly let her pass, she strode towards the entrance. "I'm glad to see you," she called, her arms outstretched in welcome. The dwarves kept pace with her, and she gestured toward them. "Don't worry. These are the Protectors of the God Sword. They're keeping me safe."

Gode pursed his lips. "You're sure you're not bewitched?" he asked.

"They're fine," said Kjell. "Everyone is fine."

Kunnegarde stepped toward Egbert and said, "Welcome, Egbert. These past many days, I didst enjoy thy company." He clicked his heels together and bowed from the waist. At Egbert's puzzled expression, he smiled. "Mayhap, you did not realize that I couldst hear all that occurred within Kjell's hearing. It was a most enjoyable trip."

Egbert lowered his crossbow, glanced at Fleta, and muttered, "I did not truly believe you when you told me you saw Kunnegarde's ring shatter and Radomil rise up from death."

Kunnegarde acknowledged Egbert's comment with a shrug and then, turning to Fleta, he made another deep bow. "Thou art Fleta," he said as he rose. "'Tis a rare pleasure to meet such a beautiful young woman."

Fleta flushed at his compliment and bobbed awkwardly in return.

Gode, who had remained silent throughout this exchange, suddenly made up his mind and strode forward with his hand outstretched. "Kunnegarde," he said, "I am glad to meet you. Kjell told us that you led us to this place."

In the body of the tall elf, Kunnegarde still had to look up at Gode as his hand was wrung in welcome.

"Gode, thou art a true champion," he said. "How went your charade with the explosive devices? That which we saw before Kjell and I didst enter the tunnels suggested thou wert truly successful."

The memory brought a grin to Gode's face, and he clapped Kunnegarde on the back sending him stumbling into Tul. "It went very well indeed!" he exclaimed. "Did you see the elves take off just after dawn?"

Modestly, Kunnegarde lowered his eyes and said, "I didst cause that. The elves bethought me Radomil, and I bethought to send them home." He grinned. "I was truly surprised when they didst as I ordered."

A nudge at his elbow stopped him from elaborating as Tul pushed past him. "I see nothing has changed in the last two thousand years," he growled. "The man still does not know when to stop talking."

Kunnegarde inclined his head, still smiling. Giving a deep bow, he flourished a hand in Tul's direction. "Gode, Egbert and young Fleta, may I present Tul of Tsaralvia, the Protector of the God Sword."

"Pleased to meet you, I'm sure," muttered Tul. Then he turned to Cwenhild. "It is time. Let us proceed with the ceremony."

"Ceremony?" asked Egbert.

"Cwenhild challenged Tul and won the right to be the Bearer of the God Sword," Flint said.

Gode's eyes went wide. He quirked his head at Cwenhild. "Is that so?"

Kjell said, "She was magnificent. It is a rare treat to see such fighting. Of course," he added diplomatically, "she needed a worthy opponent to make her look so proficient." He adjusted the silver mask and bowed toward Tul.

Shaking his head, Tul swung about and headed across the room. "Too much talk," he growled. "We need some action around here." Then, he bellowed, "Protectors, form an honour guard. Escort the new Bearer to the vault."

Expertly, the dwarves fell into two columns surrounding Cwenhild.

The captain shouted, "Protectors, stand tall. Protectors, make a wall. One, two, left, right. Three, four, left, right."

With a stamp of feet, the dwarves marched across the long room toward the doorway through which Tul was disappearing. The rest of the Hawks trailed behind, following the tramp of one hundred boots across the polished stone floor.

The procession came to a halt in front of a stone door—a twin to the one that had led them into the underground fortress.

Beside it, Tul stood rigidly. He waited until he had everyone's attention and then proclaimed, "This door was sealed two thousand years ago at the end of a long and bloody war. At that time, Abbarkov and Dworgunul charged the

Protectors of the God Sword to preserve the sword. For two thousand years, I have led the Protectors of the God Sword." He tugged on his beard braids and removed his helmet. His unlined skin and red hair showed no sign of his great age, but his grey eyes looked old.

"There have been challengers through the years," he continued, pushing the hair back off his forehead. "But never before has the power of the sword been truly needed. The world has changed. Martokallu has destroyed the balance." He scowled. "It is time to restore it."

He turned his gaze on Cwenhild and the tense lines in his face relaxed. "Today marked the final test to prove the Hawks' worthiness." He looked at Flint. "Flint demonstrated his merit when he met our comrade Gan in combat. For two thousand years, Gan stayed by the tomb of the Fifteenth Hammer of Dworgunul and guarded the secret of the map. Flint is the only challenger ever deemed worthy because he was the first one to seek the sword for righteous reasons."

Kunnegarde stepped up beside Tul. "I too didst find reason to test the Hawks," he announced. "When they didst appear before me in the mountain city of Grothbodur, they were the first to disturbeth my rest in nigh on two thousand years." He ran a finger over the top of a pointed ear and winced before shrugging.

"When I sensed the young mage in their midst, I didst test him." He grinned. "A mere novice, he wast unable to defeateth me in a battle of minds, but he holdeth power. 'Twas raw and untrained, yet full of such purity and kindness." He beamed at Kjell like a proud father. "Hence, I bequeathed mine ring, mine staff and mine mask to Kjell."

With a grimace, he muttered, "And then, I wast defeated by a Follower of my brother, Martokallu. I had no choice, so I didst join the Hawks as a passenger within mine own ring."

Straightening to his full height, he spoke directly to Tul. "In all the time of travelling with the Hawks, never didst I have cause to doubt the wisdom of mine choice. Not only art they worthy of the honour, but they hath the skills to ensureth the God Sword is used for the good of Abbarkon."

Tul shook his head and muttered, "Too much talk. As usual." Taking over, he said, "And now, Cwenhild, daughter of Orma of Abbarkon has proven her worthiness. She shall be the new Bearer of the God Sword." With that, he waved Kjell forward. "Do you recognize the pattern cut into this door?" he asked, gesturing to the circular pattern.

Kjell's shiny silver mask concealed his normally smiling face behind a fierce scowl, but his voice remained the same. "I do, indeed," he said cheerfully. Raising Kunnegarde's staff, he lined up the five protruding prongs with the five holes bored into the surface of the polished rock.

When they slid home, Kunnegarde gripped his shoulder and whispered, "Hold! Someone doth approach. They art in the throne room."

CHAPTER FORTY

Attack

"FIRST DIVISION!" TUL HISSED. "SEE to the Bearer."

At once, ten dwarves surrounded Cwenhild, weapons drawn.

"Second through fifth, move out." The command was hardly audible yet, moments later, forty elves vanished into a pair of tunnels that Flint had not noticed before. He guessed they would lead to the niches from which the dwarves had emerged earlier.

"Let's see who has come to visit," Gode murmured, striding to the entrance.

"Hold on, Gode," Fleta whispered, grabbing his arm. "Let's find out who's out there." She moved up beside him, pressing herself against the wall to peer around the corner. A look of distaste crossed her face as she drew back. "Followers," she hissed. "But only a few." Her face twisted again. "The woman who killed Dagur is there. She's with the Follower who found us in the mountain city when they killed Hackett and Hulda."

Egbert edged closer. "Let me test this crossbow," he murmured.

"Bows first," Cwenhild agreed from the center of her guards. "Then attack."

"Stay away from Velte," Kjell said. "I know her from the past. You saw what she did to Dagur."

Flint's stomach tightened as he recalled how Dagur's skull had burst like a smashed melon. The image was burned into his memory.

"She and her mages are dangerous at a distance," Kjell whispered. "Kunnegarde and I will attack with magic as well."

Cwenhild pushed her way free of the dwarves who, without actively challenging her, tried to prevent her from leaving the safety of their defensive circle.

"I defeated the great Tul in battle," she whispered fiercely. "Surely that qualifies me as capable of facing a few Followers of Martokallu."

Reluctantly, the dwarves let her through but spread out beside her. As a group, they moved closer to the entrance. Cwenhild and Fleta each nocked an arrow while Egbert checked his crossbow one more time. Flexing his bladed gauntlet, Dell drew a knife from his belt and Flint slid his swords free of their scabbards.

When everyone was ready, Gode said, "Now."

As one, they stepped around the corner and into the throne room. The intruders had spread out, so they presented a wide target only one warrior deep. Flint faltered when he saw who was among the Followers.

"Hold!" Fleta cried. "It's Hulda!"

Dell did not lower his weapons. "She's gone," he said. "Look at her eyes."

Dell was right. Hulda's eyes glowed with the same eerie light that marked all the Followers. Flint's mouth went dry.

They would have to fight against Hulda. In the next instant, arrows sprouted from the Followers on either side of her, while she remained untouched. Hulda may have been changed, but still, no one was willing to aim at her.

An arrow lodged in the shoulder of the woman who had killed Dagur. Her beautiful face twitched as she glanced down at it. When she grasped the shaft to wrench it free, Flint knew they were in trouble.

The Followers that Cwenhild and Egbert hit did not fall either. Instead, the arrows made them angry. A stream of purple flames flew from the woman's fingers. Cwenhild dove for the floor and the power blasted a smoking hole into the rock behind her.

Useless at a distance, Flint caught Dell's eye and called, "Ready?"

"I'm coming too," said Gode. "Keep out of the way of those flames. We'll come up behind them."

At Dell's nod, they darted along the outside of the room, watching the streams of magic, and refusing to look directly at Velte. Kunnegarde sent a surge of energy that shook the floor and knocked everyone to the floor.

Egbert yelled, "Easy with the earthquakes, Kunnegarde. We are underground!"

Kunnegarde gave him an apologetic grin and changed tactics. He and Kjell began throwing balls of flames at the Followers. When more purple energy streamed their way, Kjell caught it on the end of his staff and hurled it back at the beautiful woman.

She danced aside and extended her staff. The fire snagged on the silver tip and was sucked inside. Would she use their own magic against them? Keeping his head low, Flint crawled over to one of the alcoves. If only he understood magic better.

Gode was already there. "We can't get close enough to do any real damage with all this magic in the air," he shouted over the noise of the attacks.

Dell ducked to avoid a blast of energy and rolled into their alcove. "They have us pinned down," he growled.

Suddenly, the room filled with the dwarves' battle cries. The bloodcurdling echoes made Flint grateful they were not after him. The Protectors of the God Sword rushed out of their hidden niches, waving their axes and swords as they charged at the Followers.

Instantly, Dell leapt to his feet and joined them with Flint and Gode a step behind.

The Followers had no time to react. Before they could redirect their magic, the attack arrived.

Gadrith gasped at the pain in his stomach as he raised his sword to stave off the enormous axe aimed at his head. When the axe met his sword, he marshalled all his strength and pushed. But with a slight change of angle, the dwarf slid past his defense.

"No," Gadrith said. His voice was hardly more than a whisper. It should not end like this. He was meant to be a General in Martokallu's army.

The dwarf's cold blue eyes did not falter. His axe continued in a smooth line, although it seemed to Gadrith that he had time to study the razor sharp edge of the blade as it cut toward him. When it touched his neck, he hardly felt it slice through the flesh and only knew it was over when his head hit the stone floor.

Velte cast around, searching for the mage who was causing all the damage. She found two of them standing shoulder to shoulder at the far end of the room. Ignoring the dwarven warriors around her, she sent out a tendril of power, seeking an entry into their minds.

Starting with the elf, she probed the edges of his

consciousness. At first, she came up against a defense so powerful, it was as if she had hit a wall of polished black granite. Try as she might, she was unable to find a way past the shield, until she felt, rather than saw, a tiny glimmer of light.

Triumphantly, she directed a stream of energy at the opening. However, instead of sending the sweep of power into the man's mind, an overwhelming outpouring of energy blasted back at her.

Staggering under the assault, Velte lost control of her glamour. To her horror, her revolting ugliness was revealed to everyone. There was no way for her to withstand such an onslaught for long. The edges of her consciousness began to blur.

Shaking off the pain, she focused on the elven mage once more. Mortified without her glamour, nonetheless, she forced herself to meet his eyes across the room. He smirked at her and with a shudder, she understood that she had not broken through his defense. He had let her in! Cursing herself for falling into his trap, she sought a route out. She was very nearly the last Follower standing. The dwarves' barrage had flattened her force.

In desperation, Velte stretched out a wrinkled, crone hand to grasp the throat of one of the few remaining mages. As her wizened hand squeezed, an aura of purple light bloomed around her, while at the same time the helpless mage shrivelled into nothing.

When the man crumpled to the floor in a scattering of dust, her glamour returned, and she smiled in triumph before reaching out an elegantly ringed hand to grasp Hulda's arm. In a crackle of energy, Velte transported to the Master's fortress, taking Hulda with her.

In the sudden silence, Gode surveyed the carnage. He had done nothing to contribute to the battle. The dwarves had not needed any assistance. The other Hawks looked as stunned as he felt at the suddenness of the victory. And at the shock of seeing Hulda alive.

Finally, Fleta broke the silence. "Do you think we can save her?" she asked, her voice wavering slightly.

No one answered. They had seen enough Followers to know how badly Martokallu's enthralment twisted a person.

"I may be the only person I know who survived the change and I have Hulda to thank for it," Kjell said. He hoisted his staff in the air and looked around at the disheartened Hawks. "We will find her again." His face was earnest as he made the pledge. "And I will find a way to turn her back into the Hulda we all know."

Kunnegarde muttered, "And I wilt help." His attention was on the dwarves as they moved among the fallen Followers, checking for any signs of life.

"By Abbarkov!" he shouted suddenly and bolted across the room.

Everyone raised their weapons again, searching for the danger.

When Kunnegarde reached the dead Followers, he stooped. Coming up with a sword, he brandished it in the air and announced, "Mine own sword!" Nudging Gadrith's body with his toe, he murmured, "I wilt thank thee for delivering it to me, friend. I didst not expect to see it again."

Except for Hulda and the woman who disappeared with her, no Followers survived the battle. Side by side, the Hawks and the Protectors of the God Sword worked to clean up the gruesome mess. Despite the dwarves' resistance, Cwenhild insisted on helping to carry the shrunken bodies of the dead Followers up to the surface.

Outside, she was surprised to find the sun straight overhead. How much time had passed since she swung down from the ledge above the polished door? It seemed like days. So much had happened. What would it mean to take over Tul's responsibilities? Would she too become immortal? The thought was terrifying.

Tul insisted on burning the remains of the Followers and the wind carried away the choking smell. By the time the pyre had been reduced to ash, the sun was low on the horizon. Fatigue clawed at Cwenhild's eyes, and she wanted nothing more than to find a spot to sleep.

But back in the cavern, the dwarves produced buckets and mops and set to work. Unable to watch while others did the work, she and the other Hawks joined in. When they had scrubbed the last of the disgusting, glowing blood from the polished stone floor, Tul surveyed the room with his arms on his hips.

"That will do," he said. "Now, we must get on with the ceremony."

"Should we wait until tomorrow?" Cwenhild asked. "Everyone is tired."

Tul's red eyebrows shot up. "You are the Protector of the God Sword," he said, his indignation clear. "This is not something that waits for a good night's sleep."

He wheeled and stalked down the corridor to the polished stone door while everyone trailed obediently behind. The dwarves arranged themselves in two columns on either side of Cwenhild and came to attention.

Thrusting out his lower jaw, Tul studied them for an instant before waving Kjell forward. "Use the key," he muttered.

"Of course," Kjell answered, stepping forward to insert the points of the staff into their holes. When they clicked into place, he sent a surge of power through the staff, causing the sapphire to flame with a burst of brilliant blue light.

As if reluctant to give up its prize, the ground rumbled under their feet before the door slid open. At once, Tul marched into the narrow cavern where the walls glowed with the same eerie light that lit everything in the underground fortress.

The dwarves remained on guard at the entrance, but curiosity drew the Hawks and Kunnegarde into the treasure trove. Piles of gems and golden coins filled much of the space. An extraordinary set of armour was set up as if someone still wore it.

Egbert froze in front of the magnificently fashioned metal. Its polished surface shone red in the gentle light, amazingly dust-free. A matching shield leaned nearby.

"Is this what I think it is?" Egbert asked.

Coming up behind him, Kunnegarde answered, "Thou doth recognize Tsar's armour?"

"So, it is true," said Egbert, shaking his head and stepping back for a better view. "When I was a boy, my father told me stories about it all the time. He said it is our standard for everything we build at the forge."

Tsar, the First King must have been tall for a dwarf. His armour stood taller than Egbert as he stepped closer to inspect the workmanship.

Seeing that the Hawks had stalled, Tul grunted impatiently before continuing to wade through the maze of riches. Haphazard piles of gem-encrusted swords, pieces of polished plate armour, gold-plated vases, and shiny coats of chainmail were among the treasure that toppled onto his path.

"Ah ha!" he cried. "I knew it was around here." With his toe, he nudged aside a tangle of golden wire so he could reach the hilt of a sword. As he pulled it free from under a pile of golden chalices, they tumbled free and crashed against each other.

Triumphant, Tul held the weapon aloft before striding over to Cwenhild. "Here it is," he announced as he handed it over and turned back to his search with a muttered, "I know it was around here somewhere." His prodding toe pushed aside a mound of cast heads. They looked like golden skulls.

Cwenhild gaped at the weapon. The God Sword looked as though it would be too heavy to wield comfortably, yet it fit her hand as if it had been made for her. She extended her arm and tested its weight with a series of slashes. The balance was perfect. Her arm would never tire with it.

Pointing the tip toward the floor, she studied the yellow diamond embedded in the hilt. Even in the soft light of the cave, it sparkled. The fuller, the long thin channel that ran the length of the blade, glowed with yellow light while the razor-sharp edges showed glints of red.

For all that, the most stunning feature of the sword was the finely-wrought cross guard, which looked like the outstretched wings of a soaring hawk. Somehow, the maker had created an illusion of fragile delicacy. However, when Cwenhild tested its strength with her fingers, she found it hard and unyielding.

A slow smile spread over Kunnegarde's face, and he said, "I hath not seen yon blade in a long while. Thou knowst Dworgunul did maketh it for Abbarkon? 'Twas to be the blade to destroyeth Dreff." Regret flitted across his face. "Of course, it didst not work as he didst plan. 'Twas only by a whisker that we locked Dreff away from this world." He trailed off and stared into the distance as if seeing the battle of two thousand years ago.

Tul tossed a crown onto an unstable heap of treasures and Kunnegarde swung around at the crash. A long staff exposed by the avalanche caught his attention. Reaching down, he tugged it free and brought it close to his eyes.

"Why 'tis a moonstone," Kunnegarde said. Twirling it gently, he watched the play of light on the cloudy surface. "'Tis a powerful gem, and useful for channelling energy. Mayhap, I will not miss my old staff so much if I have a new one," he said, winking at Kjell. "Tul, my old friend," he called. "Thou dost not mind if I keep this for mine own?"

Turning, Tul examined him critically as if seeing him for the first time. His face wrinkled in distaste. "Kunnegarde, you are an elf!" he declared.

Kunnegarde cocked his head as if considering how to respond but Tul waved his hand, dismissing the puzzle, and demanded, "Why are you wearing the uniform of a Worshipper of Dreff?" Without waiting for an answer, he waved aside that question as well. Under his breath, he muttered, "Nothing to be done about the elf face, but no point dressing like a Worshipper."

Bustling back to a section of the room near the entrance, he rummaged through a pile of clothing. Piece by piece, he assembled a complete uniform of a Defender of the God Sword.

Finally, seizing the pile of assorted items, he thrust it into Kunnegarde's arms. "If you must look like an elf, the least you can do is to dress like a dwarf."

CHAPTER FORTY-ONE

Preparations

THE GATES OF KALLCUNARTH ROLLED shut with a clatter. Every evening, as the sun dropped low in the sky, Halvor made a point of observing the gates' closure. He felt compelled to climb to the highest tower and examine the furthest visible point for any sign of an approaching army.

Because he had been at the library of Oruk when it happened, he had not been a witness to Cadmon's death, but he had heard the stories. Halvor's unfailing belief in information told him that knowledge provided the best chance to prepare for what might happen. And for that reason, he needed to know everything about the Followers of Martokallu.

He and King Sebastien expected the Followers to arrive without warning and to attack immediately. Accordingly, Halvor had done everything in his power to ensure that no detail was overlooked as they readied Kallcunarth and its inhabitants for the defense.

Everything was in place. And it would stay that way around the clock.

Staring into the distance, Halvor recalled how the Followers had caught them off-guard at Oruk Library. It grieved him to remember how both lives and precious books had been lost due to his carelessness. It would not happen again.

With a grunt, Halvor pushed the memories aside. There was nothing to be done about the past. But he would do everything he could to prepare for the future.

Things had gone well so far. In a remarkably short time, the message had gone out to towns and cities across Abbarkon. Almost immediately, soldiers began to arrive in Kallcunarth. Almost every town and village between Martokallu's Fortress and Kallcunarth had been all but abandoned. Moving in groups of twos and threes, citizens and soldiers alike had made the trek to Kallcunarth. A month after the plan was first hatched, the city was teeming with people and supplies.

More than once, Halvor had mentally thanked the builders of the city for their forethought in leaving two huge open areas at opposite ends of the city. Tents had been set up around the perimeter of both fields after the barracks filled to the bursting point. Families throughout the city opened their homes to billet the refugees and even the palace was crowded with visitors.

After discussions with King Sebastien, who was a superb tactician, Halvor took on the task of overseeing the organization that allowed thousands of people to live in the crowded city.

His ever-present notebook was filled with lists and rosters that he shared with the deputies whom he appointed to various roles. He hardly took time to sleep as he rushed from place to place, checking on everything from the collection of wheat and oats to the filling of the huge underground cisterns that held enough water to supply the city for months.

Climbing down from the tower as the last of the light disappeared, Halvor decided to check in with Gytha. She oversaw the training of every soldier and able-bodied volunteer, setting up divisions and putting them each under the supervision of a Hawk.

The training was making a difference. Everybody was getting faster, stronger and more confidant. Gytha personally supervised the drills and with Asdis at her side, moved through the fields offering suggestions for improvement.

Making his way to the nearest field, Halvor peered around. The area had been assigned to sword and mace fighters. Across the way, targets were set up for the archers and dagger throwers. Torches flickered everywhere allowing training to continue late into the night. The crash of weapons had become part of the background noise that reminded him of his time in Halklyen.

So close to the field, it was loud. He drew a pencil from behind his ear and made a note to ensure that the division who slept around the outside of the field got the last training session of the day. They might be awakened earlier than they wanted, but at least it would be quiet when they were trying to get to sleep.

Just as he finished writing that idea in his notebook, Gytha appeared at his elbow. "Have you heard?" she asked. "There's a meeting of the Talons in the palace. It starts in twenty minutes."

Halvor looked up and smiled. "Gytha, I was looking for you." Pushing the pencil behind his ear, he shook his head. "I hadn't heard," he replied. "When was it announced?"

"Penn has been trying to round everyone up," she answered. "I've sent Asdis along to help him out." Lowering her voice, she added, "Something must have happened."

"But what?" he murmured as they turned toward the palace.

She hummed in reply and they walked in silence, lost in

their own thoughts until Gytha asked, "You were looking for me?"

For a moment, Halvor could not recall why he had come to the field but when he opened his notebook, it came back to him. "Oh, yes," he said as if he could actually see the pages in the dark streets. "The smiths just finished another twenty sets of chainmail. I thought you would know who should have them."

"Send them to me," she answered. "I'll have them distributed in the morning."

As they neared the palace, they spotted the shadowed forms of Gulner and Geir ahead. Even in darkness, they were easy to identify. Gulner walked with his distinctive springing step and Geir towered above him.

At the sound of their footsteps, they both turned, hands on weapons, only relaxing when they recognized Halvor and Gytha. With silent nods, the four fell in together and continued toward the palace.

The only place where details were ever discussed aloud was a small, windowless room near the throne room that had been designated 'Hawk Hut'. Even though Orma worked to maintain a cloak over the city, there could be no assurance that Martokallu did not have spies positioned within the walls.

As they approached the room, the number of King's Guards in the corridors increased. They snapped to attention when the four Hawks strode past.

As she passed each person, Gytha murmured, "Well done, soldier. Stay alert."

A long, narrow passageway led to Hawk Hut and the guards stationed there flattened themselves against the wall to let the Hawks by. Outside the door, Asdis and Penn stood guard.

Asdis smiled at her mother, but it was Penn who spoke. "You're the last ones to arrive," he said. "Asdis and I have been all over the city but the only person we couldn't find was you, Halvor."

He would have continued, but Gytha interrupted, "Thank you, Penn. Thank you, Asdis. As you can see, I found him. Remember, we want to know if anything unusual happens out here. If it does, knock loudly." With that, she stepped past them and opened the door to slide into the room.

The three men followed, and Halvor stopped to secure the latch. The room was crowded with every member of the Talons. They leaned against the walls around the perimeter while King Sebastien and Orma sat on chairs in the far corner.

While the late arrivals found spots to squeeze in, King Sebastien glanced at Orma. "If you please," he said.

Pushing herself to her feet, Orma gazed around at the gathered people until her eyes rested on Halvor. He saw reluctance there, but she cleared her throat and said, "I have had word from Cwenhild." A rustle of confusion swept the room, and she lifted an eyebrow. "They have a new mage. Two mages in fact. It turns out that Kjell has some power, but they have also allied with Martokallu's brother, Kunnegarde. It was he who opened the link through to me."

The murmurs grew louder and Orma pressed her lips together. "There is good news. They have the God Sword."

A raucous cheer burst out and she allowed herself a smile before raising a hand to silence her audience.

"Unfortunately, it has cost us dearly. Igon, Hackett and Dagur are dead." She paused to allow the exclamations of grief to subside. "They were good men, and we shall miss them. I am sorry to say we have even worse news. Hulda has been turned into a Follower."

Shocked gasps followed this announcement, and a disheartened silence settled over the room as people waited to see what else she had to say.

"Cwenhild tells me she has been named Bearer of the God Sword."

Halvor jerked upright. "What does that mean?" he demanded.

Orma pursed her lips and shook her head. "I don't know," she answered. "The communication was brief and Cwenhild spoke quickly, leaving no time for questions. But I understand it to be a good thing." Orma let her pride show in a small tense smile. "They will be returning home as quickly as possible, accompanied by Kunnegarde and a contingent of dwarves. Kunnegarde says Martokallu has an army already on its way here."

She drew in a deep breath that highlighted her exhaustion. "I have sensed Martokallu trying to break through my shield. So far, he has only been testing me, but I suspect that as his army gets closer, he will make a greater effort."

She raised her face to the ceiling and closed her eyes. "I do not believe I can hold him again." Glancing sideways, she met King Sebastien's steady gaze. "We have decided that I will lift the cloak today."

CHAPTER FORTY-TWO

Warning

FROM THE MOMENT SHE ARRIVED, Velte sensed the emptiness within the fortress. Weariness almost overtook her rage as she made her way through the empty hallways with Hulda obediently trailing behind.

Fleeing the disastrous battle had been her only option for survival, but Martokallu would not see it that way. He would only see the loss of so many mages. He would resent her failure to kill the Hawks. He would be angry.

Hulda was Velte's best hope to avoid punishment. It had been a huge strain on her power to bring the woman back with her, so it had better have been worth it. She felt so drained. If Martokallu could not be persuaded that it was not her fault, she was not certain she could withstand his fury.

Tottering through the familiar hallways with Hulda on her heels, she reached out with her mind. *Master?* she asked.

The reply was immediate and thunderous. *Velte!*

She winced. The blare of his voice was painful.

I have been unable to contact you for far too long, he thundered. *I had hoped you would return in time.*

Inside her head, his voice was almost jolly. What did he mean? In time for what? She did not relish the idea of reporting what had happened in Tsaralvia. Briefly, she considered hiding the truth from him, but then immediately suppressed the traitorous thought.

Outside the entrance to the throne room, she hesitated. Was she strong enough to face Martokallu? Should she wait until she had recovered her powers?

Then she dismissed the thought. She was always strong. She was Velte. Straightening her spine, she set her smile in place and said, *Master, I brought you a gift.* Before her courage abandoned her, she checked once more that her glamour was in place and strode through the door.

Martokallu sat alone but for three slaves standing just out of reach of the throne. Seeing Hulda, he sat up straight and said, *You have brought me a Hawk. Tell me what has happened.*

Despite the dread gnawing at her belly, she told him. When she reached the part about the unsuccessful attack on the Hawks within the walls of Tsarval, she felt his mood change. Cringing, she continued to narrate the chase to the open door in the Chain of Thollcrawnow.

At the point of the dwarves' attack, he exploded in rage. *You were so close. I would have been invincible with that sword.*

He poured so much anger through their connection that she feared her head would split. What did he mean? Which sword?

You and Gadrith have been all but useless to me, he hissed. *Worse than useless! Am I to understand that we lost his entire force and, aside from this one recent recruit, you have returned to me alone? Not a single mage survived? All lost after centuries spent collecting them?*

Velte lowered her head. Everything he said was true. She

had no defense. Her glamour flickered around her and for a moment, her true form in all its repulsiveness was visible. With a huge effort she pulled her magic around her again and fixed a smile on her face. She knew how to handle Martokallu.

Thrall strode at the head of his army of newly transformed slaves. Without looking back, he knew they maintained their rigid columns. They would act as an extension of himself, doing everything he ordered. Already, he had found that he could send one group in one direction and then have a second and even a third group circle around for an attack. It was like a game he had played with pebbles as a child.

Perhaps his soldiers would be even more effective than true Followers since he would not have to wait for individuals to react. The only disadvantage that he could see so far was that because the transformation was incomplete, they would still require food and water.

He had refrained from ordering them to fight, because he could not afford to lose a single body before the real battle. But he had drilled them in full armour to see how well they controlled their swords.

Thrall grimaced at the memory. Giving swords to a slave force more used to shovels resulted in a heavy-handed army. There was no grace to it. He shook his head to rid himself of the image. Graceful or not, when it came down to an actual battle, his army would triumph. There would be no giving up or running away. They would fight until they could no longer get up. That alone made them unbeatable.

Soon they would have the chance to prove their worth. Kallcunarth was no more than two hours away. As he crested a hill, Thrall turned to look back over the heads of his army to Wout's force. They were a worthy unit, highly trained and independently capable. But there were too few of them. It would be his army that won the war.

Then he returned his gaze to the valley that spread out before him. In the distance, the walls of Kallcunarth were visible. If he had real Followers with him, he would push on and arrive on the city's doorstep. But his soldiers needed food and water. The fight would go more quickly if they were rested. It went against the grain to bother with such trivialities, yet Thrall had already seen the benefits of a break. They tended to slow down if he pushed them too hard or too far.

Swallowing his annoyance, he reached out with his mind and ordered a stop before they reached the top of the hill. He smiled grimly. A few hours one way or the other would make little difference in the end.

The slaves halted right where they were and folded to their knees. As part of the efficiencies, he had instructed that the food be distributed to each slave. That way, not only did it negate the necessity of bringing along non-combatants to deal with food, but it also sped up the time it took to get the whole army fed. His next command was to eat. Given that this was their last rest, he gave permission for them to consume all that they had left.

While he waited, he rehearsed the battle in his mind. He had grown up in Kallcunarth, so he knew both its strengths and its weaknesses. He knew exactly how he would deploy his army. However, it would also be useful to know of any preparations made by King Sebastien. Unfortunately, there was very little information on the man.

Thrall debated whether to ask Martokallu what he could see of the city. A great deal of the Master's fury came from his inability to see past a cloak over the area. Perhaps though, his vision had been restored to him.

Master, Thrall called. *Can you show me Kallcunarth?*

The answer was immediate and had none of the excitement that had characterized Martokallu's earlier communications. The voice in Thrall's head was straightforward and held an edge of anger. *It remains invisible to me. But you are close now, so I shall break the shield.*

Orma felt the first fingers of power prying at the edge of her cloak. Opening her eyes, she said, "I am releasing the shield, Sebastien." She sat up and looked straight at him. "Martokallu tried to break through again. I can't hold him off. He'll be able to see everything."

King Sebastien held her gaze before carefully setting his pen beside a tall sheaf of papers. He rubbed a hand across his face. "That means they're close," he said. Standing, he strode to the window where Hrefna watched the horizon.

The room afforded an excellent view of the city and its surrounding lands. King Sebastien could see the entire field outside the gates and all the way to where the hills disappeared into the woods. As he watched, the sun vanished over the crest of the furthest hill.

Turning to Hrefna, he said, "Inform the commanders and then go to the wall. Tell them to double the watch through the night. We want the earliest warning possible. In the meantime, let the soldiers sleep."

Hrefna saluted and after knocking on the door to alert the corridor guards, she slipped out of the room.

Sebastien crossed the room to slump into the chair beside Orma. "It looks like it's really going to happen," he said. "Halvor was right." Tilting his head back, he closed his eyes. "Despite our preparations, I still hoped Martokallu wouldn't attack." Leaning forward he scrubbed his hands over his face again and looked blearily at Orma. "In the morning, people are going to die."

Orma rose from her chair and shuffled over to a table set with the makings for tea. She felt a hundred years old. Yet, without the weight of the cloak, her strength was already returning. "I keep thinking about that too," she said as she spooned leaves into the porcelain teapot. "Even one death is too many."

He scowled. "The dying will not stop with one person," he muttered. "Not without a miracle."

"Our miracle was in having enough time to prepare," Orma said. She moved the cauldron from the fire and poured hot water onto the leaves. "We are ready. And we will win." Returning to the chairs, she set a cup of tea by Sebastien's elbow. "They will not attack tonight. The best thing you can do for the people of Abbarkon is to get some sleep so you and that crafty brain of yours are ready for whatever happens tomorrow."

Sebastien picked up the tea and gave her a half-hearted grin. "No doubt, you are right," he agreed as he took a cautious sip. "After I enjoy this cup of tea, I shall head off to bed. Whether or not I get any sleep remains to be seen."

CHAPTER FORTY-THREE

Alarm

HALVOR FELT AS IF HE had hardly closed his eyes when he woke to the clanging of alarm bells. Late into the night, he had hurried from captain to captain ensuring that each one understood their role in the upcoming battle.

King Sebastien had come up with the plan, but the details had been left to Halvor. A Hawk had been placed in charge of each division and although Halvor had met with them all as a group, he felt the need to speak with each one individually.

Vaulting from his bed, he donned the armour that he had stripped off hours earlier. Over his chainmail, he wore a breastplate that Egbert had made for him. Polished to a brilliant sheen, with his helmet, it made him look formidable despite his small stature. Strapping his sword around his waist, he checked the six serrated daggers that were sheathed on the belt before hurrying toward the city wall.

The streets were clogged with soldiers moving in an orderly

fashion toward the gate. That was a good sign. People knew where to go. He called out greetings and clapped a few shoulders as he squeezed through in the opposite direction.

At the head of his archers, Penn called, "What have you seen?"

Not wanting to admit he knew no more than they did, Halvor answered with a quick grin and a shrug. "We'll know better when we get to the wall," he said.

Penn's division was assigned to the far west side. The young Hawk had been thrilled to be given command of a group of recent recruits. In a remarkably short time, using methods that had been a game to him since he was a small child, Penn had coached his archers into a force to be reckoned with. Halvor had put them on the outside position because of their inexperience, even though their accuracy was significantly greater than the division set to take the key spot close to the gates.

Penn looked as if he wanted to say something more, but he stopped himself. Halvor had talked to him about the importance of restraining his chatter when he was in charge of soldiers, and he had taken the lesson to heart. Straightening his spine, he saluted instead.

Halvor returned the salute and feeling a new sense of urgency, he jogged toward the guard tower. After climbing the stairs two at a time, he burst into the room that provided the best view in the city. Narrow, glassless windows lined the walls of the circular space.

His eyes went first to the horizon. What he saw hit him like a punch in the stomach. Lined up out of bow-shot was an army of at least a thousand Followers.

From the stories of the battle at Fasnul, Halvor knew that the primary reason for the Hawks' victory over the Followers and Martokallu came from the added numbers of King's Guards from Kallcunarth. Together with the King's Guards from Fasnul, they had outnumbered the enemy by at least ten to one. They still probably held the numbers advantage but it was more like six to one. He could only hope it would be enough.

Dragging his eyes away from the approaching army, Halvor forced himself to focus on his part of the upcoming battle. The last of four divisions of archers was moving into place along the walls. Penn had his soldiers lined up and was already distributing the arrow buckets so the archers could easily replenish their supplies. Even as Halvor watched, the archers carried in several braziers, which they would use to light the tar-coated arrows.

Six different teams worked the catapults on the top of the wall. Rocks were the usual projectile fired during training exercises, but Halvor had come up with a new idea based on Dell's grenades. He had convinced one of the master smiths to forge iron balls with a diameter of about six inches. These were filled with gunpowder and metal fragments. A short wick burned for about fifteen seconds which was long enough for the projectile to reach its target. When the bombs landed, the results were devastating. Several craters of loose earth marked the range of the catapults and the cavalry had been warned to avoid those spots.

Outside the gate, in a formation beyond the walls, four divisions of fifty mounted troops waited beside their horses. Halvor recognized Geir on the western side and his brother Gar on the eastern edge. Both men had removed their helmets, making their red hair and height visible even among the tall warhorses. The brothers had proven to be excellent captains who spent long hours training their divisions in mounted manoeuvres designed to decimate the enemy.

Four divisions of foot soldiers were lined up behind the cavalry. Many of them rested quietly on the ground, staring out toward the army of Followers that appeared to be sitting motionless in perfectly straight ranks. Halvor studied the foot soldiers, trying to pick out Gytha.

He knew she would not be sitting around waiting for the attack and sure enough, he spotted her wandering through the troops. Despite the grimness of the situation, he smiled as he imagined the reassuring words she would be murmuring to each soldier. Gytha would never be one to offer a rousing speech, but in her own way, she inspired her soldiers to fight far beyond their abilities.

Inside the tightly sealed gates, the pike-men were getting ready. Every man in the division had been selected not only for his size and strength but also for his unwavering determination. They needed brave men to brace the long pikes against a horde of Followers. Their pikes lay on the cobblestones beside them while they each worked to remove a stone from the road. The resulting holes would act as a backstop for their pikes if the Followers broke through the gate.

Four more divisions of foot soldiers surrounded them. Since they would provide the last line of defense, much rehearsal had gone into preparing for a street battle. In the square, soldiers lined up in an open formation while every street that led into the city had soldiers waiting against the walls. The idea was to allow the Followers access and then fall on them from all sides.

The squadron closest to the palace included sixty of the finest fighters in the kingdom. They carried tower shields and wore special bucket helmets that identified them as Palace Protectors. Halvor's jaw tightened. There were not nearly enough of them to be the last line of defense.

However, Orma had assured him she could cast a protective cloak over them. It would prevent arrows and swords from harming the soldiers. That was why there were so few of them. She could only handle a small group.

To accustom the soldiers to the idea of the shield, Orma had agreed to a practice run despite the energy it cost her. The sight of the arrows falling short of their targets, and sword blades being deflected by unseen forces had provided a few minutes of much needed entertainment for the troops.

The battle would have been far easier if they had a few more mages like Orma. Halvor let out a sigh and set his helmet aside. With any luck it would not come to the point where the Palace Protectors were necessary. If things went as planned outside the gates, they would never see Followers inside the city.

At the sound of footsteps on the stairs, Halvor turned to find Orma, with King Sebastien right behind her.

Dropping into a bow, Halvor said, "Greetings, my King. Welcome, Oh Great Mage."

Sebastien snorted. "Be at ease, soldier," he said with a wry grin. He strode to the window, where he surveyed the mass of soldiers visible in every direction and his smile faded. "Is everything in place?" he asked.

"Yes, sir," Halvor answered. "Every captain has performed perfectly. It is just as we practiced."

For the space of three slow breaths, they gazed out at the people who were prepared to fight and die for the freedom of Abbarkon. Then, almost together, they lifted their eyes to study the attacking army where it waited in perfect stillness.

Finally, Orma said, "The best thing that could happen is that they attack soon. If our soldiers have to wait too long, their nerves will start to fray."

King Sebastien sighed. "I hate to say it, but I agree."

And then, as if in response to his words, Martokallu's army began to move.

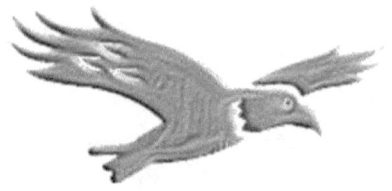

CHAPTER FORTY-FOUR

Call to Arms

THRALL STARED ACROSS THE DISTANCE that separated his army from the city of Kallcunarth. He had let his soldiers rest through the most of the night and started them just before dawn.

By squinting in the early morning light, he could make out hundreds of humans scurrying about on the top of the city walls. They had been like that since he marched his army over the top of the hill. There were thousands of people mustering outside the gates as well. Mounted troops and foot soldiers had poured through the gates. Along the top of the wall, archers filed into place. Braziers were near at hand. That would mean fire arrows.

A muscle jumped in his face. He had not expected the city to be completely unprepared, nonetheless their preparations might pose a problem. How had they known he was coming? He had left Martokallu's fortress less than a week ago and he had not seen a single person along the way.

Reaching out with his mind, he called, *Master?*

Almost immediately, Martokallu's voice boomed inside his head, *The shield has been released,* he crowed. *I can see everything.* Thrall heard Martokallu's scorn. *They imagine they are ready for us. They are in for a surprise.*

Thrall began to receive images of soldiers waiting behind the closed gates of Kallcunarth. Surprised at their numbers, he tried to determine how many people his army would be facing.

Focused on the scenes Martokallu was sharing, Thrall jumped when a voice spoke over his shoulder.

"We will send your slaves in first," Wout said. "The city dwellers can tire themselves killing the weaklings."

Thrall felt the insult of having his troops belittled, but he held his tongue. It was true.

Unaware of Thrall's irritation, Wout continued. "My men will advance around the outside of the fighting and move into position at the gates. Remember, our purpose is to rid the country of this king who refuses to acknowledge the Master."

Thrall pinched his lips together. He hated to agree with Wout, but the outline of the battle plan was just as he had envisioned it. "Let's get this done," he growled.

While Wout headed back to his warriors, Thrall drew his sword. Brandishing it above his head, he roared, "For Martokallu!"

His war cry was more for show than to excite his troops to action. Reaching out with his mind, he gathered the strands of his enslaved humans' consciousness. He tried to ignore just how sluggish and insubstantial they felt as he ordered them forward.

As Thrall started down the hill, he glanced over his shoulder and smiled at the slaves unnatural precision. They were his puppets and he would lead them to victory.

"They really are coming," Halvor murmured. He was talking to himself—as if saying it out loud would make it real. Martokallu's army was underway. They were marching in precise rows, and they would arrive in no time. He swallowed hard.

King Sebastien knew how he felt. The instant he gave the order, it would all become very real. People were going to die. This was not how it was supposed to be.

Finally, Halvor pressed his lips together and gave a sharp nod. Turning, he called, "Buglers, sound the 'Call to Arms'."

Two musicians, whose usual job was with the King's Orchestra, climbed down the stairs and stepped out onto the wall. Turning to direct their sound in opposite directions, they played the lively melody that told the waiting soldiers Martokallu's army was on the way.

Immediately, a bustle of activity followed as the cavalry mounted their horses and straightened their lines. Behind them, the foot soldiers rose from their resting spots and drew their weapons. Many of them bounced on the balls of their feet, warming up muscles that would soon be straining. Within the walls of the city, the soldiers came alert. Pike-men fitted their long poles into the slots among the cobblestones and practiced anchoring it there.

On top of the walls, Penn strode up and down behind his row of archers. "All right, laddies and lassies," he called. "It's time to teach the cavalry what the most important part of an army is." Barely stopping to take a breath, he continued. "Sure, they look grand on their fearsome horses, but in the end, it will be us who cause the most damage out there today."

When the buglers played the 'Call to Arms', the young archers had leapt into position, their excitement obvious. But even they could see that it would be a long wait before the approaching army came into range.

King Sebastien smiled to himself as he watched Penn. His

soldiers were relaxing under his steady stream of fortifying chatter. They would be ready when the time came.

Penn appeared unconcerned about the impending attack. "Watch them come across that field," he said. "They're in no hurry to get here. And, it's no wonder. I wouldn't want to have to attack us either. Just look at the defense we have in place. Halvor has had everyone out drilling for the last three weeks. I know you haven't had the years of training that the Hawks got when we were living in Halklyen, but you are the best-trained archers ever seen in Abbarkon."

Some of the boys grinned at Penn's complete lack of modesty and one of the girls called, "Penn, you've been a great teacher, but I don't know if you can say we're Abbarkon's best-trained archers ever!"

Without batting an eye at her interruption, Penn carried on. "As I was saying, you are the best-trained and we are going to prove it to everyone."

His pacing took him to the end of his archers. One of the catapult crew stopped in the middle of winding the windlass. "You may be the best archers but wait until you see what these beauties will do," he called.

"I have seen it, my friend," replied Penn. "And as impressive as it is, you can only send your bombs out onto the battlefield and hope they will hit a target. The beauty of a simple bow and arrow is that, in the hands of a trained archer, every shot is guaranteed to do damage." He rubbed his hands together as he warmed to his subject. "In fact, the efficiency—"

Penn broke off and snapped to attention as King Sebastien and Orma stepped out onto the wall. His sudden silence caused the archers and the catapulters to look. Seeing the king, they straightened up and pulled their shoulders back.

King Sebastien gazed along the line for a long moment. They were so young. Their excitement was obvious. And they had absolutely no idea what he was about to unleash on them.

He struggled to keep his face impassive. They needed him to be strong. When he finally spoke, it was in ringing tones. "People of Abbarkon," he called. "I would not have chosen to have you fight a war for our freedom. I would not have chosen to have you spend your time training to become masters of your weapons." He paused and raked his eyes down the rows of soldiers standing at attention. "But I am proud to see how ready you are to face an enemy. I am honoured to witness the courage with which you are facing this battle. I know we can count on you to find a way to bring us a victory!" His voice rose at the end and the soldiers roared their approval.

Raising his hand in salute, King Sebastien spun about and headed for the stairwell with Orma at his heels. At the bottom of the stairs, Hrefna and Gulner waited with the palace guards. This was his least favourite part of the battle plan. They would escort him to the palace tower room and remain there with him. Much discussion and argument had passed back and forth before he had finally agreed to hide at the rear.

Halvor had been the most vocal opponent to King Sebastien's participation in the coming fight, but it took Orma to convince him that he had to lead from behind. She pointed out that Martokallu could only win if he controlled the king. While she could protect him within a small room, she would be helpless out in the open. She did not have the strength.

Nevertheless, it was a bitter walk through streets crowded with soldiers. When he raised his hand in salute, they called his name and cheered his passage. It was all he could do to maintain a confident smile. He wanted nothing more than to abandon his pledge and join Halvor in the tower. The citizens might not notice at the moment, but when they thought about it later, King Sebastien would look like a coward by abandoning the fight before it even began.

CHAPTER FORTY-FIVE

War

LEFT ALONE INSIDE THE TOWER room, Halvor watched the steady approach of Martokallu's army. For the hundredth time, he wished he had been present at the battle outside of Fasnul all those months ago. For once, the stories were not enough. He wanted real life experience to give him confidence for the coming battle.

He also wished that Cadmon, or Gode or almost anyone else was here to take on the task of leading the defense. He felt the weight of the responsibility left to him. So much of his knowledge was theoretical and he could not help thinking that books might not always be the best teachers.

Tearing his eyes away from the advancing army, he surveyed his soldiers. As he watched, he took a deep, calming breath and straightened his shoulders. There was no need for panic. They were ready. The early morning sun glinted off the heavy armour of the mounted cavalry. With their helmets, it was difficult to tell, but he thought he recognized Geir and his brother Gar as they guided their huge horses slowly along the lines of mounted riders. Even from a distance, Halvor felt their calm and forced himself to ignore his own fear. He would need all his wits about him if he was going to control the battle.

Turning away from the view of Martokallu's army, he scrubbed a hand over his face and let out a breath he had not realized he was holding. At that moment, the door to the tower room opened and the two buglers entered.

They moved with the dignity acquired from years in the court orchestra. Standing just inside the wooden door, with their horns tucked under their arms, they waited for his next command. A large part of the strategy was based on Halvor's ability to instantly communicate his commands to the widespread army.

Gerasim and Afya had worked hard to create a call for every command that Halvor could imagine he would need. Then, every evening, the entire army attended mandatory meetings where he would go over the strategies with everyone.

He did not believe it was enough to tell the captains the plans. He wanted every person on the field to have a vision of how the battle would proceed and what would happen in every eventuality. One of the things he had learned from his reading was that the loss of a leader had led to more than one defeat in a war. He did not intend to permit that to happen.

Neither musician looked much like a soldier. Gerasim was a huge man, with his powerful frame sheathed in layers of fat. Easygoing in everything except music, his meticulous attention to detail had made him an excellent teacher when it came to ensuring that the soldiers knew the different calls.

Afya was his physical opposite. Barely coming up to his elbow, the thin woman had stood silently by his side while Gerasim roared out each command. Then, in unison, they would snap their bugles to their lips and rattle off a string of notes. The listening soldiers had to shout the command in return.

During the last several evenings, Gerasim had stopped saying the command. Yet after hearing the bugle call, the entire army could shout the proper response. Already, Halvor had seen the results of all the practice. The first bugle call had brought the defenders to their feet. They were ready for the coming battle.

Turning back to the window, Halvor noted that the approaching army had almost reached the markers that indicated the range of the bows. "Sound Archers Fire When Ready," he said. "And send your runners down to me when you go back up. I want you to stay on the wall. I imagine you'll get a chance to try out all those tunes you wrote."

Thrall was surprised when the cavalry made no move in their direction. He had already marched his army within bowshot, and nothing had happened. Narrowing his eyes, he tried to see if he had missed something.

Master? he called.

However, before Martokallu could respond, he heard a bugle call and suddenly the air filled with the angry buzz of arrows. All along his perfectly straight rows of soldiers, his soldiers dropped silently to the ground. Stretching out his consciousness, he raised most of them back to their feet, but a few had passed beyond his control into death.

At once, he realized that if he continued to walk his army forward, it would be decimated before they got into fighting range. In the next instant, he sent them forward at a dead run.

The first wave of arrows had been effective, but it also spurred the Followers to a run. Without turning, Halvor said, "Tell them to play 'Cavalry Charge'."

The cluster of young boys behind him shuffled in

excitement before the first one in line called, "Yes, sir!" and barrelled out the door.

Seconds later, Halvor heard the bugle call, and the cavalry nudged their horses forward. As the two hundred horses surged to a gallop, they spread out into a line to match the oncoming army.

The crash of the collision reached Halvor in his tower. Barely slowing, the big horses trampled through Martokallu's army, crashing over bodies and leaving devastation in their wake.

For a moment, Halvor thought the battle might be over before it got started. But even as he watched, the Followers lurched to their feet and began to advance again. His breath stopped as they staggered back into their straight lines. His momentary excitement curdled. There would be nothing fair about this fight. Martokallu had access to magic they could not match.

Wrenching his eyes away from the Followers as they pelted toward the city wall, he watched the cavalry rein in before swinging wide in preparation for another charge. In the meantime, a small contingent of armoured Followers completely avoided the cavalry attack. They clearly intended to skirt the fight.

Suddenly, a shower of arrows bounced off their heavy armour. Before Halvor could order a call for fire arrows, the air lit up with the bright, smoke-trailing missiles. "Way to go, Penn!" he shouted, punching his fist into the air. But the Followers batted the flaming arrows aside without a single hit.

Scowling, Halvor watched the Followers scramble past the loosened ground that marked the catapult's range. He made his voice calm as he ordered, "Have the buglers play 'Loose the Catapults'."

As he listened to the hurried footsteps of the messenger boy, the cavalry riders completed their turn and dug in their heels. The horses' muscles bunched as they gained speed. It was a thing of beauty.

The Followers continued their sprint until the entire army abruptly wheeled and brandished their swords. They were close enough that Halvor should have heard the command. But there had been nothing. His stomach clenched. Someone was controlling the soldiers. It was too unnatural.

As if to confirm his suspicions, the Followers abandoned their straight lines just as the cavalry arrived. Halvor's jaw dropped as they shifted apart in perfect coordination, leaving open space between them.

As one, the soldiers rolled away from the galloping hooves and at the same time, they swung their swords to slice through the lower tendons of the horses' legs.

Ragged screams reached him as the horses tumbled head over heels, tossing their riders. As if attached to a string, the enemy soldiers rose to their feet and moved toward the fallen riders.

Only a few of the defenders scrambled up in time to meet the attack. Bile burned in the back of Halvor's throat as Martokallu's soldiers slashed at the fallen horsemen. Most of them died before they could catch their breath.

At that moment, the first of the catapult bombs exploded. A fountain of dirt sprayed up and Halvor lost sight of the soldiers who had been creeping around the outside of the cavalry attack.

He held his breath as he strained to see past the plume of dust. Several long moments passed and he began to hope they had been hit. Finally, the air cleared. Swallowing against the sour taste in his mouth, he saw that it had not worked. The newest crater lay empty. Instead of slowing the sneak attack, the small group had sped up. They were almost upon the foot soldiers who waited outside the wall.

CHAPTER FORTY-SIX

Open the Gates

"PLAY 'READY THE PIKE-MEN'," HALVOR CALLED. "The battle is coming to the gates." His voice was not nearly as calm as it had been when he gave his first order, but the messenger responded just as quickly.

There had been no need to tell the foot soldiers outside the gates to prepare to fight. They had seen the smaller squadron move around the outside of the battle. As soon as the first of the catapult bombs sent the attackers hurrying forward, the foot soldiers knew their turn had arrived.

The two sides met with a deafening clang of swords, and it quickly became apparent that the attackers were better trained than the Followers whom they had previously met. The Hawks would have matched them, but too many of Gytha's force were recent recruits.

Any hope that the battle might remain outside the big gate was beginning to evaporate as Martokallu's soldiers mowed through the foot soldiers. If Halvor wanted to save any of them, he would have to open the gate soon.

His gaze darted to the archers. They had leaned over the parapets to watch the fight below. But they held their fire. They could not shoot for fear their arrows might hit one of their own.

Squeezing his hand into a fist, he turned his attention to the cavalry. The few horses remaining upright had wheeled around in preparation for another attack. Some of the dismounted riders continued to fight on foot. Several of Martokallu's soldiers, whose swords rose and fell in a relentless rhythm, surrounded each one. Halvor could hardly bear to watch.

Closing his eyes, he drew in a deep breath and held it. There was no other choice. "Open the gates," he said. For the first time, he looked over his shoulder at the young messengers who stared back wide-eyed. "Don't worry." He summoned a smile. "This is part of the plan. They're going to be surprised when they see what we have up our sleeves." Turning back to his windows, Halvor repeated, "Tell the buglers."

This time he heard the clatter of boots on the stairs.

In the seconds he had looked away from the battle below his feet, things had begun to change.

Gytha ducked under the short sword as it swung in a vicious arc over her head. Frantically backpedaling, she brought her own blade around seeking a weak spot in her attacker's defense. The problem was there did not seem to be one.

From the moment she ordered her foot soldiers to prepare for battle, Gytha had been looking forward to a fight. Practicing with weapons was her favourite thing and knowing that she was about to enter into a contest where she would not have to hold back the killing blow was strangely appealing. Despite all her experience with a sword, she had been involved in only the occasional skirmish. This was her first real battle.

The reality was turning out to be far more than she had

imagined. It was all she could do to avoid being skewered by the short, heavily-built Follower. For the first time in all her years of swordplay, she had met an opponent who challenged her skills and threatened her life. Neither Cwenhild nor Gode had ever tested her to such an extent.

Fighting with Flint had taught her to be wary of a dual-wielding swordsman, but it had not prepared her for the speed with which the Follower could use his two heavy short swords. No matter how she tried to put him off balance, each attempt ended with her scrambling to stay upright.

Suddenly, she heard the bugles playing the command to open the gates. She risked a glance at the soldiers surrounding her. Her stomach twisted when she saw how many had already fallen.

Her brief inattention almost cost her. Barely avoiding a lunge meant to disembowel her, she danced aside. During the spin that took her out of his reach, she saw the gate roll open. Rather than attacking again, she bellowed, "Run!"

Abandoning the fight, she sprinted hard for the opening. At the same time, the bugles repeated her command. All around her, soldiers turned and ran.

Gytha had been reluctant to agree to leave injured or dead soldiers on the battlefield and flee to safety. However, Halvor had convinced her that it was a valid part of the battle plan. He insisted that if the battle came so close to the wall and they were not winning, the best thing to do was clear the area. Then the archers could take down the attackers.

As she ran, Gytha yelled at everyone she saw to follow her. With some relief, she spotted Asdis just ahead and accelerated to catch up with her daughter. The gates were open wide enough to accommodate two people at a time and they squeezed through the gap together. As soon as they reached the safety of the city, Gytha slowed.

Turning to examine the girl who had grown taller than her,

she saw with relief that although covered in blood spatters, Asdis was uninjured. She had fought well. Briefly, she reached out and grasped her daughter's arm. The face that turned toward her was alive with exhilaration. Recognizing the look, Gytha asked, "Good fight, was it?"

Asdis glowed. "It's so much better than training!"

"Don't have too much fun," Gytha warned. "Keep yourself safe."

The waiting pike-men lowered their weapons and the foot soldiers rushed past to join the others waiting in the streets. As Gytha found a spot for her and Asdis, the bugles blasted the order for the archers to fire. By the shouts of excitement from the walls, she guessed the ploy had worked.

With a lump in her throat, she considered the people they had left behind in the field. She almost hoped that everyone on the other side of the gate was already dead.

Glancing around the square, she realized she could not dwell on those they left behind. Most of her battalion had made it safely into the city and it was her responsibility to ensure they stayed that way.

She strode into the middle of the street and shouted. "Remember, there is no shame in running. This is part of the plan. The archers will take their turn now, but we should expect Martokallu's army inside the gates. We need to be prepared!" She turned in a circle and met the gaze of the soldiers who had been with her in the field. "We will have time to mourn later. Right now, we have a duty to protect the city. See to your weapons and get ready!"

Soldiers up and down the street raised their fists and cried, "For Abbarkon!"

Gytha felt a warmth well up from deep inside. These were her people, and they would fight with her to preserve everything they knew was right. Blinking against sudden tears, she joined Asdis in her spot against the building.

Asdis gripped her arm and leaned close. "We can do this, mom," she whispered.

Before Gytha could answer, there was a thunderous crash against the gate.

Thrall frowned as he watched the last of the cavalry gallop out of reach of his army. The ease with which his soldiers had taken down the arrogant fools should have made him feel better, but instead, he was annoyed. He had hoped for more of a challenge. It was almost disappointing that the fight had turned into a rout.

It took only a small portion of his consciousness to direct the human slaves in their slaughter of the unhorsed cavalry while he studied the remainder of the field. What should his next step be? The cavalry were regrouping. It looked as if they were considering their options as well. Rocking back on his heels, he dismissed them. Instead, he turned to watch the commotion at the foot of the wall.

Wout had manoeuvred his force around the outside of the field as planned. It looked as if they were cutting through the defenders without difficulty. Many had fallen already. He frowned. The battle he had been so eagerly anticipated was almost over.

The bright call of a bugle cut through the air. Abruptly, the defenders turned and raced toward the main gate of the city. Before Wout's forces could react, the gate slammed shut again and arrows began to rain down.

Wout and his soldiers took shelter under their shields, but the archers had them pinned down.

Thrall was surprised by the good humour of the voice in his head. *They think they can hide from us within their walls*, Martokallu said with a laugh. *Show them the power of Martokallu! Take the fight to the city and kill the king. Teach these people to respect their true leader.*

Looking over to where his human slaves continued to hack at the fallen bodies, Thrall changed the orders. Immediately, the swords ceased their thrashing, and the soldiers formed a narrow column, twenty across. With a single thought, he sent them running toward the closed gate with him at their head.

Across the expanse of open field, he met Wout's eyes. The message was clear. He would wait to let the slaves take the brunt of the arrow attack. The archers could not hope to hold back so many. After that, Wout would have to figure out a way to take advantage of any opening.

They reached the catapults' range and Thrall picked up the pace. The first missile flew past on his left, exploding in a burst of dirt and dust. The catapulters corrected their aim and the next bomb exploded in the center of his column. He felt the hit in himself as dozens of his soldiers fell. But the others ran on, pounding right over the bloody bodies. Only one other bomb scored a hit on the column before they moved inside the range.

Unfortunately, at that point, the archers could reach them. An arrow bounced harmlessly off the steel plate-armour grafted onto his arm. A barrage of arrows followed that first hit and he brushed them aside. To him, such missiles posed no danger, but he had to protect his army. With a grin, he had them raise their heavy wooden shields. They had carried them all the way so they might as well get to use them.

Then, with a rush of excitement, he increased their speed to a headlong sprint. Reaching the wooden gates, he commanded his army to crouch under their shields. Through the mind link, he could feel their exhaustion. Let them rest for a moment and they would be stronger for the next bit.

After a quick glance up at the ramparts, Thrall lifted his flail and swung with all his might. The hit made a satisfying crash and left the spiked ball embedded in the hard wood. When he wrenched it free, splinters flew, leaving the beginnings of a hole.

CHAPTER FORTY-SEVEN

Entry

A SHUDDER SWEPT THROUGH HALVOR as the huge Follower bashed away at the wooden gates. They should have reinforced them with steel. If Egbert had been there—

He broke off that line of thinking. He could not look backwards—only forward. His hand went to his belt to draw a dagger, but it offered little comfort. It had come to this. Their final line of defense.

Arrows bounced harmlessly off the Follower's armour and the soldiers behind him had taken cover under their heavy wooden shield. He would break through any moment. And then what?

Swallowing to dislodge the knot in his throat, Halvor called, "Tell the buglers to play 'Prepare for Entry'."

In response, feet pounded down the stairs, while Halvor hurried to the opposite window. What should he do with the soldiers who waited inside the square? His eyes went first to the pike-men with their sharpened poles poised and ready. They would be most useful if the Followers entered at a run. Maybe they should open the gates.

Obviously, nothing would stop the monster from turning the gate into toothpicks. Halvor had never seen anyone so massive. Normally the size of the gate dwarfed everyone who approached it, but the Follower made it look like a cottage door.

Making up his mind, Halvor ordered, "Open the gate." Hearing no answering footsteps, he turned and met the boy's wide-eyed gaze.

"Do it," he said gently. "He's going to break through anyway, so let's give him a little surprise, shall we?" The quirk of his eyebrows reassured the boy, who gulped hard and ran.

By chance, the opening of the gate coincided with an enormous swing of the Follower's flail. The force of his blow sent him stumbling into the open space. Catching his balance, he pulled himself to his full height to tower over every person in the square.

For an instant, no one moved as he swept his gaze over the collection of soldiers who waited for him and his army. Then, although he made no sign, the army behind him stood and started forward, moving in perfect unison.

The pike-men braced themselves as the foot soldiers split the column to pass around their leader.

Making no attempt to avoid the sharpened poles, they impaled themselves, sticking like shrimp on skewers. When the pikes disappeared under the weight of the bodies, the Followers crawled right over their fellow soldiers.

Not waiting to send the message to the buglers, Halvor leaned out the tower window and bellowed. "Get out of there, pikes!"

At once, the pike-men abandoned their weapons and scrambled out of the way.

From above, the archers sent a barrage of arrows. The wet sucking noise of arrows hitting living targets beat out an uneven rhythm, but few attackers fell. Their relentless progress into the city made Halvor's stomach clench again.

Shaking his head to dislodge the horrific image, he called, "Tell the bugler—" Trailing off, he did not finish the command. There was no need to tell the buglers anything.

The foot soldiers stationed in the streets were already moving forward to meet the invaders. It was an odd-looking battle. The Followers swung their swords with a terrible regularity regardless of whether anyone was near enough to hit. Looking as if they were chopping wood, their peculiar jerky strokes were entirely predictable and they made no attempt whatsoever to defend themselves.

As a result, the defenders were slashing them to pieces. Yet the Followers continued to hack with the same frightening steadiness. Nothing short of a removed limb slowed them down.

The onslaught pushed the defenders further and further back from the entrance to the city. Everywhere Halvor looked, his people were falling under the attack. The streets flowed with blood. How could they hold out against such monsters?

Abruptly, the stream of soldiers stopped and Halvor rushed to the other side of the tower to see what had happened. When he leaned out of the window, he saw half of the army standing at rigid attention while the smaller force that had slipped around the outside of the first battle entered the city. Each black-clad Follower held a polished shield over his head to shelter from the archers.

Halvor stared at the motionless army. Were they breathing? It was hard to tell. What sort of powerful magic was involved in controlling so many people? As he studied the strange scene, several soldiers at the front of the column dropped to their knees, pierced by dozens of arrows.

Sucking in a breath, Halvor swung back to watch the new arrivals. They wore their chainmail over their robes and greatly resembled the Hawks. They even fought like the Hawks. Never had he seen anyone who could truly challenge Gytha in a fight. Yet, their leader had sent her stumbling more than once. If the gates had not opened when they did, she would have lost.

The new force moved like a dark shadow around the outside of the square and then onto the second street that led to the palace. None of the defenders could stop them. The Followers made quick work of anyone who got in their way. Halvor's fingernails bit into the palms of his hands as as he tried to figure out what to do next.

Gytha pushed off the wall. Beside her, Asdis straightened and met her mother's eyes. Something about the way her daughter held her head made Gytha proud. She had grown into someone she could count on in a fight. She was well-trained, fit and daring—without being stupid.

Gytha narrowed her eyes. "It's not over yet," she said. "Something needs to be done about that big Follower."

One corner of Asdis's mouth lifted and she raised her bloody sword in salute. "I'm right behind you," she said, waving her mother forward with the small round shield she wore on her left arm.

Gytha did not head directly for their target. He was charging unimpeded down the street, twirling his huge flail while everyone scuttled out of his way. Instead, she edged sideways through the crowd of soldiers who had already been pushed aside.

A gap had opened up between the Follower and his army. Many of his soldiers had died in the initial charge against the pike-men, and still more had fallen to the archers. Nonetheless, they maintained their straight rows and continued to swing their swords in that bizarre fashion.

Three soldiers in King's Guard uniforms rushed past Gytha. One struck at a mindless Follower. Dodging the mechanical blows, he darted back in to hack at his unarmoured legs. His sword cut deeply into the flesh above the knee and normal-looking blood pumped out of the wound. Yet still, the monster did not slow.

Another of the defenders stepped inside the slashing sword. With a powerful overhand chop, he severed the Follower's sword arm. When the limb dropped to the ground with a heavy, wet sound, the man bent to retrieve the sword with his other hand. At once, a second defender sliced through the exposed neck. The body finally slumped to the ground and stopped moving.

Gytha blinked. It had happened so quickly. Wiping blood spatter from her face, she stepped around the fallen body and cried, "Come on Asdis."

They skirted several more of the little skirmishes as they trailed the leader. Gytha was unsurprised when she heard the bugles over the clamour of the fight. It was the melody for Palace Protectors to the Fore. Halvor was down to his last move.

Her lips tightened in grim amusement as she recalled arguing with Halvor about tactics. She believed that fighting could only be honourable if it were done with honour. That meant no plots or designs—only skill and practice.

He would be thrilled that she was planning an attack that would keep her out of view of her opponent until the last possible moment and that she intended to use every underhanded tactic she could imagine.

CHAPTER FORTY-EIGHT

Arrival

THE IMAGES FLOODING INTO THRALL'S head only added to his sense of supremacy. It had been a glorious battle with plenty of opportunity to kill. His flail was smeared with blood, and he had relished the satisfying crunch of more skulls than he had bothered to count.

Congratulations, Thrall. You are the most successful General I have ever had. The Master's pleasure was evident as he showed Thrall a vision of the human king cowering in his palace. *You are almost there. We will end this soon.*

Without looking, Thrall sensed the fighting behind him, but he gave it no more than the smallest part of his awareness. He had set the human slaves in motion, and they would continue until he commanded them to stop.

Several minutes had passed since anyone came within range of the deadly arc of his flail, so Thrall did not have to give the scene in front of him much attention either. Instead, he focused on the images of the battle one street over.

You have done it, Thrall, Martokallu crowed. *You and Wout will sit by my side as I rule Abbarkon. Together, we will remake this country as it should be.*

Martokallu's triumph was intoxicating. Thrall wanted to pump his fist in the air. He wanted to shout and charge ahead. But he kept his stride slow and measured. He would show the humans the power of the Master.

It did not matter that Wout was getting an equal share of the praise. Their success had depended on cooperation. Wout had done just as they planned. His force had entered the city and was heading straight for the palace.

Thrall would let Wout's soldiers weaken the defense and then he would personally challenge the king. At long last, the Master would take his place as the rightful ruler of Abbarkon.

Squinting, Halvor measured the distance between the attackers and the palace. Truly, he wanted nothing more than to run down the steps and throw himself into the fight, but one more blade would make no difference. But he still might be able to help from his position on the wall.

He winced when the huge Follower slammed another defender against the stone wall of a bakery. The man slid slowly to the ground and lay still. Five more soldiers rushed forward, but they did not have the organization necessary to work together. One smooth swing of the flail cleared the street of all five soldiers at once before the Follower continued unhindered.

Halvor knew a moment's relief when he spotted Gytha making her way through the crowded street. She was unharmed. His smile faded as he realized that she planned to attack the Follower on her own. He had seen how impenetrable the man's armour was. Despite her skills, she could not win. Suddenly, Halvor wished he had a bugle call to tell her to back down. At the same time, she might be their only chance.

Switching his attention to the debacle one street over, he winced at how easily the black clad Followers were cutting through the defenders. They would reach the square outside the palace within minutes. If both groups arrived at the Palace Protectors at the same time, not even Orma would be able to keep them safe.

If Gytha stopped the leader, perhaps the Followers would abandon the fight. After all, they had run away when Martokallu abandoned the field in Fasnul. And at Oruk Library when the Followers' leader was killed, their indecisiveness had bought the Hawks valuable time.

Finding Gytha in the crowd again, Halvor held his breath. As much as he wanted to warn her away, they needed her. With some relief, he saw that she was not alone. Her daughter, Asdis and two other sword wielders whose names he could not recall followed close behind. He did remember watching them in the training yard and had been impressed with their skill.

His eyes darted to the army of Followers behind the giant. It was hard to tell, but it looked as if the defenders were winning the battle in the street. But it would not be enough to kill the mindless Followers. They had to take down the leader.

Halvor looked back in time to see Gytha make her move. Rushing forward, she held her sword like a spear aimed at the one spot on the monster's back that lacked any armour. At the same moment, Asdis and the two swordsmen sprinted toward the monster.

Without even breaking stride, the Follower adjusted the arc of his flail and smashed Asdis in the head. She flew across the cobblestones, landing at such an awkward angle that Halvor knew immediately that she was dead.

The girl had been the only one to challenge Thrall in several minutes. Perhaps the humans were gathering their courage for another attack. As if to prove him right, two more swordsmen rushed toward him, and he stopped the flail long enough to draw his sword. With his left hand, he swung hard and sheared both men in half. They collapsed to the ground in an eruption of blood.

For the first time since Martokallu started sending the images, Thrall was intensely aware of his immediate surroundings. He caught sight of a woman just as she launched herself at him. He turned and adjusted the swing of his flail, but he was too slow.

When Gytha saw Asdis smash into the wall, rage roared through her. It burned away any fear and showed her exactly what she had to do to reach the monster's weak spot. Twisting as she rose, she thrust her sword between the sheets of armour on his back and pushed.

The Follower's body went rigid. He drew himself up to his full height and moved one hand vaguely toward his back. Then he drew in a breath and his eyes snapped wide. In the next instant, he collapsed on the cobblestones. Gytha felt the moment he started to fall and rolled frantically out of the way. Coming to her feet, she settled into a fighting crouch and waited. But he did not move.

Neither did his army. Their swords dangled limply from arms gone still and their eyes stared straight ahead. In the moment it took for the defenders to notice that the threat had disappeared, many were slaughtered where they stood.

As the defenders backed away, a sudden silence descended in the street.

A stone was lodged in Gytha's throat. She could not breathe. Her baby. She had to go to Asdis. Unable to take her eyes away from the bright hair, she shuffled toward the still figure of her daughter.

Abruptly, a crackle of energy and a blinding flash of light shattered the quiet. When her eyes recovered, Gytha saw Martokallu leaning over the fallen body of the huge Follower. He radiated a light that made it difficult to look at him. Shielding her eyes with one hand, she watched yellow flecks shift eerily on the surface of his grey plate armour. They danced and flickered, illuminating his flowing black robe.

As if sensing her scrutiny, he raised his head with its fearsome conical helmet and swept his glowering yellow eyes around the square. When his gaze met hers, Gytha wavered on her feet. It was as if he sucked up all the energy.

"You have interfered with my plans for the final time," Martokallu boomed.

Unable to summon the will to move, Gytha watched with her heart pounding, as he pointed a wizened finger directly at her. And then a blast of energy streamed out of his finger.

When it hit, the blow sent Gytha flying backwards into the side of a building. Her head knocked against the brick, and paralyzed by pain, she crumpled to the ground.

With a cry, Orma rocked back on her heels. "Did you feel that?" she murmured.

"What is it?" King Sebastien asked, seizing her arm to steady her. Dizzily, she leaned against him, and he led her to a chair. "Come, sit. Save your strength."

Orma sank down. "It has come to this," she said. "Our last defense." She looked old. Tired.

King Sebastien's lips thinned as he contemplated the exhausted woman. Then his eyes returned to the square where a force of black-clad attackers had fought their way through the defenders. Under Orma's shield, the Palace Protectors had met them at the street entrance and were slaughtering every attacker who came within reach. They made it look easy.

Catching sight of motion in the second street, King

Sebastien leaned out the window for a better view. His eyes went wide, and he pulled his head back inside. "It's Martokallu!" he gasped.

Orma stretched out a hand to Gulner. "Help me up," she said.

Gulner pulled her to her feet and she leaned on him as he led her back to the window.

Martokallu strode unchallenged into the square and stopped. He swung his helmeted head back and forth before lifting his eyes unerringly to find Orma high in the tower.

Shaking off her exhaustion, Orma straightened her back and met his yellow gaze. The seconds ticked by, but Gulner and King Sebastien could only watch as the mages fought a battle entirely inside their minds.

Abruptly, Orma closed her eyes and slumped against Gulner.

He caught her before she hit the floor and said, "Bring the chair."

King Sebastien dragged it close to the window and they let her down into it.

Kneeling by her side, King Sebastien wrapped an arm around her shoulders. "Can we do anything to help?" he asked.

"He broke my shield," she murmured, her eyes closed. "I could not hold against him."

King Sebastien's heart sank as Martokallu turned in a swirl of dancing yellow light to watch the fight at the far end of the square. The Palace Protectors were no longer dominating. They were fighting for their lives—and they were losing.

The people chosen to fight with the Palace Protectors were the best of the soldiers, but they were not on the level of the Hawks. Without the aid of the protective shield, they were falling under the Followers' attack.

Martokallu crossed the square, to stand directly below King Sebastien and Gulner. Raising his head, he met Sebastien's gaze.

King Sebastien held the stare, though he could not draw a breath.

Then Martokallu laughed—a sound that raised the hair on the back of Sebastien's neck. Turning away, he raised one hand and gave a negligent flick of his fingers—almost as if he was chasing away an insect.

The result of that tiny motion was devastating. The entire force of Palace Protectors, along with many of the attackers, were swept away and hurled against a wall.

In the sudden stillness, a ball of ice settled in King Sebastien's stomach.

CHAPTER FORTY-NINE

Victory

KEEPING A WARY EYE ON THE soldiers in the square behind him, Wout followed Martokallu up the palace steps. Without stopping, the Master blew the doors off their hinges and stepped over the rubble into a magnificent foyer.

There was no time to appreciate the immense columns with their gold leaf highlights. The instant Wout and Martokallu stepped into the room, a dozen guards charged with their lances aimed at eye level.

With a flip of his wrist, Martokallu sent them careening against the wall. Drawing his swords, Wout moved in for the kill.

Martokallu growled, "Leave them. There has been more than enough killing."

Wout straightened and stared at Martokallu, his mouth hanging open. What did it mean? Was the Master going soft?

Martokallu twitched his shoulders and the runes on his robe

flickered in response. "Close your mouth, Wout. I meant what I said. I am here to rule—not to kill my subjects."

"Yes, Master," Wout agreed mechanically. He clamped down on his questions and sheathed his swords. But it did not make sense after the butchery outside the palace. Was something wrong?

"Come," called Martokallu, striding towards a set of broad stairs. "I saw the usurper watching from above. He is the one who must die so that I may take my rightful place on the throne of Abbarkon."

He led the way, almost flying up the stairs. Wout sprinted after him until they came up against a sturdy wooden door. Examining the lock, Wout considered which spell would be most effective. While he was thinking, Martokallu blasted the door off its hinges.

Shaking wood splinters from his hair, Wout raised his heavy daggers and followed Martokallu into an enormous room. The walls were decorated with banners and weapons that reminded Wout of his time as a King's Guard so long ago.

There were only three people in the room. King Sebastien and a second man stood beside an old woman who was asleep in a chair. The king's ornate red armour shone in the late afternoon sun. The second man was smaller than the king. With his dark, polished armour, he had the look of a coiled panther.

Once again, Martokallu did not leave any time to deliberate. He moved with the swiftness of a snake, charging across the room, and aiming his glowing yellow sword at the panther's head. However, the panther was not there when the sword descended.

Dancing out of the way, he placed himself in front of King Sebastien and the unconscious woman.

Rather than attacking again, Martokallu attempted a smile. The result was far more terrifying than his usual expression of disdain.

"Sebastien," Martokallu said, his voice hollow and too loud for the room. "Surrender. There is no way for you to win. No more citizens of Abbarkon need to die in this dispute."

King Sebastien sputtered a laugh. "Dispute?" he asked. "Is that what you call it?"

"It is a question of leadership," rasped Martokallu.

King Sebastien risked a sideways glance at the panther and Wout braced, expecting a desperate ploy to break free of the noose that had tightened around their necks. Prey always fought back. It was the principal joy of the hunt.

Edging away from the woman, King Sebastien said, "I do not believe your leadership is the best thing for the people of Abbarkon."

Wout smiled at Sebastien's transparent effort to delay the inevitable. No doubt he was hoping for rescue.

Martokallu's voice rose, and he boomed, "I have been ruling this country for over a millennium and the people are not suffering for it." The smile disappeared from his skeletal face and his yellow eyes flashed with anger. "What you believe has nothing—"

Whatever he had been about to say was cut off when the panther darted forward and thrust his sword through the same hole in Martokallu's armour that the boy had targeted the last time Martokallu appeared in the kingdom.

Martokallu's eyes darkened with shock. With a strangled shout, he backhanded the panther who flew across the room and crashed against the wall beside the window.

Everyone froze as Martokallu grasped the sword in his stomach by its two-handed grip and pulled. No trace of blood showed when he raised the blade above his head. Then, a shimmer of power rippled through the room and the sword turned to dust that rained down in a shower of black ash.

Lowering his arms, Martokallu pressed one hand to the

wound in his stomach. Even he appeared to be surprised to find no blood. "I am meant to be king," he said.

The panther pushed up from the floor and wiped a trickle of blood from his temple. "I speak for the people of Abbarkon," he declared. "It is not you who is meant to be king. The people have chosen Sebastien."

Screwing up his face, Martokallu extended his sword arm and stepped toward King Sebastien. "We shall see who is meant to be leader," he grated.

King Sebastien lifted his own sword in defense. Rather than waiting for Martokallu to attack, he charged forward. Martokallu caught Sebastien's blow on his blade and flipped it aside. As Sebastien stumbled backward, Martokallu lunged, striking the king's sword arm hard enough to dent the armour. Sebastien's sword flew from his hand and clattered into the corner. Desperately, the king scrambled out of the reach of Martokallu's long sword.

At that moment, boots pounded up the stairwell. Distracted, Martokallu glanced at Wout who watched without interfering. He knew better than to put himself between Martokallu and his prey.

Seizing the moment, King Sebastien rushed to the hearth where a long lance hung on the wall. Seating the butt of the staff in the crook of his arm, he charged at Martokallu, who moved aside. The tip of the lance grazed his conical helmet just as a squadron of Palace Protectors burst through the door.

Martokallu's face twisted in fury. An instant later, he vanished in a flash of blinding yellow light.

Taking advantage of the stillness that followed as the defenders blinked against the glare, Wout slipped out the door and dashed down the stairs.

Halvor raced to Gytha's side. She was too still. With a pounding heart, he pressed two fingers to her throat desperately hoping to find a pulse. At his touch, she opened her eyes.

"Oh, thank goodness," he murmured as she shifted slightly and moaned. "Can you wiggle your feet?"

Gytha wrinkled her brow, but obediently did as he requested.

He smiled. "I was afraid when I saw Martokallu throw you against the wall that you would be hurt."

Gytha groaned as she pulled herself into a sitting position so she could lean against the wall. "I am hurt," she said. Then, she looked over Halvor's shoulder and froze. What little colour she had, drained from her face.

He knew what she had seen and he shifted to block her view. He had already checked Asdis's shattered remains. "I'm sorry, Gytha," he murmured. "She's gone."

Gytha let out a long groan that turned into a sob and Halvor wrapped his arms around her despite her armour.

As he held her, he said, "You did it. You and Asdis. When you took down the monster, the whole army came to a halt. You turned the tide. They've all left the city."

Gytha pulled back. "They left?"

Stretching his lips into a humourless smile, Halvor answered, "They even took the body of that big Follower you stabbed. Right now, they're heading south again. We didn't try to stop them." He hesitated, afraid to mention Asdis again or any of the other casualties.

Looking away from her strained white face, Halvor glanced toward the palace and spotted King Sebastien and Orma. She leaned heavily on his arm as they made their way slowly down the body-littered street, stopping beside every wounded soldier.

As King Sebastien helped her rise from the side of a young swordsman who was missing a hand, Orma spotted Halvor. Their eyes met and her head drooped. He had never seen her look so weary. Then she murmured something to King Sebastien and he led her to the spot where Halvor crouched over Gytha.

As she shuffled past Asdis's still form, Orma looked at Halvor who gave a grim shake of his head. Orma knelt stiffly and brushed a hand over Gytha's cheek. "It is a terrible day," she said.

Gytha rubbed away her tears. "What happened at the palace?" she asked.

"Martokallu thought he should be king, but Gulner told him he wasn't needed," Orma answered with a hint of humour.

Halvor jerked upright. "Martokallu came?" he demanded.

King Sebastien ran a hand through his dark hair. "He did. He wants the throne." He waved his arm to encompass the injured and dying soldiers. "In Martokallu's twisted mind, he believes that all this was—" he swallowed heavily and forced out the last word, "—necessary. He believes he would be the best leader for the people of Abbarkon and it doesn't matter how many people die to make it happen." His face hardened and he turned away. "That is the last thing a king should want for his people." His voice was raw, and he gulped back tears.

A sudden rattle of hooves on the cobblestones drew their attention. A group of riders had arrived, their horses lathered and spent.

"They're back!" Orma cried, rising on her own and waving her arms. "Over here!"

The others leapt up as well. Even Gytha struggled to her feet and leaned against the wall.

A smile split Halvor's face and he planted his fists on his hips. "Welcome home," he said.

Flint rode in the lead with Fleta a nose behind. Egbert had never looked so fit. His little round belly was gone and the little man looked hard and lean. Gode's eyes were fixed on Gytha, assessing her for damage, while Cwenhild and Dell rode side by side. An elf Halvor did not recognize was at the rear with Kjell. Had they lost so many?

Before he could ask, Flint jumped down from his saddle, strode forward and dropped to one knee in front of King Sebastien. "Your Majesty," he said. "We passed an army of Followers marching south. We didn't know what we would find here." He gazed at the remains of the battle and drew in a deep breath. "I am relieved to see you well."

"I am well." King Sebastien sighed. "However, I wish there were more here who could say the same." His brow drew together in a scowl.

"It is so good to see you safe," Orma said, wrapping her arms around Flint. A moment later, Fleta and Cwenhild threw themselves into the embrace. Laughing, Gode draped his arms around the whole group and squeezed.

"A fine welcome home for the world travelers," Halvor said, standing shoulder to shoulder with Gytha. Unable to look away from her daughter's face, Gytha hardly spared a glance for Gode and the others.

Seeing Gytha's tear-stained face, Gode let his arms drop away along with his smile. He turned to her and asked, "What is it?"

Flinching from his touch, she hobbled over to Asdis and dropped heavily to her knees.

Halvor swallowed against the lump in his throat. There was nothing he could do.

Leaving Orma's side, Fleta flew to Gytha's side. "Oh, no!" she cried. She knelt beside the bloodied body. "Asdis, this wasn't supposed to happen."

Cwenhild followed and took Gytha's hand. "I am so sorry," she said.

Halvor cleared his throat. "As I said, a fine welcome. It may not look like it, but we've had a victory here," he said. "Martokallu came again. We have banished him for the time being." He looked bleakly at Gytha. "But it was a victory not without cost."

Fleta leaned forward to straighten Asdis's crumpled legs and drew a hand over the pale face to close her staring eyes. Turning to Gytha, she asked, "How can we help?"

But it was Orma who answered, "There is much to be done and extra hands will go a long way. Later, you can tell us of your adventures."

Cwenhild stepped away from her mother and approached King Sebastien. Reaching back, she drew out the long sword that rode on her back.

Dropping to one knee, she held the sword out in both hands. "It was a successful trip, Your Majesty. This is the God Sword. Forged by Dworgunul for Abbarkov during the war between the gods, it is the weapon that will help us defeat Martokallu once and for all."

His eyes wide, Sebastien accepted the sword and held it up to admire the rippling steel. "There is a story behind this," he said, reluctantly returning the blade. "I look forward to hearing it."

As Cwenhild rose to her feet, Gode stepped forward. "Your Majesty," he said, "it is true that our story can wait, but you should know the reason behind our haste to return." He pressed his lips together, obviously reluctant, and then took a deep breath and spoke in a rush. "A massive army of elves has gathered south of the Chain of Thollcrawnow. They have already mobilized and could be here in as little as two weeks."

Loved *The God Sword*? Write a review.

Review on Amazon

Review on Goodreads

Your next adventure awaits!
Grab your FREE copy of Raptor's Call, a prequel to The Hawks Trilogy today and join the fight for justice.

Scan to get your free copy.

Keep exploring the world of *The Hawks* in *The White Wolf*. Turn the page and join the adventure.

Scan to get your free copy.

THE WHITE WOLF & THE HAWKS

BOOK THREE

PAULA BAKER

&

AIDAN DAVIES

MacFay Books

The White Wolf

MacFay Books
103 Heron Dr.
Penticton, BC
V2A 8K6

Map Art by Anna-Jo Grandbois
Cover illustration by Daria 'Frealyr' Kovalenko
Cover design by Kusanagistudios

Typeset in Garamond

CHAPTER ONE

Reinforcements

WAITING IN THE MIDST OF the swirling blizzard, Wout watched a tiny speck of light grow larger. The wind on the open beach gusted hard, threatening to knock him off his feet. In annoyance, he pulled his black cloak more closely around him. As a Follower of Martokallu, the cold did not bother him, but the flapping fabric was an irritation.

It looked as if King Norgrith ben Vordrith would keep his word. When they met that afternoon within the walls of the snowbound village, Wout had been uncertain whether he could trust the leader of the Nairt. Certainly, he appeared to be greedy enough to agree to the deal, but one never knew with humans.

As far as Wout was concerned, allying with humans—any humans—was a bad idea. The debacle in Kallcunarth when the Hawks destroyed Thrall's army of enslaved humans and killed a great number of Wout's own fighting force in the process had proved that. But Martokallu had decided they needed a well-trained mercenary force.

King Norgrith's warriors would do nicely in that regard. The barbaric people who lived in the frozen island north of Abbarkon were obsessed with fighting. The king had promised he could field as many as three thousand trained fighters in return for payment. Of course, gold was not a difficulty for Martokallu. Entire rooms in his fortress overflowed with treasure for which he had no use.

Trained warriors who fought for the pure joy of the fight were exactly what he needed to put an end to the Hawks and their King Sebastien. Wout would lead them. Together, they would crush the rebellion and Martokallu would rule Abbarkon at last.

The beam of light finally reached the beach and turned to wander off in the wrong direction. Shaking his head in irritation, Wout shouted, "I am here."

Immediately, the glow changed direction. It moved toward him, growing in size, until Wout made out the bearded face of King Norgrith, hunched inside a wolf-skin coat. That was something. Wout had wondered if the king might send an underling in his place. Although, he should not be surprised. No doubt, the king of the north had not noticed the foul weather.

Bellowing to be understood over the noise of the wind, King Norgrith asked, "You brought the gold?"

Nodding to himself at the predictably human behaviour, Wout lifted a booted foot to place it on the lid of a solidly constructed sea chest—the only thing he had bothered to save when he killed the sailor and sank the small boat that had brought him across the sea from Abbarkon.

Wout had not wanted the man to return home where he might mention his passenger to curious listeners. He did not intend to leave any trace of his voyage to Nairt'kun. Even when he entered the village to find passage, he went in disguise. No one needed know that a Follower of Martokallu had ever been here.

King Norgrith lowered himself into the snowdrift that had built up around the box and fumbled with the latch on the chest. It was a struggle with his bulky fur mittens, and he entirely lost any dignity Wout might have ascribed to him.

When the leader of the Nairt finally lifted the lid and sat back on his heels to examine the cache, he let out a long low whistle. "You say this is just a sample?" King Norgrith asked from his position at Wout's feet.

Enjoying the idea of having a king kneel before him, Wout nodded regally. It did not matter that no one could see him. It had been a long time since he found humour in anything, and he would play his part for his own entertainment.

"I will fill the hold of one of your ships for your trip home," Wout answered. He waited while the big man scrambled to his feet and added, "After you win the war."

King Norgrith waved away the idea of failure. "Of course, we will win," he said. "We always win. When do you want us to leave?"

"Immediately," answered Wout.

The king's eyes strayed to the chest of gold and jewels. "And so we shall," he answered. "As soon as the storm abates.

Loved *The God Sword?* Write a review.

Review on Amazon

Review on Goodreads

Your next adventure awaits!
Grab your FREE copy of Raptor's Call, a prequel to The Hawks Trilogy today and join the fight for justice.

Scan to get your free copy.

Keep exploring the world of *The Hawks* in *The White Wolf.* Grab your copy now.

Scan to get your free copy.

Paula Baker and her son, Aidan Davies, wrote the middle-grade fantasy trilogy *Rebels of Halklyen*, *The God Sword*, and *The White Wolf*, along with its prequel, *Raptor's Call*. Their latest release, *Dirt Town* is a standalone young adult magical steampunk novel. They live in British Columbia, Canada. Learn more at https://bakerdavies.ca

https://bakerdavies.ca